COUNTDOWN TO DESTRUCTION

"Five seconds!" Larry shouted. "Five miserable, lousy..."

Larry saw the oncoming *Executioner* bearing down on him.

Three seconds...If it fired, he'd be gone. The room would tear off and shatter like glass.

Two seconds, one...

Larry's mind caught the beat. At zero his arm moved down, pulling the released switch.

Larry slammed it to the floor. He was lying on top of it when the room began to shake. The floor rippled. Larry stood as if spring-loaded. Before his eyes his ship's energy bolt smashed the *Executioner* in midflight.

Larry stood motionless, his hands clenched into fists, his knuckles skeleton white. He suddenly noticed the cheers coming from the speaker.

"You did it!" Napoleon gushed. "I can't believe it! Did you see that?"

He saw it, all right. The *Executioner* was gone. But now the *Destroyer* was moving in...

DOOMSTAR

RICHARD MEYERS

"Space Adventure...with a *vengeance!*"

POPULAR LIBRARY

An Imprint of Warner Books, Inc.

A Warner Communications Company

POPULAR LIBRARY EDITION

Copyright © 1978, 1985 by Richard S. Meyers

Cover art by Don Maitz

Popular Library books are published by
Warner Books, Inc.
666 Fifth Avenue
New York, N.Y. 10103

A Warner Communications Company

Printed in the United States of America

First Popular Library Printing: July, 1985

10 9 8 7 6 5 4 3 2 1

DEDICATION

To Steven Hartov
"We're off to see the wizard...."

ACKNOWLEDGMENTS

Al Sirois—the heart of the matter
Chris Browne—the brain
Kevin O'Donnell, Jr.—the sinew
Jeff Rovin—the guts
Ward Damio—the genes
Roy Kuhlman—the face
Melissa Nichols—the libido
Bobby London—the walleyes
Don Maitz—the facelift
Brian Thomsen—the surgery
The late great Duke of Wellington—the tail

"The more things change, the more they stay the same."

GLOSSARY

FM = Fake Man
SM = Sex Machine
TM = True Man
EM = Earth Mother
RH = Real Human
EX = Experimental Subject
ECG = Earth Central Government
ECCM = Earth Control Central Machines
Mess = Multi-unit Electronic System for Space
U.W. = United World
EX-A = Experimental Alien
WEA-War = War to End All Wars
AT = Autopsy
NAO = Noah's Ark Operation
Cirquid = a liquid circuit

* A Note on the Abbreviations *
Just keep reading. All should become clear.—R.M.

EARTH

ONE

FM Larry's back was turned when the piece of space debris sat up. He knew something was wrong from Napoleon's screeching howl and the way Mess started bellowing, "Permission to fire, permission to fire, permission to fire!"

Even if he had been deaf and unable to hear the reactions of his co-pilot and on-board compubot, he still would have known something was amiss from the way the ball of red light was flickering on the control board.

"Stinking machine," he said and started to get up, tapping the little glassular dome.

It always happens this way. They laze up from the Denver Plateau, sitting on their thumbs for the entire trip, and just as they near the Alphonsus-Moon Lab (where a modicum of skill is required to safely dump their material loads) something else goes wrong with the old bucket.

But Larry was not deaf, so he heard not only his

3

associate's exclamations but the blast of alarm bells as well. Mess had slammed his nonexistent arm across the board, setting off everything from "Broken Scope" to "Missing Engine." In one second the bridge of the E.S. *Black Hole* was turned from a majestic floating manse into eardrum hell.

Larry's spine seemed to wave like a cracking whip as he spun all the way around, winding up facing the control board again. It took an extraordinary effort of will to keep his hands from slapping over his ears and his eyes from screwing shut. Instead, he directed his hands to the control board while tightening his ear muscles.

The noise dimmed as his hands flew from one alarm neutralization to another. He couldn't keep his eyes from tearing from the din, so he let his neural ducts open wide, turning the blinding mist into a water flow on either side of his long nose.

As he reached for the switch farthest on the right (stopping the "Escape Hatch Ajar" alarm) he noticed that Napoleon had backed under her own control area, spitting and arching her back. As suddenly as it had occurred, the bridge was blissfully quiet—except for the hissing of his co-pilot and Mess' continuing begging bleats.

"Permission to fire! Permission to fire! Permission to fire!"

"No!" Larry cried, his voice higher than he would have liked. "Damper down, will ya? Uh, recheck Alphonsus entry coordinates!" If he could keep the damn machine busy, he could find out what the panic was all about.

"Coordinates checked and locked in," Mess said hurriedly. "Permission to fire now, please."

Mess had gotten businesslike; it had gotten brisk. That meant real trouble. Larry spun halfway around

4

to discover sitting up in front of him was nine by five feet of beige/brown rock where there used to be nine by five feet of prone beige/brown rock.

Larry was stunned, silent, and still. The kind of stunned, silent stillness that seemed to buzz, as if his smooth aura had become serrated. He half stood, half sat in his chair, hands gripping the edge of the control board to remain almost upright.

"Wha—wha—what," he managed to stutter.

"It sat up!" Mess shouted, suddenly hysterical. "Just a second ago! Permission to fire. Oh, hurry, quick!"

Larry's mind twisted like a gyroscope to get a grip on this one. "But that's impossible!" he noted to gain time. "Rock can't bend. What do your imputs say?"

"Oh, to the Earth Father with my imputs! Permission to fire!"

"No! One blast from you and we'll all be space debris!" (Humoring this thing was getting tougher every day.) "Just damper down, will you? Look, there's nothing to shoot. This must be a new element, or something. It's simply reacting to the atmosphere in here, that's all."

Larry was pleased with himself. His reasoning was sound. After all, that was why they had brought this hunk of space junk onto the bridge in the first place: a subject for further study when they were back in Earth orbit. In all the *Black Hole*'s years of scavenging they had never come across a piece like it. Although it was small as ore asteroids went, Mess had judged it extremely rich in rare materials. And although it looked exactly the right size for an ancient satellite or a second-stage rocket hunk, it was bumpy and jutted like a rock.

But not like any rock they had ever seen. All the bumps and ruts were smooth. Even where a grade looked to be ending in a point, the edge felt rounded to the touch, like a living optical illusion.

"I don't like the looks of it," Mess had said.

"You don't like the looks of anything," Larry had retorted. "Bring it in." At this stage of the game, Larry and Napoleon couldn't afford to pass anything up.

So they had watched as Mess maneuvered above it, reached down with his only working arm, and pushed it into the bottom hatch. But they were all so intrigued with it that Larry had the compubot drag it into the back of the bridge area for further examination after reentry orbit.

But now it was Alphonsus entry time and the piece of space something had sat up. Five feet of it was still parallel to the floor, while four feet were bent up at a right angle. Moonlight, coming from the front port, dappled the top foot and a half, which looked ominously like a dome all of a sudden.

Larry rose slowly, completely to his feet. "Yeah," he said with a nod and a frown. "It's just a molecular reaction." Napoleon looked at him from under her seat like, "What the hell is a molecular reaction?" "Surprising," Larry agreed with her expression, "but probably not dangerous."

The crew seemed willing, even desperate, to accept his reasoning. Napoleon edged out from under her co-pilot's board and rubbed her back across its underside. In the same movement she rose to her hind legs and swished her tail. Its very end continued to wave, like a stalking cobra head. Mess stopped begging, but its biomechanical doubts still hung in the air.

"You see?" said Larry with soothing command. "Nothing to worry about."

That's when the rock stood up.

One moment it was still sitting passively, the next

6

all nine feet of it were at ninety degrees to the floor.

Larry couldn't keep his arms from crossing before his face, his first thought being that the huge thing was going to topple forward onto him. Napoleon threw her body backward, twisting around in midair to land on all fours and scurry back under her control board, her hair standing on end. Mess took a moment to redirect its empty interior weaponry, then started in again.

"Permission to fire, permission to fire, permission to fire!"

Larry pulled his arms down angrily and stared at the monolith before him. His mouth wanted to snap open and let his vocal cords rip, but Larry regained control. He stared hard.

The space debris had seemed solid. Mess had said it was solid, but that didn't mean much. Twice it had moved, once changing shape. Even now, though, it seemed to have an uneven surface. It stood completely level with no rocking or tipping. What did it do, re-organize its molecules? And if it did, what would it change into next time?

"Permission to fire, by the Earth Father, permission to fire!" Mess shouted.

Larry found his voice. "No! For the last time, damper down, you paranoid pile!"

"Then let me contact Earth Control," the voice wheedled.

That got a rise from Napoleon. "Noooo," she howled. "Any trouble here we handle ourselves." Mess listened to her. Its suggestion had drawn her up to her hind legs. "What do we do, Larry?"

Larry slowly raised his arm and moved to his left. "Go get the beamers. If it does anything else, we'll bathe it."

7

The debris remained silent, rooted to the floor. Napoleon began to pad over to the beamer compartment.

"You're not going to let me shoot, are you?" asked Mess.

"What do you think?" Larry replied tightly.

"I don't think. I make logical conclusions based on core information ingrained on my liquid circuits by Dr. Palsy-Drake at the date of my conception."

Larry moved left, resisting the urge to roll his eyes or gag. "The Earth Father you do. Now quiet."

Mess continued, oblivious. "I respond to new stimuli either spoken, viewed, or 'cirquided,' and based on your spoken information I conclude you're not going to let me fire."

Larry now felt he was far enough away from the thing that if it did change or fall it wouldn't hit him. "Correct," he said with a sigh.

Napoleon had reached the compartment and retrieved her own padded beamer with the extra-large trigger guard to fit her foreclaw as well as Larry's beam rifle with the quadra-lens barrel, and was even now returning to cover the thing from her side.

"Well, if you're going to shoot it, why can't I?" Mess complained.

Larry hopped over to Napoleon in an exaggerated tiptoe and got his weapon. "We are not going to shoot it if we can help it," he said quickly. "You, on the other hand, would blast it, us, and the ship to kingdom come if I let you."

"I have no kingdom come on my cirquids," it sniffed.

"No one likes a smart computer," said Larry.

"Then what good are we?" replied Mess.

Napoleon remained tense, every feline sinew locked on to the space debris, but Larry felt himself relaxing, not certain whether Mess was bantering to relieve the tension or simply reacting to and by its unreprogrammable psyche. That is, the core information impregnated on the compubot's cirquids by Dr. Palsy-Drake, the infamous final scientist executed under the Lasser-Welles Act of 204 A.N.D. (After Natural Disaster).

Somewhere along the line, the good doctor had rejected the ancient robot laws and decided that a machine's main concern should be for itself, since man was too stupid. Therefore Mess' rule of thumb was self-preservation. Thankfully (or unfortunately, depending upon one's point of view), Mess was created just before Palsy-Drake's nervous breakdown, trial, and execution, so the man's programming was not airtight. Mess thus emerged aggressive but very considerate.

Even so, Mess had managed to kill three FM engineers before they got him dismantled and stored away. And there it lay until Larry had smuggled most of it aboard to be the *Black Hole*'s compubot: a guidance computer with the capability to manifest itself into a variety of small robots. It would have been a real good defense computer as well if Larry had been allowed near any *real* weapons.

As it was, even the beamers Larry and Napoleon held were essentially baby's toys. Imagine, the very idea of letting FMs and EX-As have real weapons! Why, they could hurt someone with them.

Instead, Larry let the newly dubbed MESS—Multiunit Electronic System for Space—think it was fully armored. For months it had navigated and computed while trying to blow up anything within a parsec of the ship. Naturally it thought its guns were empty, or worse, thought they had no effect on the target.

Larry managed to survive their first trip with the speakers blaring, "Emergency! Mayday!" before demanding that Mess ask permission from either pilot before trying to destroy anything. Mess had argued eloquently that either of the living beings could be asleep or unconscious when danger struck, but Larry stuck to his empty guns.

Further modifications were necessary as time went on, but somehow Mess never got wind of the deception or at least never let on. It was tough to tell with Mess. It even had an "Escape Hatch Ajar" alarm when the *Black Hole* didn't *have* an escape hatch. But all the difficulties were worth having an illicit computer not tied in with the ECCM.

Besides the privacy it assured, the Earth Control Central Machines were also unaware of the ship's extracurricular activities, like these scavenger runs. All sorts of junk was floating between the Earth, the moon, and Doomstar, and Larry could buy more time for Napoleon and himself by trading the greatly loved raw material to the United World scientists directly, rather than going through the Earth Central Government, which sought to control all things through its U.W. chapters.

Confused? Larry usually had to spend his evenings thinking it all through in order to keep it all straight. Time was running out for Napoleon and him, so as long as this *Black Hole* black market in raw materials kept the U.W. scientists from their door, he would continue risking the wrath of the ECG.

But now his regular, official supply run from the Denver Plateau to the Alphonsus-Moon Lab was disturbed by a nine-foot-high hunk of contorting space debris.

"You want to know what you're good for?" Larry finally answered the machine. "I'll tell you what you're good for...."

A hum filled the room. Larry's words stopped in midsentence. Napoleon's hair bristled and her tail lashed. She held her beamer tighter and brought it up as Larry managed to keep his hands from gripping his own weapon too tightly.

"Mess, is that you?" he inquired.

A pause accompanied the hum.

"No," the answer finally came. Quietly. "Permission to fire, please, please, please."

"Uh," said Larry. His grasp of vocabulary surprised even him. "Better check the ship's cirquids for the problem, then." Napoleon had begun to crouch, her tail straight up, ready to pounce. Larry was glad she was wearing her tight EX-A I.D. suit. She had a habit of going naked on the ship.

"All cirquids functioning properly," Mess reported without a pause. "Permission to fire."

Larry's mind struggled with the situation. As an EX-FM, he wasn't really equipped for leadership (at least that's what they had told him again and again). All he could think of doing was to buy more time from Mess. "Did you really check it?"

"Yes, permission to fire."

"Then check again."

"Rechecked, permission to fire."

The top foot and a half of the debris began to turn to the left.

Larry shouted, "No!" and both he and Napoleon pulled the beamers' triggers. Orange bands of light streaked from the barrels, widening perceptibly as they crisscrossed the room. The beams hit the debris, broke into two, and coursed off around it. All they left on the rock was an antiseptic stench.

"Permission to fire, permission to fire, permission to fire!" Mess cried.

"Fire!" Napoleon howled.

Mess shut up for just the second necessary to engage his empty weapons.

"They have no effect!" it screamed. "We're in deep yogurt now!"

Larry lowered his gun and watched helplessly as the top of the debris continued to turn. "What's happening, Mess? What do your sensors show?"

"Look for yourself!" Mess yelled back. "I'm getting out of here!"

Larry stepped forward as a section of the computer bank slid aside and a triangular box with two balls of sensors on the back, three levitators on the bottom, several flashing system analyzers on the top, and a slashing ariel flew out. It circled the room crazily, just missing the pilots, then sped out the rear bridge hatch.

"Get back here, you compu-coward!" Larry shouted after it. "Sensors! Damages! Coordinates! You tin-plated tube, get back here!" He glanced at the still-turning space-junk top, then ran over to the snarling Napoleon.

"Keep it covered," he said, scratching her neck roughly. "I've got to override the cirquids of the esc-globes before Mess can jettison itself." Napoleon shook off his hand and nodded curtly. She knew what was going on here. All the beamers did was bathe the target in a mild tranquilizing light. They were good for a second of pleasure, that's all; a relaxing spark. As a weapon, their only use was intimidation—if the target was ignorant of their use or too unintelligent to care.

Larry stabbed some buttons on his co-pilot's console, then returned his attention to the space debris. The top section had risen two inches during the previous action. Napoleon understood before he did.

"By Cheshire," she said, "there's something in here. It's unscrewing itself."

Larry bent over to retrieve his dropped beamer, for all the good it would do him. When he had straightened, he saw the turning top had risen another half inch. *What an astonishing development. A hunk of rock that could sit up and stand, but then had a screw top.*

As suddenly as it had started, the turning stopped. The room was silent once again, but only for a second. Then the top foot and a half rose smoothly and dropped backward.

Napoleon managed to remain perfectly still, but Larry could not keep his legs from propelling him back. He lost his balance and fell, his beamer skittering across the floor. Extremely upset with himself, he leaped to his feet and the first thing he saw was a human face crosshatched with throbbing blue-green-gray veins. It was sitting on top of the space debris.

The human's mouth opened and a small voice at Larry's waist said, "Greetings. What language do you speak?"

TWO

Harlan Trigor was a space bullet. After climbing out of his nine-foot suit and pulling off his exoskeleton, he explained in unaccented English exactly what that was: a self-contained armament and space vehicle created for the purpose of defense in the upper atmosphere of the planet Destiny.

It was simple enough for him to say. It was extremely hard for Larry and Napoleon to understand. Napoleon had kept her beamer on him during his complicated disembarking, an act that seemed to give him some amusement.

"What's so funny?" she growled at the humanlike figure, who was peeling off his blue-green-gray body suit from just above his slim black eyebrows.

"You mean, besides a cat who uses contractions in perfect speech?" he asked rhetorically. "Your weapon, for one. It's fairly useless." He pulled off the exohood, exposing a rugged face haloed by a rich, black beard.

"I'm not a cat," hissed Napoleon, which left her the awkward task of explaining just who she was. "I'm a feline. A female feline from the planet Mandarin. Who are you?"

Trigor repeated his preliminary introduction, which made about as much sense as Napoleon's declaration, then elaborated eloquently, "A piece of jade in the black velvet of space, Destiny is a mythical garden world, long ago prophesied to be populated by a superior human race and long an inviting target for all manner of space vermin and scum. I was born for the sole purpose of becoming a soldier—a space bullet created to protect the lush planet surface from the scars of battle."

Napoleon scoffed, "In that?" She pointed at the open-space debris with her beamer.

"The weaponry in my suit is so abundant and advanced that I can neutralize and/or destroy any known spacecraft in seconds. This suit enables me to withstand the terrible pressures of space and battle, but I must say that I am the best at what I do."

Trigor completed his theatrical dissertation as he took off the last of his bulky outerwear, leaving his short, wide body encased in a skintight black shirt and hose. He touched the no longer pulsing exoskeleton with his toe. On the floor it looked like a pile of dirty laundry.

Napoleon scowled, but Larry's face was wide open in amazement. "What you say must have some validity since the translator"—Larry lifted the thin bar, grated at both ends, from his belt—"knew what language you were originally speaking."

"It is an ancient vocabulary created for the early space travelers," Trigor explained. "Once other inhabited planets were discovered, we needed a universal language."

"You know English well enough," said Napoleon.

"My ancestors came from Earth," Harlan repeated. "Did yours?"

Larry looked over to his shipmate quickly, but her only reaction was a pause and a slight squinting of her eyes. "No. I learned the tongue the hard way."

"You say you're from Destiny," Larry interrupted quickly. "We have no evidence that the planet actually exists. The legend goes that it is vastly powerful and also hateful toward the rest of the galaxy. If you're from there, why didn't you just blast us when we picked you up and continue on your way?"

"The legends have grown melodramatic with age," Trigor said simply, humbly. Changing the subject, he inquired, "Your ship was unlike any I had ever seen. I was curious."

Larry could understand why. The Earth Ship *Black Hole* had been designed and built, in a manner of speaking, by Larry himself in the miserable years of his youth, while in orbit in space. It was a patchwork quilt of junked spacecraft he had requisitioned from the Providence Space Center garbage heaps.

He had done it for therapy, and the U.W. scientists let him get away with it as a test. It wound up rescuing him from the Galactic Pool. No other FM had his own space vehicle. No other FM had been given as much freedom and responsibility. Larry had avoided FM slavery by becoming the ultimate gofer—a glorified messenger transferring precious materials from one lab to another and running end products up to Alphonsus for use on the Doomstar.

Trigor interrupted Larry's thoughts. "I would be pleased if you would show me around," said the squat, muscular man, looking slightly ridiculous in his tights.

Napoleon flashed Larry a feline frown, but he could see no harm in it. It was obvious the man was unarmed unless he had mazers under his fingernails. Besides, it would give Larry time to think out the uncomfortable situation. What was the man doing here? What did he want?

Might as well give him the grand tour, Larry finally figured. If nothing else, they could retrieve Mess.

"What the hell are you doing up there, Larry?" an unfamiliar voice suddenly interrupted. "Are you going to land or what?"

"Taplinger-Jones," Larry exclaimed under his breath, using the strongest curse then known. He invoked the name of the man who had started the WEA-War. "I forgot all about the run." He ran to the console, leaving an annoyed Napoleon near the space bullet. She looked at his racing figure, then sneered back at Trigor, hefting the useless beamer with an assurance she didn't feel.

Larry jumped into his seat and engaged the audio communications link. "Uh, hi, Julius," he said sheepishly.

"What's going on up there?" Julius, the FM in charge of incoming shipments, demanded.

"Nothing," Larry assured him. "You know, the usual garbage."

"The *Black Hole* acting up again?"

"Yeah. You know, the usual."

"You really should get U.W. accreditation," Julius harped. "They wouldn't let this sort of thing go on. I mean, if it was just you, I wouldn't trouble myself, but hell, Larry, you put my boys in danger every time you dump here. And the Earth Father knows the ECG puts them in enough danger as it is."

"Yeah, I know, Julius," Larry apologized. "This trip, I swear. I'll take the test."

The United World accreditation benefits were far greater than the ECG license that Larry had. If he passed the U.W. science test, the local chapter would keep the ship in shape for him. The ECG didn't really care what condition the *Black Hole* was in as long as it did the job.

"You say that every trip."

"This time for sure, Julius. I swear."

Neither FM said anything for a second and when Julius came back on he was apologetic. "Listen to me, will you, Larry? I'm sorry, bro, it's just that..."

"Yeah, I know," Larry commiserated.

"You scheduled for the AT yet?" No matter how emphatic or sympathetic a fellow FM was, he couldn't help bringing it up. I mean, they were only human, weren't they?

"No," Larry sighed, a catch he could never get rid of in his voice. "Not yet."

They were all brothers under the skin because of their mutual plight. Still, they had to hold on to whatever humanity was offered them. Julius was trying to be considerate, but he couldn't help feeling good about not having an AT hanging over his head. All he had to worry about were the shameful Alphonsus working conditions.

"Well, if you could, Larry. Not for me. For my boys, you know? The U.W. accreditation?"

"Next time, Julius," Larry said heartily.

"All right then!" Julius' voice matched Larry's briskness. "To business. You landing or dumping?"

"Dumping this time, I think."

"Larry, gee...."

"Get Stan and Dean," Larry suggested. "They've done it with me before."

"You sure you want to dump? You can't see your way to land today?"

"Dump. Really, Julius, it'll be all right. Stan and Dean have done it with me before."

"All right, Larry, if you say so. But I'm telling you, bro. Only with you, brother, only with you."

Larry broke the connection and slumped in the chair. Julius meant well, he supposed, but maintaining the farce exhausted him.

"What is it?" Harlan asked. "What's the matter?"

Larry turned toward the two. Napoleon's furry face was concerned. "Are you a TM?" Larry asked quietly of Trigor.

Harlan's head shook slightly, as if Larry had sneaked in a Swahili word. "I don't understand," he said. "A tee-em? A tem?"

Larry laughed. "We do have an alien here, don't we?" He looked away at the floor, freeze-dried in his misery.

Harlan looked at an angry Napoleon. She hated to see Larry hurt this way. "A TM, space bullet. True Man. See that?" She pointed to a mark on her nearly sleeveless outfit. It was a stitching of three letters. "EX-A. Experimental Alien." She jabbed a paw at Larry. "He's an EX-FM. Experimental Fake Man. Julius is a straight FM. Everybody at Alphonsus-Moon base is an FM."

Harlan frowned in wonder. He didn't want to inflame the situation by asking for any clarifications Napoleon didn't want to give, but he couldn't help himself. "Then what's an AT?"

Napoleon growled, glancing furtively at Larry. He smiled wanly and waved the question away as if it didn't hurt.

"An Autopsy, idiot," Napoleon hissed.

Trigor was completely confused. "I don't understand."

"How long have you been away from Earth again?" Larry asked, looking over.

"Eons," Trigor said. "Millennia."

20

"Lots has happened since then, friend," Larry explained tiredly. "There was the WEA-War, the War to End All Wars. The only ones that survived that were the military men and the politicians. Between it and the Natural Disaster, Earth is not a very nice place to visit. So they made up an army of FMs from the cells of long-dead men to build themselves another home on the other side of the moon. They call it 'duex ciel'—second heaven. We call it Doomstar."

Harlan nodded sadly. "I know of this."

Napoleon ignored his distrust long enough to spit, "Do you know how many of them died building that thing? Do you know how many die mining underwater on Earth for the ore, how many die shipping it between the moon and the Doomstar? But the TMs don't care. They just make up more."

"Enough, Napôleon, enough," Larry said weakly. He turned toward Trigor with a pathetic little smile. "You wanted a tour?"

The trio went from the bridge to the storage area. One-half of Larry's mind was used to point out the solar panels and the sensor scopes, while the other half considered their predicament. By the time they discovered Mess' manifestation blinking wildly in one of the escape globes as it tried to get the jettison mechanism to work, he had boiled it down somewhat.

What they had here was a refugee from the most dreamed of planet in the galaxy. He had finally wound up, rational and communicating, in Earth orbit somehow, just as the *Black Hole*'s crew was getting desperate. They had maintained a living by the skin of their teeth for years, but their rope was running out.

Soon neither Larry nor Napoleon would be good for anything else but AT. They would be worth more to the U.W. scientists as ATs than they would to the ECG as messengers. It was just a matter of time before

Weinstein-Hubbell's AT request wound its way through the tortuous ECG procedures and back on his desk with a large Y embossed across it.

Now all Larry had to do was figure out where the Destiny soldier fit in. He tried while showing the man the engines. Napoleon trailed behind, looking bored but holding her beamer as tightly as ever. Trigor nodded, smiled, murmured, and just generally showed innocent appreciation.

"Tell me," he finally inquired, "where are your weapons?"

Larry shot a glance over his shoulder where Napoleon's face hardened. Turning back, he took the subtle approach. "Oh, the usual places. Why?"

"It just seemed strange that an Earth ship would have no weapons."

"We have weapons, we have weapons," said Mess' manifestation defensively, hovering in, nearly taking a piece of Trigor's ear off.

"Why should you be interested in our weapons if your suit is so powerful?" Napoleon snapped.

"It just seemed to me..." Trigor said defensively.

"What do you want to know for?" the feline demanded.

"All right!" Larry barked over the din. "All right," he said again quietly. "Let's all go back to the bridge and do some serious talking."

"Right," Napoleon agreed, pushing her beamer barrel into Trigor's back. "Just keep a safe distance away from that suit of yours."

Larry entered the area first, feeling proud. He had handled the situation well, he decided. Mess' manifestation shot by his head and slammed into its console opening. The wall slid back in place as the triangular box with the slashing antennae disappeared inside.

Larry sat in his pilot's chair and pulled his beamer across his lap. He looked at his control board to see that Stan and Dean's ship was getting into range. He dumped their load with the press of a button.

"Make sure everything cleared," he told Mess. Stan and Dean would scoop it up like the garbage it was. Julius would have preferred their unloading it on the moon's surface.

"All clear," Mess assured him diffidently.

Trigor entered, guided to the left of his nine-foot enclosure and exoskeleton by Napoleon's prodding. She brought him to within ten feet of Larry, then stopped.

"Now, I'm not much for clear thinking. . . ." Larry began.

"Weinstein-Hubbell saw to that," Napoleon said bitterly.

"But it doesn't take a TM to see something's wrong here. A soldier from the most loved and sought-after planet in the galaxy just doesn't up and come to Earth for a vacation. At least not in uniform." Larry motioned toward the suit. "How many light-years is it to Destiny anyway?"

"Approximately or exactly?" asked Mess.

"Keep out of this."

"Approximately or exactly?"

"Never mind!"

"I don't have a position for Destiny," Mess suddenly complained. "Let's say a lot."

"Damper down!" Larry roared.

"Don't you want to know?" Mess asked.

"It doesn't make any real difference," Larry maintained stridently, amazed he was getting into a fight with the compubot.

"Then why did you ask?"

"I didn't ask *you*."

"Then you should have told me that," Mess huffed. "How difficult would that be?"

"Damper your egocentric electrodes!" Larry screamed at the compubot console.

Silence suddenly hung in the air, so Larry was able to turn his attention back to Trigor, who looked as if he were imprisoned in the hyena country of the Zoo World.

"Now you've had the crash-course tour of the ship," Larry continued reasonably, "so it's time for some straight answers. What are you doing here?"

Trigor spread his arms beseechingly. Napoleon danced back, growling. "I was only curious."

"And don't repeat your old story," she snarled. "That lame tale wouldn't fool a booger."

Trigor stiffened at the mention of the word. He turned toward Napoleon, horror cracking his countenance. "Do you have Mantases here as well?"

Napoleon's beamer remained level with the man's chest. No one spoke.

"Yes," said Mess. "But not as many as many other planets. We have less land area than many other planets. Then again, we only have the Mantases' word for any of this."

Larry was taken aback by the change in Trigor. In less than a few seconds the soldier's strong face had degenerated into wrinkles of despair. His mouth hung down, his brows rose to a point, the lines on his forehead made a succession of peaks, his chest caved in, his shoulders hunched, and his knees buckled.

"Then all is lost!" he cried and dropped to the floor with a resounding thunk.

Larry looked up at Napoleon in surprise. Napoleon moved nimbly back, her weapon still aimed at the prone Trigor, expecting a trick. They both stared at the man cringing on the floor.

"Dramatic," Napoleon mused.

"Something is definitely wrong here," Larry said, stepping around the fallen man. He stood by the feline, still looking over his shoulder at Trigor. "What do you think this is all about?"

"I don't know," she said simply. "I really don't care. You figure it out. I just want to be ready for whatever it is." Her weapon remained steady and centered on the man's back. Larry knew her. First she'd shoot Trigor with it and then use it as a club to crack his skull.

Larry nodded and scratched her back three times. He moved to the back of the bridge and leaned against the wall. If "a" is an alien crying on the floor and "b" is the Alphonsus-Moon Lab waiting for supplies and "c" is the administrative Mantases, then what is "x"? Larry was quickly content that he couldn't make heads nor tails of it.

He stood and walked back to Trigor. "I'm afraid I'm just going to have to ask for an explanation," he apologized politely.

The Destiny soldier raised his head and Larry plainly saw the tears cascading down into his black beard and beading up. Noise wasn't causing this, he marveled. Wow, emotions. Real deep ones at that. Trigor rose to one elbow and wiped his arm across his face. "I will not apologize," he stated.

Larry shrugged. "I don't know what your problem is, but maybe..." Larry let the words trail off. What could he say? That he'd try to postpone his autopsy long enough to help? How could he help? With a weaponless junk ship good only for orbital travel? That was hardly an impressive start.

"It's all right," Trigor maintained. "I'm making a fool of myself."

Napoleon nodded in agreement. Larry looked at

her in silent reprimand. "Talk to me," he suggested. "Make me understand."

Trigor stood abruptly, nearly knocking Larry back. The military bearing had returned. He finished brushing the tears away. "No. No, no, no. You could be of no help. I must be on my way."

"Great," said Mess. "Go out through the hatch, take a left, then a right, then another left. Stand in the middle of the floor and I'll dump you."

"Be quiet, Mess," said Larry, approaching the soldier. "Now, Harlan Trigor, you can't just go like..." The space bullet moved threateningly toward Larry. The pilot moved quickly back. "Well, maybe you can," he decided reasonably.

Harlan stepped over to his exoskeleton, ignoring Napoleon. "I can assure you that even without my suit I could tear you both to pieces. Do not attempt to stop me. For your own good."

"Considerate," Napoleon decided.

"I'm not surprised," said Larry to Trigor, "but that's hardly the point."

"I must insist you allow me to leave without incident," reiterated Trigor.

"Let him leave without incident," Mess cried.

Napoleon spat a sharp hiss. Everyone stopped talking and turned toward her. She was curled in a ball on the floor, her beamer still held level with Trigor's chest. "Larry was nice," she said. "I'm not so soft-hearted. You are not putting on your suit, you are not getting into your rock, and you are not leaving this ship. You either tell us what this is all about or I'm going to slice you in half."

Larry ran backward away from Trigor, cementing the impression that Napoleon's beamer was actually a fully charged mazer. Trigor stared at her for a second, then his face began to crumble again.

"And don't cry," she moaned. "It's disgusting."

Trigor could sense she was serious. As with an ancient cat, one could feel its energy rising to a crescendo instants before it attacked. Trigor sobbed and his hands rose to grip the sides of his head. He sat heavily on the floor. He looked at neither Larry nor Napoleon. Instead he looked out the front port.

He saw the rim of the dark blue and blackened world, Earth. It could be just made out from the sparkling blackness of space beyond. He knew that within his sight were several other habitable planets, planets with creatures discernible to the human eye and within understanding of the human brain. Creatures with problems they imagined were as insurmountable as his own. He stared and tried to pinpoint when his life had become so complicated. He opened his mouth and spoke to the stars, finally telling his story.

THREE

"Long before Holocaust II and the Natural Disaster, Earth was a decent planet, full of life and hope. Scientific advances were being made constantly. Incredible advances in medicine, transportation, and communication seemed almost commonplace, but the fallout from them was bitter and widespread. These discoveries were paid for by businessmen who were more interested in profit than humanity. The wealthy prospered while the rest stayed desperate and disease-ridden. Those who tried to interfere soon found the cost of resistance too great.

"If a new energy source was needed, it was soon harnessed. If new food sources became necessary, they were created. If faster transport became imperative, new ways were conceived. If more living area was a priority, larger space colonies were funded. Thus spoke our teachers.

"The United States and Euro-China prospered while everyone else begged for charity (which was plentiful). The cost of charity was the country's soul. Soon all animosities were broken down into the United States and Euro-China. They each moved into their new territories, teaching the inhabitants either English or Pinyan, each force spending as much as it needed to keep one step ahead of the other. Ships were launched farther and farther into the galaxy in a strange game of 'One, Two, Three, Red Light.'

"Many ships were never heard from again. My ancestors were on one such ship. Generations were born and died on that great ship, which finally found a home on the planet Destiny (name by Kevin O'Neil). That was from whence the last of the O'Neils, Craig W., triumphantly returned to Earth to share his family's legacy. He found only wholesale destruction.

"Huge swaths of this third planet from Sol were uninhabitable from the wrath of war weapons. Formerly teeming space habitats circled the world, broken and burned. Storms of broiling death swept the planet's surface—radiation and the monsters it spawned—killing all in their wake. They mingled with clouds of deadly bacteria that unknown warriors had unleashed. The only places left for civilians to live were areas bombarded by neutronic devices.

"Craig W. found unscathed survivors in the mountains and under the deserts. Most of them were military men and scientists, the ones with the warning and knowledge of the shelters' locations. Only they knew how to protect themselves from the war that only they knew was coming. What O'Neil heard from them destroyed the hopes of his soul.

"They had not changed; rather than learning, they rationalized; rather than seeking peace, they plotted; rather than rebuilding, they struggled for power. Insanity, radiation, illness, loneliness—all could have contributed to their state. Whatever the cause, it mattered little.

"Women were at a premium and were treated accordingly. Not as people, but as prizes and as prisoners. They satisfied lusts and created new beings. That was all. After death, they were studied and used for reproduction experiments. Craig W. sent a transmission back to Destiny saying he would return. He was frightened. He was afraid of what the survivors would do with the faster-than-light engine that he had created on the journey from Destiny.

"He never came back.

"Years later we received another transmission from an Earth ship outfitted with a variation of O'Neil's engine, the O'Neil Faster Than Light Drive, called the OD. The ship insisted on landing on our planet to offer the same opportunity it had presented to other inhabited planets in the galaxy. The Earth Ship *Opportunity* landed and greeted my forefolk with what they called an offer of a 'simple business transaction.'

"In return for certain natural elements to be chosen after a thorough study of Destiny had been made by their on-board experts, Earth would consider inviting us to join their Brotherhood of Planets. As members we would be supplied with humans for whatever purpose we required. Slaves, we asked? No, they replied. They would be humans, but not really humans. Living but not truly living. People made to conform with the host planet's wishes.

"My forefolk discovered the truth. Holocaust II was followed by the Natural Disaster, where nature rebelled against human abuse. The scientists and soldiers went underground again, stealing women in lightning raids made possible by their OD variations. During the Natural Disaster, the floods, the tornadoes, the volcanoes, the earthquakes, etcetera, the scientists did their jobs too well, using the human material with as little feeling as they had for their lab animals before.

"'It was for the ongoing good of their tortured world,' was the reasoning. 'We must save the human race,' was their battle cry. After nature's fury calmed, they returned to the surface to find the Northern Hemisphere almost entirely sunken, save for a circle of land that created a rough zero shape. On this ground they built a new fleet of space cruisers to bring their message of coexistence to their descendants in the stars.

"My forefolk killed the members of the Earth Ship *Opportunity* and destroyed their ship. We did not send any message, leaving their superiors to conclude that the dangers of space had done them in. But after six other Earth ships disappeared in our sector, the message became clear. We would have nothing to do with Earth or its people. Thus our planet became the stuff of legend.

"Earthens continued to struggle on their shrinking, violent world. As hard as the scientists worked, they could not supply all the 'humans' the other planets required. Soon all Earthens could do was make their inhuman humans simply try to save themselves. The Brotherhood of Planets collapsed, while Destiny became a myth.

"Destiny. Never reached. Only dreamed of."

Trigor's head sank. His feet were crossed and his hands lay palms upward on his knees. He sat on the bridge, which was suddenly cavernous and bathed in the dark blue light of Earth below and the gray light of the moon above.

Napoleon sidled over and rubbed herself against Larry's legs, settling down at the base of his chair. She closed her catlike eyes and her normally serene face showed great pain. But she would not cry. They had not made her cry when they had destroyed her planet, killed her parents, or tortured her brothers and sisters to death. She had not cried then, and she would not cry now. Tears marked a feline's face forever. She would not scar herself for anyone.

Larry sat straight and tense, trying to share her pain. He could not feel it, no matter how hard he tried. He had opened his eye ducts wide but no tears came. Instead, his eyes were washed with lubricant. He looked out the viewport, his lips turned down in sadness. Stars marched out toward infinity, blinking their wonder at him. He saw one bunch that looked like a blade-wielding warrior, another like a gem-breathing monster. He watched the tableau drift by and wondered why feeling never came to him.

He set the coordinates for their return trip to Earth and listened as Trigor continued.

"We have survived many generations untouched by other worlds. Our females ruled with their wisdom, our men protected the planet with their strength. We cherished our world, and it repaid our respect with seemingly endless bounty. But we instinctively knew it was finite. We had learned the lessons Earth had ignored. Our population was still small enough to control our desires willingly. We developed planetary systems as best we could, but we needed help. That is where my story truly begins."

"You mean there's more?" Mess blurted.

"Damper down," Larry groaned.

"There's more?"

"Damper down or I'll disconnect you," Larry said evenly. He had done it once before. Mess remembered and shut up.

Trigor rose from the floor and went over to where

his exoskeleton lay. He reached down and lifted the gray mass, holding it before him. Napoleon didn't even tense at that. She, like Larry, was completely under his spell. Trigor spoke as if alone, floating in space.

"We had been unique in the universe until the arrival of the Mantases. They said that they were named different things on different planets. But by humans, the description 'Mantas' was most apt. They said all this through their interpreters, the tiny, friendly, furry creatures that negotiated for them."

"The foozles?" Mess asked. "You've got foozles too?"

"We do not know them by that name," Harlan said. "We do not know them by *any* name. They simply said that they would speak for the Mantases even though it might be wiser to deal with the Mantases directly."

"That's a foozle, all right." Napoleon grimaced. "Polite and honest to the point you want to shoot your foodstufs."

"Foozles, then," said Trigor.

"Stupid name," said Mess, "but memorable."

"They had much to offer a thriving world in terms of organization. The Mantases could evaluate and solve complicated problems ingeniously. They offered their services as a show of good faith. We accepted them. No one knew then, no one knows now, what I know."

Larry and Napoleon looked at him at the same time.

"What?" Mess beat them to it.

Harlan Trigor was not born a soldier. He was made one. It was not enough that his ancestors had genetically adapted themselves to the tougher surroundings of the forest and jungles. It was not enough that his father was a premier space bullet, as his father was before him. It was not enough that his mother and sister were among the most respected on the beautiful planet. That would not help *him* survive.

Only he, and he alone, could guarantee his future, through strength, stealth, intelligence, and training— years of training starting from when he was born through the time he rose to his hind legs.

Strength he developed. Stealth nature provided. Intelligence was handed down genetically. Training was gained from every living person and every living thing. Life was a struggle where only the masterful excelled.

His childhood games were amended to tests. A sort of kickball was played, but one where no limb was ever used twice. Fingers, wrists, palms, elbows, fore-arms, shoulders, neck, forehead, nose, skull, chest, stomach, ribs, sides, hips, thighs, knees, backs of knees, legs, calves, ankles, feet, toes, soles were used to move the ball. Incredible contortions were possible through natural and developed double joints.

His formal education stressed cerebral exercises as well as the more subtle physical ones, such as motor coordination of the eyes and every muscle in the body.

Students spent hours each day in tubes, with lights in their eyes and sounds in their ears. Calibrations of stimuli were learned until they knew every facet of their reactions. Then followed serious physical train-ing of another kind. Fighting arts of several worlds were adapted for two arms, two legs, one head, and twenty digits, and with them, the philosophy, the energy-concentration techniques that made them all possible.

The secret of his success and the mark of an ex-traordinary man was to take all that had been taught him and improve upon it. That is what Harlan Trigor did. Already a young man of breeding, with warm eyes, a wavy black mane of hair, and a tightly muscled body, he not only garnered the unanimous respect of his fellows but stunned his teachers with his abilities. His blows were simpler, his muscle control more precise, his judgments more incisive, his reasoning more exact, his innate abilities seemingly fathomless.

On a world that constantly fought for survival, the Earth-normal of envy was almost negligible. The final proof came in his defense against the Skull Planet Pirates, whose ships had only begun to accumulate over the central city of Destiny when a team of space bullets led by Trigor was dispatched.

It could hardly be called a battle. He personally moved into the thickest area of their ships and dispatched five within seconds. His speed, use of specific weaponry, and aim were surprising even to more experienced veterans. Years of practice were united and improved upon within his body. His legend was born and grew immediately.

His stature would have been assured if not for the creatures who had appeared before his birth. In various cities the small, soft, sweet creatures appeared to kindly offer the assistance of their ugly mentors. After a suitable interim of preparation, the Mantases themselves appeared: six-feet-tall creatures with large triangular heads, two antennae, large, cylindrical bodies, two long, double-jointed hind legs, and two long, double-jointed arms with three surprisingly dexterous mandibles hanging underneath. They looked to be giant insects specifically suited to live in a human environment.

The humans instantly understood the need for the puppylike creatures. Organic mistrust would have been impossible to quell, even for the temperate Destinians. Even so, initial "misunderstandings" resulted in the wholesale slaughter of entire Mantas settlements. They continued until the creatures' innate intelligence and problem-solving abilities were discovered. They had a remarkable ability for mathematics and logistics and were invaluable during the Second Great Forest Problem, conceiving a far more consistent and satisfactory solution than the one the Destinians had solved the human-created First with.

Through cooperation a mutual language was devised and was soon phased out once all Mantases had mastered English. When one learned, they all learned. Other adaptation problems were solved through political and architectural means, with the patient, polite "translators" standing by to serve as bridges between the two races. In general, a Queen-approved plan was put into effect making the Mantases' transfer into human society as easy as possible. Soon their presence was accepted, their appearance commonplace, but interaction with them was never accepted as completely natural.

Still, it was not unusual for Harlan to find a Mantas waiting for him outside his consignment center—the blockhouse where he was launched from. Trigor had been promoted to the central takeoff location, the best-defended one, where the first bullets were almost always projected through the atmosphere. As always, the Mantas had one of the nicer-looking aliens by his side, which moved forward on its stocky, lightly furred hind legs.

"Although it would be wiser to speak directly to Ministic, the Queen's aide," it said in its rough voice, "you could still talk to me and I'll mediate."

"That's fine," said Trigor. "I would be proud to speak with Ministic...." He paused to get the doglike creature's name.

"Don't worry about me right now," it said, walking briskly away. "You talk to the Mantas. I'll be around."

Trigor watched it go until the Mantas spoke. "A fine battle," it said. Across its chest was a wooden medallion with a sparkling stone—the seal of a Queen's aide. It was a high honor for the Queen to send the insectlike advisor to him.

"I take greater pride in your presence," Harlan said, well aware of the eyes of his associates and passersby, who had all rushed over to congratulate him.

"I would be honored to join your return home and share your happiness," it said formally.

"Your wish makes the happiness greater," he said just as formally.

The two set off together, the walk at odds with proper conversation. The city was celebrating and not even Ministic's presence would temper the human exultation. Other soldiers bounced the bottom of their fists off Harlan's shoulders and chest. Women would smile and nod their approval, offering him their future company. Harlan moved easily through the adulation, the Mantas at his side making his steps all the more impressive.

The city was built to be harmonious with the environment. Wood begat wood, stone begat stone. Vehicles were simple, needing only the O'Neil variants to become practical. Roads connected towns, paths connected houses, channels connected cities. The highest technology was created and fostered by the natural waves of energy in the atmosphere and earth. Power generators, arrived at through a cunning combination of human and Mantas science, were housed in one-story stone buildings.

Even the most opulent of dwellings consisted of wood—treated wood made as strong as any Earth steel. Destiny was a stunning combination of the arcane and sophisticated. At surface, a quaint, rural existence, but just below that was a spiral of the supranatural.

Harlan moved through his town, admiring it all the more from the knowledge that this was what he had saved today. Here was something indeed to fight for. He loved the feel of the solid ground beneath the soles of his boots and his chest swelled with clean air. His hide shirt and pants felt good against his skin.

He came to the house where his friends and relatives had gathered; among the crowd were two Mantases who lived in the neighborhood. His sister, Hana, got to him first. She too had black hair, but hers was long and lustrous, with curves throughout. Her eyes too were brown but deep, wide, and rich. Her skin was not pale or pink but light brown and smooth. Boys all over the city dreamt of her as their partner.

She wrapped her arms around Harlan's neck and assailed him with a long kiss. The other space bullets there chanted raucously in unison until Harlan smacked her on the rear and swung her across his shoulders. He bore her into the center of their home—the huge, open main room—with the others following laughingly behind.

He set her down on the great wood banquet table, where he greeted his mother and father. He kissed his mother's forehead in a self-conscious show of respect, then hugged her to him. After a few seconds she stepped back, looked him over in mock disapproval, and said, "That's no way to treat your sister, young man."

The crowd roared its approval as his father spun him around. Arthur Trigor was a huge man with gray beard and mane. A more classic picture of Norse-like grandeur could hardly be envisioned. He had his hands proudly on Harlan's shoulders before they embraced.

Another roar went up from the gathered throng until Harlan made way for Ministic, the Mantas. A hush fell over the crowd when they spied the royal seal. Ministic was steel blue, the color of a female. She shone among the brown hues of the home and its rugged occupants.

"The Queen bears with me her greetings and congratulations," the creature began. "She also extends an invitation to be her honored guests during the next moon at a dinner honoring all the brave space soldiers."

The house was once more filled with the joyous thunder of the guests' voices. As the din died down, the Mantas concluded its speech. "Now you have a celebration of your own. I will return to the Queen to tell her of your happiness and approval."

The crowd gave way as Harlan accompanied Ministic to the street. As they passed, animated conversations started in their wake. By the time they reached the outside, the house was ablaze with exultation. The Mantas turned to Harlan. "This is for your knowledge only. At this dinner you will be awarded the Destinian Star."

Harlan was at a loss for words. The pompous reply he had been formulating disintegrated. He was expecting some sort of reward, but not the highest honor the planet had. That was reserved for people with lifetime achievements! "I cannot... I do not know how to express my wonder," he stammered.

"Accept the honor," Ministic advised. "Grave situations arise. You make them easier to bear. You shall deserve what you shall receive."

With that mysterious farewell, the steel-blue insect moved into the night with another puppy-dog assistant suddenly at her side. Harlan stared after them for a moment, trying to organize his thoughts and wipe her news away lest a friend read it on his face. It was swept away in a wave of pride that threw him back into his loving home.

The night was a jumbled haze of warm images. It was a sea of pleasure, building a fire's glow in his heart and soul. They ate, they drank, they laughed, they loved, and they sang. The bullets gathered by the fire with plenty of mead in them and full voice.

> We came from the world
> All rotted with death;
> To a garden like Eden
> Given Life's breath;
>
> Protect it we must
> For the Queen that we serve;
> In the air above us
> The land to preserve;
>
> Space soldiers all,
> Bullets shot into the deep;
> We outdive all others
> The planet to keep;
>
> From the womb we are born,
> It is what we must be;
> We're divers of glory
> And the sky is our sea.

FOUR

"I think I'm going to be sick," Napoleon said. The spell had broken. Trigor's unblemished memories of his idyllic planet were too much for the abused feline creature to bear.

"Shh."

Harlan continued.

Humming their song, the last of them left. The parents decided to wait until later to clean up, and went to their bed. Hana went to her brother and stood before him, the top of her head just reaching his brow. She looked him in the eye for a moment, then lightly tapped his chest with the bottom of her fist.

It was the most beautiful day of his life. Harlan encircled her with his arms and they held each other for minutes. When he finally released her, she stepped back. She let him look at her for a moment before turning toward the stairs. In the middle of her ascent she stopped by an open window and turned back to him. The illumination from outside made soft shadows across her face and along her hair.

Harlan knew from that moment on what the angels must look like. The love between a brother and a sister is a strange thing, made more wonderful by their strong moral heritage. She turned and continued up the stairs as he resisted a powerful urge to follow her. He wanted to take her away, keep her in a high tower, and protect her for the rest of his existence. Such beauty and grace no man deserved. No pain, no heartache should ever come to such a one.

Harlan went outside. He looked toward the Destinian sky, the aqua-colored sky no Earthen had seen for many years. He felt the mild rays of their system's sun.

All preparations for the next moon dinner had been made. Destiny's large moon would only appear in the night sky once a week. Harlan was ready when it showed. He wore his finest tunic, boots, and breeches, all made from the painstaking interweaving of a certain jungle tree's bark with the classic worm larva that had been bred on the Earth ship that first discovered the world. On one sleeve was the green encircled dot, mark of the space bullets.

Ministic's adorable canine aide had appeared earlier in the day with strict instructions. "Since you're the honored one," it said quickly in the creature's normal clipped, almost bored tones, "you should arrive early at the southeast entrance of the Mile Long Castle. We'll be waiting for you. Ministic, the Queen's aide, will see to you personally." Again the little canine left before Harlan could get its name or anything else.

By the time Harlan reached the southeast point, darkness had almost returned to Destiny. This world orbited around its sun, giving the planet day and night on roughly the same scale as Earth. But the moon swung around the globe vertically, making the light hard to come by. Even with the sun in the sky, the night would be gloomy.

Harlan pounded on the heavy wooden door. It opened in a few seconds and Ministic stood before him, her insect body shrouded in a garment of rose. Having been accustomed to the Mantases since birth, he was not put off by their customs or proximity.

"Welcome," came her voice. "Come. We will prepare you."

Harlan had been in the castle only once before, and that was for his official induction into the space bullets. It had occurred in the mile-long throne room, which occupied the center of the palace. Although the population lived simply (sometimes austerely) no one begrudged their female ruler her pomp and ceremony. In fact, they demanded it.

So this second visit held only wonder for Harlan. He was led through stone corridors with wood floors and wood corridors with stone floors. All were illuminated by ceilings that shone with soft white light. Like rivers emptying into the sea, the Mantas and the soldier emerged into a large room with tall windows. On the floor were clear bubbles the size of Destiny's personal street vehicles. They were recreations of nature in amazing forms—three-dimensional representations of Destiny: its forests, its cities, its jungles, its seas. There was one full-size recreation of the planet and a final globe with a working model of Earth inside—the Earth that Craig M. O'Neil had died on.

"Our room of wonder," said Ministic. "Here we see how different things are actually alike. Here we chart the many possible fates of our world."

Harlan did not completely understand, nor did he notice that he was the only human in the room. The others were blue, black, and gray Mantases. Even as the Queen's aide led him away, the fact that there weren't any foozles did not completely register.

The two moved into a corridor of great opulence. The walls and floors were carved wood except for a path down the center that led to all the rooms. The ceiling was not uniformly illuminated—rather, half globes of light were interspersed among more wood carvings. The work was exacting and must have taken ages to create.

Harlan was speechless. Even a Destinian male, and an accomplished warrior at that, was still very much a yokel when it came to wealth. Harlan only knew comfort and personal accomplishment. He did not know, but was not made uncomfortable by, this sort of luxury. His mouth did not hang open, but he was hard pressed not to stumble about, staring at everything in the hallway.

Ministic stopped before a door on the right and motioned. "You must wait here until called. There is illumination if you wish it and refreshment. Please help yourself. It will be a long time before you eat."

Harlan stepped in and Ministic closed the door behind him. The room was fairly large but no longer than a normal living room. To the left, against the wall, was a large, soft bed. To the right of that was a table with a dial that controlled the illumination's intensity. The only light coming into the room was from the window where the moon shone. In that temporary light Harlan also saw a beautifully carved wood chair with an interlocking branch design and a broad, strong table on which sat a round stone mug.

Harlan lifted the cup. Inside was a rich purple liquid. The art of wine making had not been lost in the colonization process. The fruits of the food-rich planet made excellent brew. Harlan breathed its aroma deeply, his stomach gurgling. He realized that he had not eaten all day. As he raised the cup to his lips, his stomach tightened. He then realized that he was too nervous to drink. It would do him little good to start spitting up during dinner. Best to wait until he had food in him. He moved to the window while trying to calm down.

He took in the family of trees embracing just outside. Below was the central city, alight with orange warmth and brown yewn security. All around were the stone factories and the security settlements in the forest and jungles beyond. Harlan realized he would gladly risk his life in any way for this still-virginal world. When a society is growing right, it becomes bigger than its occupants, and all their thoughts go out to it. When the society grows cancerous, all human thoughts drool selfishly inside.

Harlan also realized he was still holding the drink in his hand and someone was coming. He did not want to risk insulting Ministic by not partaking, so he quickly emptied the liquid out the window. In the many long days of anguish that followed, he often wished he had drunk it.

The door opened and Ministic's foozle entered. "You drank it?" it asked. Harlan showed it the empty mug. "Good. Just a matter of time now." And it closed the door.

Harlan's nervousness was not helped by the furry creature's appearance. It was hard not to love the cute, direct aliens—they established a natural subconscious attachment through human memories of pet dogs in the past—but there always seemed to be so much the terse aliens weren't saying. Harlan sat down on the bed. The nervousness continued to claw at his stomach pit.

He decided to lie down. That decision saved his life for the second time that night. He felt his heartbeat slow. He felt his respiration slow. He felt his mind clear. He felt the door to the room open.

He did not have to see it. He felt it as surely as if he had opened it himself. The delicate atmosphere in the room was disturbed by it, the darkness of the room blending with the strange darkness of the hall. It had not been dark before. The illumination had been eliminated so that whoever was entering would not be discovered.

The odor of the drink refilled Harlan's clean brain. He felt the sensation over again, his mind having "recorded" it. There was something special about this wine, all right. Something had been added to it. He did not have to see it or smell it clearly (he was a space bullet, by Destiny!).

The small figure moved toward the bed. It was not a foozle or a Mantas. It was a hunched human carrying something in his right hand. Harlan's other senses kicked in. Then his feet kicked out.

One foot expertly knocked what the man was carrying onto the table. Then both feet were at the man's throat. The top of one foot was behind the man's neck. The other foot was stepping on the man's neck.

He died with a small wheezing sound, as if air were being pushed out his ears. Hardly two seconds had passed. Harlan lowered the man to the floor with his legs. He released the head, which flopped down like a deflated balloon. Trigor wiped his feet on the fallen man's shirt. The killing had not made a sound.

Harlan was up and at the thing sticking into the table. It was as he had thought. A disruptor. A pencil-thin, pointed blade which used energy waves to hemorrhage internal organs. If the man had plunged it into Trigor's body, his interior would have been so much sludge in a matter of seconds.

Harlan had to kill without raising an alarm or allowing his attacker to. Who knew how many associates were with him? All he knew was that someone had entered the room intending to kill him. Disruptors had been outlawed on Destiny as needlessly sadistic. An attack force had somehow avoided attention, reached sacred soil, and even infiltrated the Queen's palace.

His eyes were already adjusted to the dark. He went to the dead man and searched him. Nothing but Destinian clothes and a human, though bloated face. He went to the door and listened intently. Hearing nothing, he hazarded stepping out. The hallway was empty, but the illumination was not as bright as it had been. Could the pirates have taken control of the energy sources? And why hadn't their landing ships been spotted? Did they have some sort of new weapon that rendered Destiny's first line of defense inoperable? What madness was it that they were in the castle trying to kill him in silence?

His training eradicated his reasoning. Questions that could not be answered should not be asked. Harlan had to act on what he already knew. He moved back to his doorway as he heard a sound ahead. A group of black and gray Mantases had come around the corner, several of them rubbing antennae. With an inward sigh of relief, Harlan came out of the shadows.

"Quick," he said sharply, "protect the Queen. I will notify the space bullets of . . ."

That was as far as they let him get. A gray Mantas to his left suddenly rose into the air, its wings sliding open and pushing down. It came directly at him and he instinctively dodged. A mandible ripped across his cheek. His brain kicked over to automatic. Without wanting or meaning to, he switched on the disruptor and threw it into the pasing gray Mantas. Even before that action was complete, he was already running down the hall toward the others.

The flying Mantas crashed to the wooden floor as Trigor leaped onto a black Mantas, both feet landing solidly on the alien's chest. It was like slamming onto a padded hard board. Harlan stopped in midair and the Mantas was hurled back. It fell as Harlan landed on his feet, crouched, and spun right. He came up under the remaining Mantas' chopping mandible to smash his forearm against the creature's eyes and antennae. He dropped it like a stone.

Harlan retreated quickly then, trying to organize his attack and thoughts. The war haze cleared, leaving horror in its wake. He surveyed the scene with confusion. His lurching stomach made him spin and hold the sides of the doorway for support. There was no doubt. The Mantas trio had meant him harm. A space bullet could recognize physical threat in any known creature instantly.

But why? The question ripped across his mind like a hacksaw blade. Still, the first thing to do was to alert the others and protect the Queen. Every battle had to have a central point. He mustn't disperse his energies. He unerringly turned toward where he knew the throne room must be. His thoughts of Destinian protection were overridden as half a dozen other Mantases came around the corner. All he could think of then was escape.

They swarmed at him. He knew their purpose, as unbelievable as it seemed. With a single leap he was back inside his room and over the bed. Another step and he was on the windowsill, then in the air, soaring through the night toward a tangle of trees thirty feet beyond.

He felt the rush of air across his body, the flash of star and moonlight, the jumbled haze of light, wood, ground, stone, and fire. Then his feet smacked a wide branch. He had landed standing. He was a space bullet, what else? There was a crunch of loose bark as his body hurtled forward. He dove through a small frame made by several trees, then grabbed another round branch, which gave as he swung beneath it.

He fell, his middle slamming into another branch. He curled around it like a gymnast, spinning, his legs moving up and over, the top of his figure following. He was rising, his body arching, his arms in an upward swan dive. He brought his legs forward and dropped twenty feet, hitting the twig- and leaf-packed ground. He rolled, somersaulted, and was on his feet again, running through the brief forest, toward the city beyond.

Now let the Mantases come! he thought in his haste. No gray fliers or float-belted pirate could navigate this tangle of trees. And no weapon could be fired without raising an alarm, and by their actions he knew that was the last thing the attackers wanted. Although the blood pounded in his ears, he could not tell if anything else was unusual. The castle was ominously quiet, as was the city beyond. He could scarcely believe he was their only target.

Two Mantases came at him from both sides. They were trying to keep pace with each other, but Harlan knew the one to his right would reach him just before the other. Those few seconds would be all the time he needed. He moved even faster toward them. Their arms were up and their sharp, triangular mandibles faced him. He hurtled at their skittering figures.

Just before the right Mantas' fore mandible seemed destined to be part of Harlan's face, his ankles locked, his knees bent, and he hurtled sideways through the air. His feet dove into the Mantas body and he swung the broken branch, which he still held. The wood broke the creature's antennae and Trigor used the alien torso as a backstop. He vaulted headfirst into the left Mantas. He ripped the antennae from the creature's skull as it fell, somersaulting over its oozing head.

He was back on his feet and running, dread mingling with his war frenzy. He knew he stood no chance alone, but his fellows were either at the palace dining or dead. And if they were innocently eating, they would be without weapons in the Queen's presence. The idea of treacherous Mantases was incredible, but not unthinkable. Any thing had desires and anything could be turned.

He needed time and he needed weapons. He needed to be at his home or at the launch center. Proximity made his decision. Before he had decided completely, his legs were pumping him home. He sped through the woods with an incredible animal grace, making split-second decisions and adapting his mobile ankles and feet to ensure each step landed solidly on the uneven forest surface. His route was as straight and swift as possible. It didn't make any difference. He was already too late.

The Trigors discussed their daughter as they lay in loving darkness on the bed. Grayle lay with her back to Arthur, who held her to him, their body warmth more than a match for the night air. They had decided to let Hana decide her own pubescent fate naturally. Such family perfection could not be marred by a father's obtuseness or a mother's overprotection. It was this very perfection that made their destruction seem so preordained.

Arthur became aware of the presence first. He jerked up in bed, seeing the clear silhouette of a foozle in front of the window. He looked to his right. The sweet, trusting face of another foozle stared at him. The creature was at its best. Its fuzzy head was cocked. Its long ears hung to its rounded shoulders. Its mouth was wide with a sad smile. Its black, shining eyes were soulful.

Then it all changed. The lips moved back off the yellowing teeth. New eyes, like full-sized lenses, dropped over the black globes. These were tinted eyes now, re-formed to enhance the evil, dangerous expression. These were the creature's second eyes, which only came down when the monsters were ready to attack. This was the second-to-last image Arthur saw.

He felt Grayle move beside him. He looked at her. A disruptor was in her neck. It was the image of her horrible, inflated expression and bubbling skin that he took with him. A disruptor sunk into his own neck from behind.

Hana opened her eyes suddenly and sat up to scream. Something flew into her mouth. Something grabbed her tongue. A Mantas held her tongue in its pincers as other insects and their foozles moved quickly around the room. All that was required to keep her captive were the needlelike pincers over and under her tongue. It paralyzed her voice and limbs. She sat up in bed, drooling and grunting as a foozle beside her communicated with the ship outside by way of a collar transmitter.

"You all set?" it asked. "We're all set." It listened, then started to argue. "I don't want to take time for that. The guy got away, didn't he? Who needs him coming back here? Hey, you made the deal, I didn't. I don't have to abide by the rules. All right, all right. Just be ready," the foozle barked at its comrades. "They want her dressed up."

All the other foozles groaned. They said things like, "Oh, come on," "Do we have to?" and "This is ridiculous!"

"She has to be decked out or we can't go," the head foozle whined, like an adolescent camp counselor. The others all whinnied again. Hana thought she was going mad.

The Earthen moved slowly from foot to foot. He breathed into his cupped hands, even though it was not cold. Ministic had little use for nervous posturing. She simply kept track of the passing moments, making sure they stayed within their strict time schedule. The Earthman stopped rocking and rubbed the sweat off his palms onto his pants.

"What if he gets back here?" he asked like a boy on his first date. The Mantas did not deign to answer, checking instead on the compact craft crewed by the Earthen's assistants. It was dark in color and unmarked. It was capable of silent flight at any altitude. It was but one of the Earthman's private fleet.

The Mantas turned back to the Trigor home and looked up. The girl would be nearly prepared, she thought. If Ministic had looked up a second earlier, she would have seen Harlan jump from a tree into the open window. Instead, she saw his shadow recede into the room but did not recognize it for what it was. A noise made her look down. The back door opened and the foozles came out with the girl.

She had been done up like a human foozle. The tiny creatures had pulled one of their own pairs of thin, blue, shiny, legless shorts over her haunches. It just barely covered her pelvic region. Across her chest was an intricate swash of bandage, which held her breasts in place without covering them unduly. From her shoulders were draped the clear, clingy, sparkling capes the foozles wore on special occasions.

"You happy now?" the foozle with the leash asked. "She's dressed."

The Earthen smiled, hard pressed to contain his excitement. They stopped her before him.

"This is really an EM?" he said in awe. "Are you sure?"

"Don't waste time," Ministic said. "Can't you see?"

The Earthen placed both his hands on Hana's perfect breasts and squeezed. She reared back.

"You satisfied?" asked a foozle in exasperation. "Let's get out of here."

All Bishop-Fortune did was turn to Ministic, nodding and smiling. Oh, yes, they definitely had a deal.

Harlan moved with utmost skill, his way totally silent. To a normal man his presence would not be felt even if he were directly looked at. His body was in shadow at all times, as if he carried the darkness with him. He heard movement everywhere in and around the house but could see nothing.

He moved into his sister's room. Empty save for a bed unmade, the covers half on the floor, her nightclothes in a corner pile. He moved slowly to the doorway, sniffing for danger like an animal. He formulated his plan. His family must have joined the other residents in celebration of the space bullet dinner. They must have all gone to the castle. He would have little chance of finding allies in the empty neighborhood. He would have to go to the consignment center.

Harlan slipped into his parents' room. He bit his tongue, then clamped his teeth down to keep from screaming.

The two grumbling foozles raced up the stairs. Kill the parents, kidnap the sister, dress her up like a slave doll, clean up. It never ended. Why not just burn the place down? They trotted into the parents' room, opening the large body bags. On the floor were two corpses. Both seemed to loll against the wood beneath them as if their skin could barely hold their insides. The skin was unnaturally rounded and smooth, with nary a crease. The faces were slack, limp, longer than before, the eyes big jelly balls.

The foozles started to pull the bags over the squiggly bodies. One kicked the male corpse's hand, which felt like a gelatin sausage. It was the doglike creature's last thought before its head became mush. The other foozle became aware of the dark shape dropping from the ceiling just before the human foot rammed its alien jawbone into its alien brain.

Harlan bounded to the window. He looked down. Ministic looked up. A dozen stingers were fired at him from the dark shape of the space vehicle. Harlan was driven back into the room by chips of flying wood as the spatting stinger needles spun through the air. Bishop-Fortune dragged Hana Trigor toward the ship. She heard her brother's cry and tried to call back, but the sodden packing choked her and the gag tore her skin. Her arms were numb and her legs sought some sort of purchase, but the leg hobble snapped taut.

She heard shouts as Bishop-Fortune carried her into the ship. He ordered others to move outside. She heard Ministic tell them that Harlan must die for the plan to take effect. Then she was thrown to a couch and covered by a soft body. The air was forced from her lungs. She tried to squirm out from beneath the weight, but she was too weak, unable to breathe.

"Relax," a strange voice whispered in her ear. "It's over now—at least for you."

A sudden whirring noise and a hiss of sealed air.

Then the ship took off. Thus was she stripped, pinned by her buyer's body, and abducted from her world.

Harlan had given up trying to comprehend. His parents had been murdered, his sister shamefully assaulted and kidnapped, and the Queen's most trusted aide was trying to kill him. He did not understand and he did not care to. The beauty of the planet held no more meaning. It might as well have been the surface of the sun.

He tore the disruptors from his parents' heads, jumped over the still-quivering bodies of the cleaning foozles, and ran out the bedroom door. From the top of the stairs he heard feet running toward the front door. He switched on one disruptor and sent it spinning down the stairs. It sank into the front wall with a humming thunk. As the door below it sprang open, stinger-armed pirates entered and fell over the escaping foozles.

The next disruptor flew from Harlan's hand onto the floor. Other pirates pushed over their fallen comrades only to drop into the cellar. The disruptors could rend wood as well as mulch flesh. The wrenched-apart wood fell all around the routed attackers. Harlan catapulted from the top stair to the disrupted entrance. He rolled outside, grabbing a stinger from a fallen man's hand. As he rose he sent four needles into a pirate's neck. He took not one backward glance at his home, now a sagging, rotted structure. His home was forgotten. His parents were forgotten. Ministic was forgotten. His only wish now was to get his suit, stop the ship, and save his sister. He fired madly, rushing toward the launch center.

The Queen's Mantas appeared from hiding once he had gone. "Make certain the bodies will never be found," she instructed the survivors. "I must return to the castle." The foozles went with her.

The pirates needed no elucidation. They would do as they were bid and get off the well-defended planet through the hole the Mantases had made. Once back into deep space they could dump their casualties and the Trigor parents into the vacuum void, where they would implode and disintegrate.

Harlan gained entrance to the takeoff center with the key he always had with him. He moved down the sloping hallway to his compartment. He was not even considering an alarm. He didn't have time. He would raise an alarm once in space and explain when he returned. He could not wait. The pirate ship already had a head start. Within Destiny space he could find and cripple it. In deep space he would be lost.

Drastic times called for drastic deeds. He ran to the lab. He mounted a force crane on his shoulders. The device fit over his shoulders with armrests that ended in hand grips. Place any object between the grips' forks and energy waves would lift it, whatever the weight. Harlan lifted a space bullet O'Neil Drive. It was fashioned as his suit was: curved, bumpy, rock-like.

The launch center was operational at all times. Each piece of equipment had its own power supply, so even in the event of the central energy source being knocked out the space bullets could go into action. Harlan placed the O'Neil Drive near the rear of his suit. The molecules adhered automatically. The suit had a hump.

Although he had not exerted any effort lifting or installing the Drive, Harlan's body was covered in sweat. He released the force crane with an effort, his hands slick and his muscles tight. He had to get into his exoskeleton and then the suit. More precious time. It was running out from all sides.

Ministic slid out of her vehicle at the castle. She checked to see if her rose draping was sufficiently rent by wood chips and stained with her brethren's liquid. The foozles took the vehicle away without a word. She entered the palace and raced to the throne room. The Mantases, like the foozles, became totally alien when they ran. Both kinds reverted to their original heritages: insects and dogs. They were fast and they were frightening.

As she grew near, she heard the sounds of the celebration. All the city's residents must have been allowed into the mile-long room to join the reveling. Several human guards noticed the Mantas' condition but did nothing. They were not bidden. Ministic reached the door without help and waited until the cheering inside had quieted. Then she entered screaming.

"Traitors! Insurrection! They have tried to steal your life and your rule!"

Harlan was scared. He had always been launched by his team. Masses of input were always fed in to him as he was launched, preparing him for battle. The enemy's location would be pinpointed, the men were lined up like bullets in a rifle magazine, waves of calming information pumped through, and they were shot into the atmosphere rapid-fire.

He was ready. His eyes did not see, his limbs did not feel. He was safe inside his suit. Warm, at peace, supremely powerful. Each time was like being born again. The wonder, the agonizing, terrifying wonder!

He floated across the floor until he was centered in the launch chamber. After switching to operative, he would be automatically secured into position, the chamber would be locked, and he'd be shot into orbit. When the entire team was there, all the chambers seemed to blast at once. The entire city felt the powerful throb.

His suit arms set off a tiny beam of force, lightning fingers. The chamber came alive. Instantly he knew all. The ship he wanted was almost out of orbital range. His muscles danced. The launch center equipment readjusted the chamber's aim to the proper calibration. Harlan blinked. The hunk of space debris, the lone space bullet, blasted into the sky.

Information burned into his senses at a rate beyond his comprehension but just within his understanding. He did not know how he accrued all the material, but his mind worked without him. Automatic movements of obscure muscles controlled everything. His speed multiplied by the millisecond. He exulted in his power. His sister was not helpless. He could not fail. He had to save her. He must. He would.

There was no doubt here. Inside the suit Harlan Trigor was a god. The kidnappers thought they would slip out into uncharted space. They would maintain their lead until they were lost among the stars. No chance. One minimal burst of the O'Neil Drive and Harlan would be in front of them. He lanced toward the ship. A muscle moved to initiate the drive.

Red, the universal color. Then more colors, more warnings. They crowded his consciousness, elbowing out the rescue. He had been hit. Damage. Impossible! No other ships were in orbit or launched. Damage. From below. Only Destiny itself had the ability to circumvent a space bullet's powers. Damage. His planet, his own people had fired upon him just as the O'Neil Drive was taking effect.

Harlan Trigor, space bullet, spun into warp space beyond the speed of light.

In the wrong direction.

FIVE

"I don't believe it," said Mess. "The science doesn't work."

"One thing you should've already learned," said Larry with disgust. "Scientists know nothing about life. They only know science."

The stars stared on impassively as Harlan neared the end of his discourse. He remained on his haunches, arms upside down on his crossed legs. He looked like a swami of fortune.

"I sped for light-years, overwhelmed in a space bullet's form of unconsciousness. An overload. After I regained my senses I could not shut down the O'Neil Drive. I could not change course. I traveled for six months."

"Six months!" Napoleon cried. "In that thing?" She pointed at the suit. The idea of even an hour in an environment as small as that made her tail curl.

"After the O'Neil Drive turned off, I drifted for months more."

Napoleon fell to her forepaws and shook.

"A year! A year in that thing," Larry said in wonder, looking in confusion at the rocklike uniform, then at Trigor. For him, used to the *Black Hole* and its company, not to mention huge expanses of space always in eyeshot, a year in the space bullet suit seemed like being buried alive. Why wasn't Trigor hopelessly insane? Or for that matter who was to say that he wasn't?

"You do not understand," Harlan told them. "Inside I am at peace, at one with the universe. Sensory imput never ceases. It is always changing. All aspects of my brain and body are stimulated and treated. A man drifting alone in the vastness of space would surely go mad. But I can see myself as anything, anywhere. I am nourished, cleansed, and exercised."

The looks on their faces told Trigor they still didn't completely buy it. "My psychology has been adapted," he shrugged. "I am motionless but always moving. Neither my mind nor muscles atrophy."

Larry still couldn't comprehend it, but he couldn't deny the reality sitting before him. Trigor was betrayed, defeated, and lost, but he did not seem insane. "But what was the Mantases' purpose?" he asked when Harlan remained silent. "Why did they kill your parents and not your sister? Why not kill you in a more certain way?"

"I have thought on this long and hard," Harlan said quietly.

"You've had the time," said Napoleon.

"My family had done nothing to them, so revenge could not be the motive. The Mantases seem uninterested in humans, so lust could not be the motive."

"Profit?" Napoleon suggested.

"They already have great wealth," said Harlan. "The only thing that makes sense is that they needed ... what is the word? A person to take the blame."

"Patsy," said Mess. "Fall guy, pigeon, dupe, tool, sucker, gudgeon, cat's-paw."

"What's that?" said Napoleon sharply.

"Cat's-paw," Mess repeated. "You want the antonyms?"

"I want you to damper down!" Larry directed at the omnipresent computer. "Fall guy for what?"

"Nothing short of a takeover," Harlan summed up. "Destiny is a lush jewel, a shelter, a home, the ultimate prize...."

"Enough already," Napoleon moaned.

"Many races would do almost anything to possess it," Trigor continued. "The Mantases have shared this with us for years, only to have treachery in their hearts."

"Mantases don't have hearts," said Mess. "They have brains, though. Only the thought of treachery would fit...."

"*Damper!*" Larry suggested warningly. "So why kill your family? Why not kill the Queen and get it over with?"

"I wouldn't want to take on the space bullets," Napoleon mused. "I'd keep the populace in the dark and for that I'd need a..."

"Pigeon," said Mess. "A patsy, a fall guy—"

"Enough!" Larry barked.

"Sucker," said Mess.

Larry ignored the final gibe. "You mean they would kill the Queen and say your family did it, then set up a new government which they would control?"

"Isn't that what I just said?" Napoleon complained.

"She is right," said Harlan.

"Well!" Larry exclaimed. "It's obvious they haven't succeeded."

"How can you be so sure?" Trigor asked hopefully. "It's been a year."

"A year with six months' faster-than-light travel," added Mess.

"Mantases are all over the place," Larry explained, ignoring the ramifications of Mess' statement. "Or at least on every planet I know of. If they had taken over Destiny, it would have been wide open to galactic trading by now. We'd have heard about it."

Harlan pondered Larry's theory. "Keeping it all for themselves does not seem consistent with their history," he reasoned.

"Your escape crimped their action!" Napoleon suddenly realized. "They don't dare move ahead with you still at large."

Even so, Trigor's head remained low and his tone glum. "Still, I am helpless. My suit is damaged, the O'Neil Drive is now useless, my sister is lost to me, and my planet is ultimately doomed."

"Wow," said Mess. "Mr. Self-pity."

Larry slapped down on the compubot connection. Mess was not off but they could not hear him. There had been no great grief in Harlan's monotone, just empty failure, but that apathy made his declaration all the more chilling. Larry sat with Napoleon curled at his feet. His mind lobbed Trigor's story back and forth.

If "a" was the conspiracy and "b" the catalyst and "c" was the takeover, then "a" minus "b" did not equal "c." Now, given that, if "d" was his sister and "e" was Destiny, then "e" minus "d" equaled "x." This was fun, but what was "x"? And what about the why? Larry's eyes drifted to Earth. It was a molten blue marble in a black eye. That did it. He had the solution. He took on his role of captain of the ship.

"You can repair your suit here. Your O'Neil Drive can be replaced with an OD. We'll find your sister somehow. And as for your planet, well, we'll see what we can do when we get there."

It had taken awhile to quiet Mess down and convince him of the plan, but finally, as the two pilots prepared to drop back to Earth, the machine had dipped into its spare parts and manifested itself into a four-wheeled, four-armed vehicle. A mobile toolbox.

It begrudgingly assisted Harlan in what he foresaw as at least a day-long tune-up job (even with computerized cross-checking). When any damage was found, it was a toss-up whether Mess could repair it with the *Black Hole*'s equipment. Napoleon and Larry had returned the beamers to the compartment, much to Mess' disapproval.

The machine had fallen right in line with the exodus concept; that was no problem. In terms of long-range preservation, getting away from Earth was a priority. Once Larry and Napoleon were ATed, the dismantler wouldn't be far behind. Working with Trigor seemed to be the main stumbling block. It made sense to Mess for the pilots to take their beamers along in case they could get any real ammo for them, but Larry knew the guns would be confiscated as soon as they landed.

Larry looked down at his blue, long-sleeved, U-neck top and gray pants over his tall, thin body. He wriggled his toes in the brown socboos, the "sock and boot all in one!" It was what all the well-dressed EX-FMs were wearing. He smiled a wide, reassuring smile at Napoleon as the two moved to the esc-globe.

"We had better go separately," he suggested. "In case of trouble."

"No, let's go together."

"Nap, it would probably be better—"

"Let's go together, all right?" Napoleon snarled, her voice tight. Larry suddenly realized that she was scared. He wondered why he wasn't.

"All right," he answered, pulling himself into the globe, coming up behind two seats and the U-shaped control board. As Napoleon rose behind him, Larry sat and pressed a button.

"All systems checked and ready," came Mess' voice. "Come back soon. Don't leave me with this creep too long."

Larry pressed another button as the feline sat down next to him. The globe rolled down the chute and out the hatch Mess had opened. Larry pressed a third button and instantly the opaque ball became clear and the vastness of space stretched around them. They had felt no queasiness from the roll and the rug suddenly going out. This was space and they had been through the routine many times.

Mess maintained a vacuum for the second it took them to roll out, and then the proper atmosphere was attained inside the ball. If anything had gone wrong on rollout, the two would have boiled and imploded inside the globe, but those were the chances you took as an EX or FM. The first time the glassular pod went clear, Larry had cracked his head on the ceiling when he jumped in surprise and Napoleon had tried clawing back into the *Black Hole*. But they were used to it now, more or less.

Napoleon looked back as they floated away from the ship. Every time she did this it seemed something new hung on the outside of the large, cylindrical hunk of spaceship. From the cone-shaped bridge area to the variety of shacklike compartments jutting out of its sides, there were balls, squares, antennae, pans, mirrors, fans, grids, and holes, all signifying something. Only a few were important. Most had largely been forgotten.

When a young Larry had first started working on it, he meant to build a ship for every occasion. In back was the gridlike housing for the four reentry escglobes, two more than the U.W. scientists said he needed. Larry said company might drop in. Then there was the huge cylindrical engine area, which housed only the tiny motor. The rest of that space was taken up with storage and catwalks.

She turned back to look at Larry, hardly believing that the sandy-haired, lanky young man with the big nose, the big bright gray eyes, and the body seemingly fashioned from irregular metal bones had made it all work. If not for the years of punishment etched in his skin, he would look almost goofy. Instead, he looked like a starving innocent who wasn't quite aware that he was hungry yet.

Napoleon tugged at her one-piece suit's crotch and settled back in the chair. "Where are we going to get an OD?"

"I don't know," said Larry. "We'll have to look."

"And how are we going to find his sister?" She was expecting the same reply. She was surprised.

"By Trigor's description, she was kidnapped by an Earth ship. How many Earthens are there capable of trespassing on Destiny simply to steal some flesh?"

Napoleon sniffed. "All right, smart guy. How do you expect to get to Destiny? Earth isn't about to let us leave and the Destinians kill all Earthens!"

Larry looked over at his co-pilot slyly. "No one in their kindest moments could call us Earthens. Come on, Nap, tell me how much longer are we going to last down there?" His thumb jabbed downward. Napoleon mirrored his action as answer.

The world of black and pinpointed white changed

to overwhelming blue as they came through the clouds. Everywhere was the incredible variety of ocean; here some choppy gray-blue, there some wavy blue-green, then a sparkling yellow-blue. Only in a few places was it black or orange. There was hope for the planet yet. Only the sun reflecting off the water and off the ball was frying the pilots' eyes. Larry jabbed another button, which tinted the globe yellow so all turned deep green.

"Thank Cheshire," Napoleon breathed as the globe dropped across the coast. They sped over a wide strip of land, then over the sea again. The United States were united now in a doughnut shape, crossing a great chunk of what used to be Canada along the top, sweeping down into a thinner band that used to be hunks of California and Texas, then wrapping up through pieces of Kentucky, Ohio, and New York.

Larry's hands were over the board as they neared the Denver Plateau. The boys at the Providence Spaceport were supposed to handle everything from there, but if the TMs were on duty they had a nasty habit of being real lax with FM esc-globes.

The commlink crackled and the commercials began. They were nearly home now. They had hit the Adband.

LOW, INVITING VOICE: Tough trip? Relax and visit Providence's best Dreamport, the Lush Siesta, where your every wish is our command. *(whispered conspiratorial tone)* Your ... EVERY ... wish. *(music cue)* SINGING GIRL CHORUS: Your every wish is our command at the Lush Siesta. QUICK VOICE: See our representative at the entry bay.

HEARTY VOICE: Need your valuables handled with personal, individual care? Then just press I.D.

01141 and your circash number for *(echo effect)* Space-port Transfers. *(voice normal)* The only service with style! If it's THAT important, you need *(echo effect)* Spaceport Transfers!

SONG: Hungry, thirsty, bursting for love? FRIENDLY VOICE-OVER: You dream it, we do it! At Dream Universe! See what you want to see! Do what you want to do! SONG UP FULL: If you want to eat hearty, if you want an orgy party, you don't have to wait; in by four, out by eight! There's no rush—at Dream Universe. There's no crush—at Dream Universe. Take your time, relax, be still, gorge yourself, plunder, and kill. At *(big finish)* Dream Universe! QUICK VOICE: Look for the red dots on Providence concourse C.

"They must have spent a lot of circash for that one," Napoleon figured.

"Actually, the opening spot costs more," Larry told her.

"Really?"

"Sure."

They were a captive audience, so they tried to enjoy it. After the always touchy reentry maneuvers, after the problem-fraught landing procedures, the ECG Industry Division hit you with everything they had. The commercials ran every second in the spaceport but those could be mentally phased out. Businesses used cutthroat practices to get on the Adband, the worldwide blanket of commercials that assailed every landing ship.

SOLEMN SONG: Look for the FM label. Whatever you're doing, wherever you are, in P-shop, restaurant, or bar, look for the FM label and you won't—go—

wrong! REASSURING VOICE: Have a wonderful visit. Enjoy our beautiful planet. But be sure not to do business with anyone but an authentic TM with the proper RH factor. How to be sure? Just look for the FM label. And remember, if you have any doubts, call the Comps! QUICK VOICE: This has been an important message from the United World Brotherhood, a division of the Earth Central Government.

Napoleon and Larry looked at each other.

FAST, STRIDENT VOICE: It's a great land out there! It's a great world! It just makes you want to shoot something! Take it from me, I'm the one who knows. The minute you leave your weapon behind—the things you see when you don't have a mazer! It'll drive you crazy! But don't worry; I've got what you need: mazers, tazers, spitters, beamers with new Fulblast ammo, shafters, crinklers, tumblers, complete Cremor Adjusthunks, and the new, brand new, Maghawk Strepper! I'm talking Maghawk Streppers here, REAL Maghawk Streppers. Come to me, come see me first! Here! Now! Providence level J. You can't miss me. I won't miss YOU!

Larry shook his head. "What that guy can do with fifteen seconds," he marveled. Morgan-Fullmer took up all of level J with his weapons store.

TEMPERATE, WISE VOICE: It's a great life here on Earth. It's a wonderful world. Anything you ever wanted is right here for the taking. But I know. I know. Sometimes things can get out of hand. Sometimes...well, you know what I mean. You're ready for things, but...things aren't quite ready for you.

At times like this you need FulBright, the pharmaceutical company with you in mind. We carry a full line of relaxants, temporers, and libaids for whatever the difficulty. Look for our products everywhere. And remember . . . read the label.

Napoleon was ready to scratch something. Her teeth were on her lower lip. She had wanted to hug Larry earlier. He wanted to hug her now. They didn't touch each other. Ah, the life of an FM. Larry looked helplessly at his feline friend, who looked ready to spit at the speaker.

But finally the esc-globe locked down on Providence Bay FM3 and Napoleon practically leaped for the door. As Larry stepped out a machine with a small hole in its middle rolled up on treads. Larry pulled the translator from his belt and stuck one end in the machine's hole. The machine clicked recognition. He had been acknowledged as an official messenger of the Weinstein-Hubbell U.W. Laboratory.

The machine ground itself next to the esc-globe. If Larry wanted his translator back, he'd have to pull it out and the machine would automatically prepare lift-off. The pilot and Napoleon walked off toward the L-shaped spaceport building. They passed a variety of other ships and tread machines in the dingy hangar. At least it was peaceful in here, since the commercials that still barked through the ships' commlinks were not intended for FMs. This small, gloomy hangar was a rusty oasis from the media bombardment of Earth life.

The doors of the terminal building opened as the two approached, and with it came "the rush." Commercials blared on speakers everywhere. Glass and silver metal gleamed in their eyes. The spaceport was maintained, as were all TM outposts, by an army of busy FMs, who worked slavishly to keep it as clean as possible.

That is not to say that there weren't women about. There were women everywhere. Astonishingly beautiful women of all kinds. There was one blonde sitting on a man's lap right across from where the pilots stood. An unconscious redhead over a man's shoulder went by. Napoleon saw another being dragged, screaming, into a store on the balcony level by two men. Even one raven-haired girl lay in the middle of the floor, facedown.

Larry went directly to a panel in the wall. A wide orange beam was between them and the wall. While Larry rechecked his and Napoleon's Galactic Pool status, Napoleon watched life go by. Advertising was everywhere and every advertisement utilized the same kind of voluptuous female fantasy image—most of them naked. What was being sold came under the category of pleasure. SM women, drugs to keep the SM women pliant, and weapons to shoot the SM women with when the buyer tired.

There was only one poster without a female. It was a white poster with a photo of two figures. One a Mantas. The other a foozle. They held hands. Underneath them were three words: "Man's Best Friend." There was a theory about why the Earthens had accepted the creatures so readily. Besides needing their abilities (at least those of the Mantases), many said that the human subconscious responded to the concept that the aliens were the mutated brethren of the original Earth insects and puppies.

The official dictum was: All aliens came from Earth originally and mutated among the stars. Napoleon didn't know what to make of that other than the fact that she hated foozles with a passion.

But this Earth couldn't compete with the wealthier planets, whatever their residents' origins. So this planet's artificial pleasures had to be grimmer to get what audience it could. The adjusted went elsewhere to get the princesses. The jaded came here to use the Sex Machine women. SM women—even the name connoted robots. But like the FMs, they weren't. Clones, yes, people produced from the cells of those long dead, but not programmed androids. These were "fake" people with complete minds who were made for specific reasons, *but not tailored to them*.

Conditioning from birth and drugs kept them in line, for the most part. What Fulbright Pharmaceuticals couldn't do, the Comps (combination TM, FM, and machine police) could. Each with a memory of every TM on the planet. Everyone else came under the heading of FM or EX. All were treated the same— except for those few with special, temporary dispensations. Like Napoleon.

The orange band disappeared. Larry rejoined his companion, his face blank. "All set?" she asked.

"Trouble already," he said. "We report to room A."

"Taplinger-Jones," Napoleon said with exhaustion.

The custodial FMs looked at Larry with hate as he crossed the floor. They couldn't help it, but they quickly looked away. Survival came with speed. If you worked fast, a TM couldn't catch you. Continued life depended upon not coming to the attention of any TM. No eye contact, no expression, no mistakes, no nothing. When any TM could do anything to any FM or SM, life was a series of small triumphs, like existing through an entire day.

Just as they reached the plain door on the other side of the enclosure, a body slammed into the floor just behind them. Both whirled around. Staring up at them was the SM who had been dragged into the store upstairs. A pool of red began to grow under her head. Her eyes were open and staring. Her chest wasn't moving. The fall had killed her.

"Don't look up," Larry said tightly. Napoleon didn't listen. The two men were staring down at her indifferently. They walked away as if nothing had happened. Napoleon smirked. "Taplinger-Jones," she muttered. Larry looked at the floor. The feline noticed the raven-haired girl was gone. They'd clean up this one by the time they got out as well. Napoleon couldn't feel much pity for either of the SMs. At least their torture was over.

They entered the large room with no windows. There was a table near the opposite wall. Two men stood behind it. Two men without FM labels. They had the RH (Real Human) factor. "Well, if it isn't our favorite Fake Man and his pet pussycat," said the dark-haired one. He shuffled some plastic cards.

"Yes, indeed," said the blond-haired man standing beside him. "It's our hardly human and his meow-meow." He stared at Napoleon and barked, "Woof, woof."

Napoleon did not react. She stood beside Larry, who was also expressionless. The men before them wore khaki uniforms with the sparkling letters EG in a diamond patch emblazoned on both sleeves and one breast. These were Earth Government officials—as was every TM on the planet.

Everything was the Earth Government. Their job seemed to be to abuse their power. Even the U.W. lab employees were not safe, but at least they were familiar with the routine and prepared for the sarcasm and humiliation. Knowing this, the leading officials tried harder every time.

"Well, let's get the chores out of the way so we can have some fun," said dark hair, grinning. He picked out a card and slid it into a pocket. "Time for a reexamination of your Pool standings. Have to keep them up to date, what?"

Neither pilot reacted. Dark hair rubbed his lower lip. "Oh, playing hard to get, are you? Name!" he suddenly barked at the EX-FM.

"Larry."

"Larry what?"

"No last name. Just Larry."

"You have a last name," warned blond hair. "Use it!"

"Larry nothing," the pilot said.

"Age?" asked brown hair.

"Twenty-seven."

Brown hair framed the next question carefully, enunciating each letter. "B-o-r-n?"

Larry let nothing show. If they saw anything on his face—if they wanted to see anything—it could be a long night.

"No."

Both men cracked up. "Good!" announced brown hair. "We finally taught you! You do not have a date of birth. You were not born. What do you have?"

"Made-day."

"Louder?"

"Made-day."

"That's right. Made-day because you were made. For you we have a special form. Just so you won't have to answer that question. Ready? Here's your new form. Name?"

"Larry. Nothing."

"Age?"

"Twenty-seven."

"Made?"

"May seventh—"

"No!" exploded blond hair. "On this question you

reply yes or no! Understand?" he raged.

"Yes."

"Very, very good," soothed brown hair. "Made?"

"Yes."

"Parents?"

That was a new one. Larry answered quickly, to get it over with. "None."

"No!" said blond hair.

"That will not do," said brown hair. "Our files will be incomplete. You must answer truthfully. Repeat after me. 'I have no parents.'"

Larry repeated it.

"Only chemicals."

"Only chemicals."

"I was not born—come on, come on."

"I was not born."

"I was artificially created in a lab."

"I was artificially created in a lab."

"I am not a man."

"I am not a man."

"I am garbage."

Larry did not echo. It was a useless and stupid gesture. Blond hair hit him in the stomach. Then he threw him on his back.

"You see?" said brown hair. "That proves it. A man would fight back."

A no-win situation. If he fought back, they could kill him without concern. If he did not give them sufficient reason (read: any reason) they would have to answer to Weinstein-Hubbell for his death.

"I am garbage," Larry said through his teeth, gasping in pain.

"Good," said brown hair. "Now answer all your forms just that way. I'll be seeing them."

It was blondie's turn. He walked around the table and faced Napoleon. "Don't worry, *peach fuzz*, you need a new form too. You left such a big blank in the middle- and last-name section of the old one." He reached back and took a card from brown hair. He put it in his pocket before continuing. "Not to mention date of birth, parents, age, and hair color. So we made up a new, tiny little section for your name. Name?"

"Napoleon."

"Last name?"

"None."

"Middle initial?"

"None."

"I'll put that down as 'N.' Now, Napoleon N. None, if you only listened to us you could have had a nice long name. Earth Ship *Napoleon,* that has a nice ring to it, don't you think?" Brown hair smilingly concurred. "How about you, darling?" blondie asked her.

"I have no choice," she said tiredly. She had learned from Larry's examination. She was going to lay it all out for them. "I was named for the ship I was brought in on. So were my eleven sisters. I don't know my real name or original language. I don't remember my parents. I was taught English in school and in church was told my god was Cheshire."

The men laughed as if it were choice humor. "Don't you at least have a number?" blondie asked. "With eleven sisters all named the same, they at least had to tell you apart. You know, Napoleon One, Napoleon Two...."

"They didn't have to tell us apart," she said. "They used us all for the same experiment. I was the only one that survived." Her voice was empty of emotion. It helped that it was a long time ago.

"What was the experiment, sweetie?" blondie inquired.

"The experiment was in reproduction."

"Hmm, boy, those scientists are plenty smart, aren't

they?" blond hair inquired of his fellow TM. "Maybe we should have a reproduction experiment of our own, huh?" Dark hair smiled widely. Blondie started rubbing Napoleon's arms.

"Not tonight," said Napoleon flatly. "I've got a headache."

Blond hair looked directly into Napoleon's eyes. He stopped rubbing and moved back. "No need to get testy," he said casually. "You're not like your fake friend, you know. You're precious. Oh, yes, they told us you're precious. There aren't any of you left, baby. We're supposed to take real good care of you. We're supposed to see that you're not damaged. But do you know why, dear?" Blondie moved in again. "Because the lab wants you in perfect condition when their new experiment is ready." Blondie towered over her. "So just remember, darling. You're coming to the end of the line. You're getting real close. And remember— no U.W. lab's going to help you if you attack an EG official."

With that, blond hair began to search her. He fondled her head, stroked her shoulders, rubbed her back, and caressed her chest. He got down on his knees and rubbed her legs. "Pretty kitty," he cooed.

Larry looked from dark hair's smiling countenance to Napoleon's passive one. He did note that her claw muscles were spazzing. The claws themselves had been pulled and her fangs were blunted years ago.

Blondie finished and moved back. Suddenly they both were all business. "Listen," said brown hair. "You've reached a new plateau. Your space license has been revoked. You're now on twenty-five-hour call at the labs." The men handed the cards in their pockets to the pilots. "When these go off, you are to report to the nearest U.W. lab immediately."

Larry and Napoleon moved from the room stiffly.

They walked down the hallway slowly, commercials blaring; TMs, FMs, and SMs going about their business. That was it, then. The ATs were coming through. Larry fought the urge to start running and Napoleon fought the urge to clean herself with her tongue. They walked away as the two EG men watched from the door of room A.

"So," said the feline calmly, "when do you want to steal that OD?"

SIX

"Quiet, quiet," Dr. Weinstein-Hubbell instructed as Larry entered. "It's prom night."

Larry stood patiently by the entrance, watching his creator as he was engrossed in this day's episode of "Ah, Glorious Youth." Lucky me, the EX-FM thought. It's prom night.

The VU series hero Sam Stone was in high school. In fact, today was the big day: prom night. Sam had dumped his "true love"—virtuous Sarah—for Kathy Anastasia, who had done everything but a strip tease to get the boy's attention. She had used almost every other underhanded ploy to wrest Sam from his steady girlfriend.

Weinstein-Hubbell had a big smile on his face as he watched the result of her deviousness. Kathy was resplendent in her frightfully low-cut, incredibly tight, shimmering gown. Sam had encircled her smooth, naked shoulders with one arm and was pulling her skirt up over her white-stockinged legs with the other when she stopped him.

"Please, Sam," she said. "I'm not that kind of girl."

"What?" Sam said, confused.

"Please, Sam," she repeated, pushing him away as they sat by the gym wall. "Just because I let you take me to the prom doesn't mean you can paw me."

Weinstein-Hubbell giggled in anticipation.

Sam was confused. A great actor, Johnson-Finlay was. He had been playing Stone since birth. In fact, "Ah, Glorious Youth" had been running on the P Channel every day since he was born.

"What do you mean?" Sam said quietly. "Are you insane?"

"Now really, Sam," Kathy said, as if lecturing a child. "Be a gentleman and let's enjoy the dance, shall we?"

"Come on, Sam boy," Weinstein-Hubbell murmured. "Let her have it."

"Are you out of your mind?" Stone exploded, standing, his confusion turned to rage. "You come on to me like a bitch in heat, you wear those clothes, you do everything but throw yourself at me, and then you say, 'Please, Sam'?"

"Please, Sam," Kathy said nervously, looking around. "People are watching."

"Then let's show them something worth seeing, baby!" Sam shouted, grabbing Anastasia by the hair and throwing her under the refreshment table.

Larry looked around the room purposefully and thought about other things as Sam forcibly had his way with Anastasia under the table to the cheers of his fellow prommers.

He had been indefinite with Napoleon. She had been ready to take on the Comps, the TMs, and even the entire planet to get the O'Neil Drive at that very second. Larry liked to think he was the more temperate of the two, the wiser, but he had to admit to himself that he probably was also the more frightened.

He did not want to die and he saw no way of getting
an OD without getting killed.

In short, he was more willing to wait, hoping the
AT orders didn't come through before he had devised
a foolproof plan. The sound of Sam's triumph from
the VU monitor coarsened his thoughts, but he managed to keep his eyes from the screen. The images
didn't sicken him. They embarrassed him. Instead of
watching the latest Sam triumph, he looked around
the orange room (orange for scientific services). Upon
entering the building, Larry had walked through the
red military section, the blue administration section,
and the green laboratory section to reach his lord and
master's office.

Here, as on every inch of wall space throughout
the complex, were advertisements. The walls were
completely covered by advertisements. Ads for foodstufs, toys, P-Shops, and drinks, among many others.
They were changed monthly, for the most part, but
there hardly seemed a day when Larry couldn't see
something new among the adverts.

In fact, there was something new that caught his
eye right away. "Cyanide-brand Mixers. Guaranteed
Cumulatively Fatal." That was their trademark catch
phrase. Ten drinks, dizziness. Twenty drinks, illness.
Thirty drinks, death. Double your circash back if dis-
satisfied. For use with FMs and SMs only. TM use
strictly prohibited.

Finally Sam Stone finished with his date and rose
from beneath the refreshment table to the applause
of his classmates. Larry glanced back just in time for
a shot of Kathy lying under the table—her tear-
streaked mascara making lines across her face. Larry
looked away quickly, rolling his eyes and sighing.

Weinstein-Hubbell leaned back and nodded in contentment as "Ah, Glorious Youth" ended for the day.

The doctor had been hooked on the continuing saga ever since Sam's dad had taken his third mistress and Sam had humiliated his first girlfriend.

"Be with us tomorrow on 'Ah, Glorious Youth,'" an announcer intoned, "when Sam steals Sarah back from her new boyfriend. Now stay statted for Killerball. Today's match? The Oakie Stallions meet the York Bulls. Coming right up over these VU stations on the P Channel."

Weinstein-Hubbell turned the set off and turned to Larry. "Ah, you don't like these shows, do you?" he said.

Larry didn't answer. He didn't have to. It wasn't really a question. Although Larry never actually said anything on the subject, both knew that the FM couldn't stomach the P Channel. From its most popular show, "Ah, Glorious Youth," through its sports presentations, with all FM teams literally tearing into each other, to its single public-service show, "Men Are Just Beasts" (featuring an all EM—Earth Mother—panel), Weinstein-Hubbell declared Larry too sensitive to appreciate the positive nuances of the tension-relieving programming.

"It's just fantasy, Larry," the doctor soothed. "We would never do those things in real life." Naturally FMs and SMs weren't part of "real life." Only the male actors on "Ah, Glorious Youth" were TMs. The EMs were too precious to risk any sort of damage. The actress playing Sarah had originally been an EM, but when she reached maturity she was replaced by a team of identical SMs.

"I've told you before, my boy. It's just entertainment. True Men and Real Humans require this sort of release in our True Female—starved world."

Larry was noncommittal. But he knew that to the TMs the very idea of having a relationship with an

EM was the same as having sex with Mom. So the land was overflowing with SMs and the P Channel.

As usual, Weinstein-Hubbell's attention span was insultingly short. As soon as the VU set was off, the entertainment was out of his mind. It was back to business time. The doctor, like so many other scientists, had the annoying habit of talking to himself more than anyone else and introducing any subject that came to mind. He seemingly existed in a world of his own.

Larry imagined it was from creating so many people himself. He imagined that the doctor could not accept that anything made from his own hands or mind was equal or superior to him. Weinstein-Hubbell couldn't pilot a spaceship to save his life. But his creation, Larry, could not only pilot one but could build one too.

An amazing thing for any engineer, but unfortunately Larry had not been created to be a super-engineer. He had been created to be a biochemist, essentially Weinstein-Hubbell's protégé, maybe even his FM "son." So in the U.W.'s eyes, in the ECG files, in the doctor's mind, Larry was a failure.

The scientist touched a tiny flesh-colored circle on his neck. "Cormundin?" he said. The Mantas in the white lab coat appeared behind Larry. "Good," said Weinstein-Hubbell to it. "Go with Cormundin like a good lad, will you?" Weinstein-Hubbell said to Larry.

That could only mean one thing: test time. Larry had taken many different exams over the last few years, at approximately quarterly intervals, but lately the doctor had a project for him weekly, then twice a week, and then nightly. Was this the final exam before the AT? The Mantas gave no indication as it led Larry to his cubicle.

Officially, it was an FM sleeping enclosure. Actually,

it was a comfortable rectangular room at the very top of the U.W. complex. It was a spartan efficiency studio apartment, but one not without a modicum of warmth. It had a tiny AU monitor and two rectangular windows that nearly met in the far corner, giving Larry a nice view of the Citiden (City-Denver), which took up the central portion of the plateau and was separated from the lab by a swath of vegetation.

Cormundin motioned Larry to his single table and chair just beneath the corner windows. The FM walked past the text-lined walls and stood before the three beakers of liquid. He knew the routine. The three vials were one of the simplest applications of the cirquid discovery (an invention that matched the OD in influence).

The beaker on the right held the test. The beaker in the middle enabled Larry to give the answers. He would urinate into the right beaker the following morning to hand in the exam. Weinstein-Hubbell would pour the urine into a machine that would grade the FM. Larry looked back. Cormundin waited in the open doorway. Larry hefted the exam vial and drank. Hmm. A pleasant orange taste.

The information flowed through him. Was this how the space bullet felt on lift-off? Larry drop-kicked any thought of Harlan from his consciousness just in case it appeared, doodlelike, on the test. Hmm. A solid core of biology questions. Maybe not an AT prelim. Maybe Weinstein-Hubbell was still trying to fire Larry's biochemical origins—trying to save his protégé from the what-went-wrong operation.

Bless him. It was the doctor's paternal desires that kept Larry alive this long. Taplinger-Jones, it was Weinstein-Hubbell's influence that got Larry everything: the ship, the feline co-pilot, the extraordinary freedom—everything.

Larry prepared himself. He used all the relaxation exercises he had found in the textbooks that decorated his walls. Weinstein-Hubbell was not only fatherly, he was sentimental. Although the cirquid had replaced almost all books, he could not bear throwing away his favorites. They were kept on Larry's wall. Larry had read them all.

Just when he felt the time was right, Larry drank the second vial. Chocolate. It mingled with the orange still coating his throat for a disarmingly pleasant taste. Only when Larry set the second beaker down and swallowed did Cormundin leave. Fine, just fine. He didn't want the Mantas to see the effort it took him to cheat.

It was tough, but it wasn't impossible. For Weinstein-Hubbell had succeeded in making a powerful new form of FM, an FM who knew that survival depended on *not* displaying his ability to control his body and mind. He didn't use his biochemical knowledge for he had let it diminish while excelling in mechanical engineering.

Larry concentrated on the test. It was harder than usual. Not in terms of the scientific questions, but in terms of the psychology behind them. They were getting wise to him. At least they were getting suspicious. Pretty soon his charade would become obvious. Larry got nervous. He'd have to calm down or tomorrow would be the day his semisecure existence would end.

He turned on the AU and listened to the ECG station—the crap that passed for music. Eliminate all effort and give TMs everything they could possibly want and the creative edge completely disappeared. Without suffering or self-control, TM art and music became the worst sort of mental masturbation.

Larry quickly tuned to the FM outlaw station in the area. That at least had some heart and guts. Although the Comps were constantly shutting the renegade FM stations down, the ECG had an unofficial understanding with them. As long as they kept the FM mass pacified, they could continue to pop up.

That helped. The music here was more hearty.

Larry looked across the landscape, which was a monument to nature's strength but empty of humanity's grace. The coil of foliage between the lab and the Citiden was treacherous and vicious, requiring an army of custodial FMs every day to keep the paths clear. Down those paths, deep in the city lay no safety. Only through the invitation of deep space to Destiny was there a chance. Maybe out there was some sort of answer. Or at least some sort of decent question.

Larry gripped the sides of the table, gritted his teeth, and began to cheat.

The hot lights flashed across Napoleon's face as she moved down the street. Here, by the spaceport, dozens of P-Shops made a decent living, even after their ECG fees. And some eliminated that headache by being part of the ECG. Napoleon was on her way to one such establishment.

Meanwhile, the various signs, speakers, lights, and psi messages spelled out the same thing to Earthens and tourists alike. Here! Here is the place where your wildest dreams come true! Here is the place where your secret passions take life! Rape! Murder! Enjoy! It will all be real. The blood will spurt, the flesh will give, because the victim is real. Really made of flesh and blood; muscles, organs, brain, and veins. It is really life and death. And it's all for you. Buy! Buy!

But even on such a street, lined with human and semihuman creatures, Napoleon got unwanted attention. A feline of any sort was rare, and a female feline was unique. And sadly, her short-haired, calico-furred form was attractive to every Earthen-oriented race.

A round Abyssinian dove forward and gripped her arm. She stiffened in place and jerked her head around to look at his short figure. Napoleon growled, her irises becoming black slits.

The bald Abyssinian ignored her attitude. He knew her claws and fangs would have been blunted. The ECG would not allow a wild feline to walk free on the streets. He fingered her arm, then looked around, shouting, "I will pay anything for her!"

Napoleon slapped him on the side of the head. "Hey, whiffleball," she said. He blinked, seemingly seeing her face for the first time. "Nobody owns me."

It was clear from the Abyssinian's expression that he didn't believe her. "I will pay anything. Anything!" he cried.

Napoleon shook her head. "Not for damaged goods," she said. "Look what you did to my arm."

The short fat man bounced back from her, his fingers leaving her limb. "What? I did not do anything."

"Look," she said, holding her elbow out to him. "Look at the marks you made."

The Abyssinian leaned in and peered at her elbow. "I see nothing," he said defensively.

"Look closer," she suggested. He did and she threw the back of her paw into his face with the power of a pile driver. The Abyssinian went down like a bowling pin. His two hulking bodyguards jumped forward from the curb, their hands out to grab the female. Napoleon's spine bent until her body looked like a question mark.

Then two clear blue, three-foot walls came down from the sky between the feline and the guards. The men ran right into them and were thrown back to the sidewalk. Napoleon skittered quickly away. She straightened before a hovering Comp team. The machine shield was in front of her.

"Assault," said the FM behind it.

"Self-defense," said Napoleon automatically.

"We could contain any situation arising from his personal contact," came the smooth voice of the TM. "There was no need for violence."

"Have you ever been pawed?" Napoleon smirked, then cut the conversation short. "You see this?" she said, showing her EX-A emblem to the machine shield. She continued without waiting for confirmation. "You know what it means. Move aside."

"Destination?" said the FM, just to be troublesome.

"Pleasure Palace One," Napoleon said without hesitation. "Stand aside, or do you want to talk to Grossman-Smith?"

The Comp got out of her way. The unit was a surprisingly versatile one, with both street and hovering capability. The FM rode it, the computer unit was installed throughout the craft, and the TM was in direct sensory contact with it while still safe in Comp headquarters downtown.

Napoleon looked back at the Abyssinian, who was being helped to his feet by the guards. He pointed at her and they moved forward, only to be hurled back again by the Comp's blue ray. The crowd watched their humiliation, gasping and oohing at the appropriate moments. Otherwise, they paid no undue attention. After having their fantasies realized in the P-Shops, nothing surprised them on the streets.

Napoleon turned away and nearly walked into three foozles. She immediately jumped back, her face twisting in a scowl. The doggies stood impassively staring at her. One held an ice cream cone, which was melting over its paw. Her back began recurling of its own volition. Napoleon felt her legs wanting to bolt. Instead, she spit at the trio. They turned and ran away.

Lordy, she hated those things.

Napoleon's back straightened and her expression was haughty until she came to the opulent opening of the dream factory: Pleasure Palace One. The automatic door automatically let her in and immediately a lion loped toward her and asked, "Can I be of service?"

It stopped her in her tracks. Her hair stood on end and she visibly shrank back in fear. "Grossman-Smith," she managed to mew. "I want to see him."

"Certainly," the male feline said pleasantly. "And after your visit with him, perhaps you would care to see me again."

Napoleon was near hysterics. Years of self-control saved her the embarrassment, however. "Yes, perhaps," she choked. She tried to smile. "Perhaps I shall."

"Wonderful!" he roared. "This way, please." The lion moved down the hall and up the stairs on all fours.

Napoleon didn't really see the ornate surroundings, the levels of sculptured glass, the entries to different environments for different alien types. She only saw the lion. She ran after him, feeling an exhilaration she had never experienced before.

Where had Grossman-Smith found him? Could he be from Mandarin? If not, was there another planet that could be Napoleon's home? Her thoughts dissipated as the lion slowed, turned, sat, and gestured.

"In here," he said. "Grossman-Smith awaits." Then he disappeared.

Napoleon felt herself sinking to her forepaws until she heard laughing from inside the room. She snapped to her full height and kicked the door in. It was unlatched so it swung in without damage. Before her was Grossman-Smith, convulsed with levity. She only felt dark hatred.

"You should have seen your face!" he hooted, his dark eyes alight with moisture and mirth. She looked around the large room filled with curtains and pillows. She looked at his white desk and the molded white VU screens over it. She stood in the doorway for a second, then grabbed the door and slammed it shut behind her with both hands.

"What do you love most in this room?" she demanded of him.

Grossman-Smith's laughter subsided instantly and he smiled. "You," he said.

Napoleon grimaced. "Nice try." Her eyes picked out his favorite reclining pillow. She marched over and tore it apart. She leaped for his desk and tore a VU monitor off it. She hurled it at the far wall with all her strength. It slammed into it, cracking, bounced off, and slid across the floor back to Grossman-Smith's feet.

The doors flew open again as guards swarmed in. Grossman-Smith stopped them with a motion, and with another he sent them away. He looked calmly at the heavily breathing feline. "Feel better now?"

"I do not like being humiliated," she said.

"Few creatures do," he replied. "That is what makes it so much fun." He sat behind his magnificent white desk, which was covered with glass sculptures. Artifacts and tapestries from the known worlds were on one wall. A chair for every alien type was positioned before him and four translators were on the desk top, angling off in every direction.

There was a panel of equipment just below the desk lip on his side. From it he was able to see her entrance and movements outside the room. She stared hard at his countenance. His lips were upturned, but there was no humor in his eyes. He was pleased that he could shock, embarrass, and anger her. It gave him the edge.

Grossman-Smith liked edges. Anything he could hold on to made him feel better. Anything he could use as a pry to tear something apart made him feel at home. He needed an edge over Napoleon because she knew what lay behind the black wig, fake mustache, and false goatee. She knew Pleasure Palace One's owner was actually the noted Dr. Dundon-Little, ECG official.

But that kind of edge was a dangerous one for the feline. It could turn at any moment. Her uniqueness was her only protection. She moved forward until she stood directly before him. "You knew what effect that would have on me." He smiled. "Hardly a friendly gesture," she considered. "How was it done?"

"I thought it best to take a little starch from your stride," he said lightly. "You may be an EX-A and all, but you're still an adaptable biped female."

"I am not an adaptable," she said angrily.

"You are a flesh-eating mammal," said he. "Large, well-developed brain. Acute sense of smell, touch, and hearing. Slightly color-blind."

"Don't change the subject. How did you do it? What was the method of my humiliation?"

"Not childbearing, no," Grossman-Smith replied, iron in his voice, "but capable of intercourse. You can supply sexual pleasure, and all such females should do so!"

"We've had this discussion before. I have not come here to beg residence. I ask you again: how did you create the lion?"

Grossman-Smith looked prepared to rage on, but he calmed himself. "As a gentleman," he said, bowing slightly from the waist, "I shall reply. A three-dimensional image perfected in the ECG labs. One that I couldn't resist testing when I heard of your impending visit. We will soon use them in the P-Shops and through the VUs. Please sit down, my girl."

"Don't," Napoleon warned.

"You act like a girl, you look like a girl, you dress like a girl, and physically, you can react like one. I see little point in being defensive. Sit down anyway, your feline highness." She decided not to deny his hospitality any longer. His patience would only go so far and she was prowling around the edge already. "If not for my luxurious, secure sanctuary, what have you come for?" he asked. "Surely not the pleasure of my company?"

She ignored his obvious insult bait. "I am interested in your associates," she said. Then it was her turn to be pleased. Though she had never surprised him, this was close. He stilled for a split second before leaning over his desk.

"Whatever for? After your repeated rejections of my sanctuary, surely you are not interested in theirs."

Napoleon lived alone in the ECG EX-A blockade, a nondescript, two-story, previously heavily guarded dorm. She had lived with her sisters until they all died, and after many years of catering to her alone, the staff had been reassigned. Now the place was empty and quiet, with a single guard at all exits who signed her in and out. Once under Dundon-Little's protection, she was given ample freedom.

"I have said nothing of sanctuary," Napoleon said. "I have not even framed the nature of my interest yet."

Grossman-Smith's expression became dark. He ruminated silently for a moment. "What else could it be?" he suddenly blurted. "Information is not my trade. The only thing you could hope to achieve is to enlarge the scope of my protection by setting their offers against mine."

"My dear sir—" Napoleon began.

"I warn you," said he. "I could only tolerate your freedom when I knew you were mine alone. I will possess you or no one will!"

Though his reaction was part of her plan, the intensity concerned the feline. "I tell you the question of my possession is not involved," she maintained.

"Who is it?" he suddenly raved. "Taylor-Barnes? A life of drudgery, one freak after another, I can assure you. Perry-Hirsch? His illusions are not half mine. Nor are his dividends. Nor are his quarters!"

"I'm not interested in Citiden small fry," Napoleon said. "My question concerns far more powerful—"

Grossman-Smith sprang from his chair, lightning striking his face. His finger was a metal knife pointing at her. "Bishop-Fortune!" he spoke. "You have discovered Bishop-Fortune! Of all the females on all the planets, he would have to spot you. I thought he would be satisfied with the raven witch. I thought she would preoccupy him for weeks, but—"

"The witch," Napoleon said quickly. "A girl?"

"Yes, yes," he replied. "Of course. A beauty he pirated. But it doesn't make sense! He already has her. He can't have you!"

"Where is he?" Napoleon knew it was the wrong question as soon as it slipped out of her mouth.

"What is this, woman?" Grossman-Smith snapped out of his reverie with a nearly audible sound. "Have you been toying with me? Me? Have you been trying to raise your worth in my eyes?" He was around the desk, standing before her and yelling. Suddenly he hugged her fiercely, his voice cracking. "But you are already a goddess to me! Do you know how many catwomen I have created in my labs? Do you know how many times I have tried to satisfy myself with them? Do you know what I would do for your company?"

Napoleon rose quickly, snapping his hands apart and shrugging off his grip. "There is no competition for a body not for sale," she spat. "I have no interest in your establishment, your business, or your desires. I require only information. I do not require it if the price is me."

"I am the power on this planet!" he shouted in her face. "I control your destiny! I'm the only thing between you and an AT table! If there were but one more like you on this world, I could do whatever I wanted to you! But there is not. It has to be you. I must have you."

"Get your paws off," Napoleon said flatly.

The words seemed to slap him. At first he looked hurt. But his arms did not release her. "By the Earth Father," he whispered, "I will have you." Then he bellowed, "I will have you now!"

He seized her shoulders and pushed back, falling on her.

Her reaction was instinctive. She grabbed his chin with one hand and his hair with the other. His back snapped just before his skull cracked on the desk edge.

SEVEN

"I'm telling you that man's work is sacred." The blond man with the cleft chin stared directly out at the masses for a petrified moment, giving the VUers a clear shot of the big beads of heavenly sweat across his blessed face. "God has given us a clear dictum!" he pronounced, chopping at the black book in his hands several times. "Be not led into temptation, the great book declares! What is that telling us?"

He didn't so much talk as bombast. He would shout and then query, his voice rising in an audio question mark. He did not really want an answer, since he wanted to set up his own.

"It is saying that we must bless our own work and reject the false images of those who are untrue. Those who are false, those who are not real, human, living creatures of the union of man's body with woman's. Thee of no living flesh cannot be living flesh no matter how warm and smooth and yielding."

Weinstein-Hubbell had switched from the P Channel to the E Channel. Twenty-four hours of evangelists pounding out the new-time religion, mounting justification after justification of FM and SM abuse, backing it with the New Testament II.

"There are those," the blonde began on a new tack, "who would say that those of false flesh were actually children of flesh long dead. That once their fathers lived and once their mothers lived, so they are, indeed, of the true flesh." He seemed to mull this supposition over. But then he shouted, "But I say that the children of those long dead are just as dead. They are the living of the dead and their true home is in death, which we do not keep them from. Oh, no, we do not keep them from rejoining theirs in death. Therefore ours is the blessed work of eternal peace, I say yes."

"I say I'm finished," said Larry, holding the third beaker out to his creator.

His good creator had given him the talent to control his body more than other FMs. Whether he wanted to or not, whether he knew it or not, Weinstein-Hubbell had allowed Larry to cheat by flooding his system with oxygen and adrenaline. He could control his biological answers.

It took him months to complete his experiments, but now he could subtly alter his test results to gain more time. Before, he didn't know why he bothered. At least now he had a reason. There are no coincidences, Larry remembered. Only postponed reasons.

The container was becoming heavy in his hand. It seemed to carry the weight of all the other poor, pathetic FMs too conditioned or drugged to use common self-control to fool their bigoted master/creators. It was simple for Larry now. He hardly needed to think about it anymore, comparatively speaking.

"I'm finished," he repeated.

Weinstein-Hubbell looked at the FM from the VU

screen, his expression wondering whether Larry was trying to make a joke. Bad move. If Weinstein-Hubbell truly suspected, the U.W. would observe him day and night with a battery of scientific checking and re-checking his every move for any sign of aptitude. Tests would fall from the sky like rain every day.

Larry would lose then, no matter how much internal control he mustered. Stealth counted, not sincerity. And now that an opportunity had arisen for him to escape the Doomstar and the shadow of the AT once and for all time, he had to be extra cautious. "I'm tired," he told the doctor.

Weinstein-Hubbell looked at the evangelist and at his creation. He turned down the VU sound. "It's been a long day, hasn't it?" he said in sympathy. Larry nodded. "Well, you've been a good boy. You finished early. You didn't have to hand that in until the morning. You've done a good job...." The doctor faltered. He looked toward the floor. "Lawrence," he finally said. "I want you to know something." Weinstein-Hubbell couldn't look at Larry. "I want you to know I've always been proud of you. Now go to bed like a good boy."

The doctor turned away and turned the VU up. "...does not smile on these creatures. The Lord does not bless them and give them life. He blesses us and we give them life. He trusts us to take care of our own house and not bring these creatures into His house. They are not of His creation, they are of ours. We must deal with them, not He...."

Larry's mind felt muddy back in his room. What was Weinstein-Hubbell trying to do? Confuse him? What was that—a farewell? A death sentence? Was that what Weinstein-Hubbell was giving him? What would pride mean on the AT table? Larry quickly moved out of his room and down the hall. He made for the exit, thinking about Napoleon.

He cursed himself for suggesting she try to get information from her protector. It was the only thing he had been able to think of to get her mind off the OD. He remembered when she first came to him, desperate for a way out. Having survived the twelve years of experiments that killed her sisters, she had the unappealing choice of living with other guinea pigs or succumbing to the corrupt demands for sexual services.

It seemed that everyone was jockeying for her. Only political infighting in the ECG and with the U.W. kept her from being claimed. She had been offered a life of relative comfort if she would a), undergo a variety of genetic operations to salvage her insides, or b), copulate with every known galactic creature.

But as a "special case," she had heard about Larry's ship and the open co-pilot position. He had originally no intention of filling it, but when he heard her plight, he made an exception. In an attempt to escape, Napoleon had registered with the Galactic Pool, but no ECG official had any intention of processing her application. Between deals cut with Grossman-Smith, requests of Weinstein-Hubbell, and a little unofficial work by Mess, which Larry never told her about, she was assigned to the *Black Hole*.

Larry found himself outside and moving toward her abode. He'd have to walk through the foliage along the paths, but that was worth risking. His concern for his friend was directing him there. Grossman-Smith was moody at best, power-mad at worst. Any personal visit, whether social or light business, was risky. No one had heavy business with Grossman-Smith. He had it with them.

"Going somewhere?" came the hiss. Larry turned in the entrance of the foliage, strangely calm. The voice had surprised him but had not frightened him.

Mingling with the plant curls was Cormundin, Weinstein-Hubbell's Mantas assistant, minus his lab coat.

"Out for a walk," Larry said blankly.

"The doctor thought you might be nervous tonight," Cormundin said. "He suggested I accompany you."

"Fine," said Larry, his mind working. "I'm going to visit my co-pilot. You want to walk that far?"

"I wouldn't mind," said the Mantas. "If you wouldn't mind my asking another friend to join us."

"Who?"

"Me," said the foozle, emerging from the darkness at the edge of the foliage archway.

"You don't mind, do you?" said the Mantas.

"I don't," said the FM.

"You should," said the foozle.

The three walked through the foliage archway and down the path. Its inside was like a tunnel, an ominous tunnel filled with night silence. Unless one walked by the spaceport, it stayed quiet. Legends of murdering mutants—made from the WEA-War—wandering the countryside were big at one time and the P Channel had a very successful series depicting their atrocities, but they had long since been eradicated. Now these new "mutants" wandered down the road side by side, seemingly ignoring each other.

As he walked, Larry acquired a strange sense of peace. It was from the knowledge that he could leave this place, a place he had called home, and not miss it in the slightest. It was a storybook land created by adult men in their own image, just to feed their ego. It was a world of every emotion but love. And into the fairy tale world came death. Real death, not the kind packaged on the VU or exercised on the SMs.

Larry turned to Cormundin just as five holes

erupted in a neat row across its head. It nodded violently and its entire body spasmed and crumbled, its mandibles clacking. Before Larry could even accept the reality of the horrible event, the foozle was speeding away, whining at the top of its voice, holes erupting in the ground, nipping at its heels.

Suddenly its way was blocked off by a leaping form. The foozle fell to all fours and circled around the other slinking shape. Its lips went back from its unblunted teeth and the second eyelids slipped down to shield its pupils. Larry had never seen such a complete transformation before. The foozle had changed from an innocent puppy to an attacking beast.

All at once it shot forward as if propelled. The other figure fell and a third arm grew from its torso. This third arm shivered and the foozle floated in midair, jerking. The third arm stilled and the twisting foozle dropped in an ugly heap in the middle of the path. The other figure rose and turned toward Larry, its eyes glowing.

Napoleon approached the FM, who cowered on the ground, close to the foliage wall. She kneeled down, laying the spitter—her third arm—down, pulled his right arm up, and forced his fingers to wrap around a second spitter's grip. Larry looked at the weapon as if it were a magic wand.

"I killed him," Napoleon said. "You should have seen the look on his face."

The look on Larry's face was pretty hard to take as well. "What happened?" was all he could stammer.

Napoleon didn't know whether he was asking about then or now. "He attacked me. I didn't stop to think. It just all burst inside me, I guess. My natural heritage." She grinned without humor.

Napoleon grabbed Larry's arms and shook him. "Wha-Wha, wha-wha, wha-wha what happened?" he repeated, shivering. "This isn't happening."

"Yes, it is, Larry," she said. "You have to accept it. All of it. The space bullet, the O'Neil Drive. Grossman-Smith is dead, Larry. I killed him. His eyes were open. The look on his face was like this was the biggest surprise in the galaxy. Imagine, a female killing him. And an experimental alien at that."

Larry came back to life. Death, real death, was a horrible sight. Even more horrible was the realization that he hadn't seen the death of his fellow FMs as real until that moment. The horror of Earth fell on him all at once. He could see all the corruption and perversion clearly for the first time. His brain shut it off almost immediately to protect him from madness.

"Oh, my God," he breathed. He had to get off the planet. They had to get off the planet. Taplinger-Jones, they had to get out of the galaxy! Napoleon had done the undoable. She had killed a TM, an RH, and a top-ranking ECG official all in one! There was no way to know what the ECG would do to them, because there was no precedent. This had never happened before.

He knew better than to soothe Napoleon at this point. Her tail was lashing back and forth like a scythe. "Could they figure it was an accident?" Larry asked feebly.

"Sure, if they accept that he threw himself backward so violently that his spine broke and the top of his head was shaved off."

"Oh, my God!" Larry said in horror. "I'm going to be sick."

"Stop," Napoleon whined.

Then they just sat there. With a dead Mantas and foozle lying around, they just sat there looking at each other. Larry tried to think. He tried to dump all the warring emotions clanging against his skull and ribs to figure out their next move. It wasn't easy.

The ECG would divvy up Grossman-Smith's empire and cover up the particulars of the crime. That much was assured. They couldn't let anyone else know that an EX-A had killed a TM. Other cities and worlds would have to be put on alert. Be on the lookout for a dangerous female feline wanted real dead.

Naturally Larry would come under suspicion through association with her. It wouldn't help that his master's Mantas and his master's Mantas' foozle were both dotted with spitter holes. That was pretty much it for them. They sat across from each other in the dark Earth night, bound by friendship and someone else's blood.

Larry looked up at the moon. Beyond it was the Doomstar. He knew that when the morning came they would have to be on another planet. Or the morning would never come.

Wolf-Hoover led his six FMs out of the palace where the seventh remained stationed. Just one uniformed man with the M in the red triangular patch was enough to keep curiosity under control. Bystanders knew that behind that patch lay all of Earth's strength—a literally endless supply of soldiers ready to be unleashed on anything in their way. Many would die, but the ECG hardly cared—there was more where those came from.

The sentry turned when he heard Wolf-Hoover approach. The other half dozen encircled their leader protectively while he thought. He deserved his name. Like Grossman-Smith, his moniker had become his way of life. His face was long and his dark hair was streaked with white. His smile, on the rare occasions it appeared, was thin. His eyebrows naturally arched down, giving him a perpetually angry look—a look that turned demonic when he smiled.

He was not smiling now. Just the opposite. His strong body was tense, his hands were clamped to his waist, his eyes were down, and his jaw muscles clenched. "Seven," he said tightly. The sentry saluted. "Go to the EX-A rooms. Cover the place with psonic traps."

"Yes, sir!" the man said sharply, ordering a Comp down so he could ride it to the blockade.

"One through Three," Wolf-Hoover said sharply. "The spaceport. No one goes in, no one goes out. Keep tracking that ship, the *Black Hole*." The three saluted and turned. Three more Comps served as their chariots.

"Comps down," he ordered. The remaining machines landed. "Break the FM connection." The Fake Men were instantly cut off. Wolf-Hoover communicated directly with TM-Comp headquarters. "Inaugurate NAO. Repeat, NAO."

Tyler-Merrick, the TM-Comp in charge, was stunned. "Are you certain? I mean, couldn't it have been an accident?"

Wolf-Hoover was used to incompetence. "Not unless he was able to throw himself back so violently that his spine broke and the top of his head was shaved off. Do not question my orders. Initiate NAO."

"The ECG will have to clear this," Tyler-Merrick stammered.

"Then clear it!" Wolf-Hoover snapped. "You'll have to contact them to start the plan anyway, fool! Get busy!"

"I'll...My entire squad is at your disposal," said the TM-Comp, trying to make amends.

"Idiot," sighed the military man. "The Comps will be part of the NAO. We don't want anyone, I repeat, *anyone*, involved in tracking the EX-A besides myself. We can't have any FM or SM even guessing what has happened. Understand?"

"Y-Yes, sir."

Wolf-Hoover broke the connection. "Report back to headquarters," he told the now undeafened FM-Comps. When they left, he shook his head. He blamed the politicians for this mess. Wolf-Hoover was a direct descendant of the best military minds in the field and damned proud of it. If only the politicians hadn't been allowed in the underground shelters, this Earth wouldn't have the P-Shops or the P Channel or this ungodly mess.

But Wolf-Hoover *was* a military man. His was not to reason why, his was to do—period. He didn't think about the corruption or the perversion. He followed the orders of his superiors, and their orders in this eventuality had been very clear. If ever, and they meant ever, a TM or EM had been killed by anything other than another TM or EM, the Noah's Ark Operation had to begin.

The world was to be cleansed and then started over again.

But that was not his concern anymore. His concern was finding the one who had started it all, and the way he figured it, she was a cat, and no matter how independent, when in pain or in trouble a cat will always return to its master. Wolf-Hoover led his remaining three FMs to the Weinstein-Hubbell labs.

Larry ran down the hallway, sweat beading his brow. The floor was deserted. The scientists had gone and from the evidence of his closed door, Weinstein-Hubbell was otherwise occupied. So, with a certain degree of skill and massive amounts of luck, they could find an OD or the necessary parts thereof, load it into a salvage vehicle, and get a message to Mess to prepare for immediate departure.

If they could do this and *if* the drive could be adapted to the *Black Hole* and *if* it could be installed in time and *if* they could find Destiny before Earth and/or its allies found them and *if* they could take care of the problem there, then everything would turn out all right.

Napoleon sped around the corner after Larry, holding her spitter tightly. It was a long-barreled, two-handed weapon, which required great control if the owner was to avoid waste. And they had to avoid waste, because whatever ammo was inside the spitters was all the ammo they had. When the trigger was depressed, small bands of light were spat, one after another, like a laser machine gun. They were sadistic killing weapons made by men who liked to see targets in tatters.

Larry pushed the grip deeper into his palm and moved into the scientific-services maintenance area. This was the labs' warehouse, containing all sorts of meaningless junk. The pair went over to a table littered with metal and glass devices. They recognized some tools, but most of the stuff was totally alien to them. Napoleon lost interest in the table and started to scan the rest of the area for anything that might be a spaceworthy faster-than-light O'Neil Drive.

"Remember," whispered Larry hypertensely. "It could be any size, any shape. As far as I know it could be made of any material."

Napoleon thanked him for his "help." Except her retort was not humorous. It had the ragged sound of hopeless despair.

Larry returned his attention to the table. A large hunk of machinery at one end looked promising. He moved over, noticing various materials he recognized from his own ship's engine. Maybe somewhere in that hunk was an OD. He couldn't lug the whole thing away, but maybe he could take it apart.

He didn't want to make undue noise, so he went about it manually. Occasionally he would glance up for any sign of Napoleon, but she was nowhere in sight. Once he thought he saw some movement atop a pile of boxes, but he couldn't be sure whether it was her or his own overwrought imagination. Ever since the death of Cormundin and the foozle, he had been hyperthinking, hypertalking, and hyperventilating.

He continued his work, obsessed with this single piece of equipment. Finally he came to the core, which was a bunch of welded-together sections surrounding an item he couldn't see clearly. At no point was there a grip or nut he could loosen, so he tried to pry open a section. His fingers were too weak; he couldn't get any leverage.

The longer he took, the worse things would be. That much he knew for certain. He looked around for something, anything he could jam the thing apart with. His hands skittered around the table until the left fingers encircled a closed section of tubing, which had another band of some sort of metal around the middle. It was a foot long and perfect for leverage. He stuck one end in the hunk and started to push down.

"Don't move."

Larry's heart leaped into his neck and his head rose so quickly his neck audibly cracked. He stared at Weinstein-Hubbell with confusion. That hadn't been the doctor's voice. But then, like a living optical illusion, four men seemed to fan out from his master's back. There was only one who could've spoken: a muscular man aiming a beamer right between Larry's

110

eyes. At this range it would cut the FM's head in two down the middle.

"What are you doing, Larry?" asked Weinstein-Hubbell.

"Nothing," said Larry as nonchalantly as he could. The doctor just stared at him. "Nothing, really. Well, not 'nothing' in the literal sense. I, uh, come down here all the time. To look around. To relax and tinker, I guess. You know the AU can get pretty boring. What's going on?"

"Nothing," echoed the muscular man with no nonchalance. "Nothing you should know about." The beamer stayed motionless between Larry's eyes. "Literally or figuratively."

Larry fought the urge to look wildly about for Napoleon. Instead, he stared straight ahead, letting his fear come to the fore. Anyone would, staring straight at a military man's beamer. Wolf-Hoover did not weaken his stance, but his eyes darted about, scanning the darkness.

Larry tried not to think about the moment when Napoleon would show herself or when anyone would take a good look at the table. For just beyond the torn-apart machinery lay Larry's spitter, the clinching evidence of his duplicity. If anyone saw that, the charade would be over.

Weinstein-Hubbell spoke again, further closing the coffin on Larry's fate. "I was looking for you when these men arrived. I have some questions about your test."

"Oh?"

"Later, Doctor," cut in Wolf-Hoover. "You! Have you seen your co-pilot recently?"

"No," said Larry quickly—too quickly, Taplinger-Jones it! "Why?"

"You're lying," said Wolf-Hoover with an edge of triumph in his voice. His instincts were unfailing. He not only now knew that Larry was lying but that Napoleon was somewhere nearby. If only Wolf-Hoover had X-ray vision he would have seen the spitter and acted faster.

"Separate," he ordered the FMs. "Search." The second word had just left his brain en route to his mouth when the hole went through his head.

Wolf-Hoover jerked in place and then stood at attention. Only after his body began to topple were the beams of orange-yellow light visible. They swung to the right and literally perforated two more military Fake Men.

Larry was rooted to the spot, his mouth agape until the third Fake Man swung to his left and brought his beamer up. Larry wanted to dive for the table, but he knew he wouldn't make it. He threw the pry bar instead.

His aim and speed were remarkable. He controlled all his muscles beautifully (killerball vets—survivors of two games—would have admired the speed with which the bar sank into the military FM's face). He fell back as Larry whirled around and down. He was already calculating the angle the spitter would have to be to hit the prone man. Larry's right hand slapped down, curled across the spitter trigger, and turned the weapon.

The beams went through the machinery, through the table, and into the last FM's hip. Another beam from above cleaved his head. Larry collapsed to his haunches, turning away. Even in the dim light the sight was too disgusting to take.

Weinstein-Hubbell had no trouble after years of the P Channel. He surveyed the scene in amazement more than shock.

"You killed a man," he cried. "A real man!"

Napoleon appeared atop the boxes. She jumped off, landing easily. She strode purposefully up to the scientist. "Not like Larry, huh, Doc?" she said, brushing by him.

Weinstein-Hubbell's mouth worked as she helped Larry up. He needed both hands on the table to stand, gulping. Blood had begun to make lakes across the floor.

"Come on, Larry," she said softly. Trying not to think, he quickly grabbed the spitter and moved toward the door.

His numbness was shaken when he heard a scuffle behind him. Both he and Napoleon turned to see Weinstein-Hubbell sliding across the scarlet liquid to tear at the beamer in Wolf-Hoover's dead hands. Napoleon automatically brought up her weapon to center on the doctor's torso. Larry pushed it away.

Suddenly their eyes met; the maker and his invention. The demigod and the Fake Man. Larry remembered the wonder of his birth, the sudden awareness, the powerful love he had for his father figure. They had long talks about the philosophy behind what Larry was learning. He did not experience; he learned second-hand. He knew things; he never did them. But he was witness to mass birthings. He was closer to his creator than any of the others.

Larry hesitated while Weinstein-Hubbell aimed the beamer at his protégé. That second was enough for Larry to see that the doctor was not firing. He started to smile but then couldn't. Weinstein-Hubbell was not firing because he felt something for his creation, not because of some sort of responsible emotion flickering in his deadened brain, not because he wanted Larry to have a single second of dignity, a moment of anything approaching humanity. He wasn't firing because he didn't know how to work the weapon.

In that second Larry wanted to die. To be paralyzed, then cut up, then reborn into thousands of others, then drugged and set to work, too stupid to know anything.

But that endless moment ended. The doctor concentrated and the beamer shaft cut into the floor. A line of yellow-orange tubes sped by Larry's side and disappeared into Weinstein-Hubbell's chest. He fell back simply, without ceremony, dead. A human god gone on to whatever higher reward was destined for a creator. But meanwhile the creation had to continue.

Napoleon lowered her spitter (it having served its purpose). She had no love for scientists or doctors. She took Larry's elbow and pulled. "Come on," she said. "It's not worth any thought."

Larry shrugged off her paw. He walked slowly to Weinstein-Hubbell, who lay with his head on the chest of the FM Larry had killed. Larry sank to his knees, picked up the pry bar that lay nearby, and pounded the doctor's face with it until his tears finally started.

EIGHT

The slaughter had begun. Everywhere TMs with the proper RH factor did their patriotic duty. They got guns or knives, or simply used their bare hands and went out and killed everything in sight.

A precedent had been set. A non-TM had killed a TM, and if other non-TMs discovered that, they might kill TMs too. No TM could afford any FM finding out. So every FM was to be killed and then they'd be able to start all over again.

The FM-Comps were killed in their machines by the machines themselves when the TM-Comps gave them the orders. The TMs stayed off the streets until all the FM-Comps had crashed. All the military FMs were either lined up and shot or blown up in their barracks. All the SMs were locked in their rooms and gassed.

The ECG went about it systematically. They were very proud of their system. It worked. Every FM or SM was lorded over by a TM somewhere. And every

TM did what he had to do. It was only at the very end of the campaign that things got out of hand. It was only at the very end when the few FMs and SMs who got through the first dragnet panicked.

There was no place on Earth they could escape to. So they had to go somewhere else. And the only way to get someplace else was through the Denver Plateau Spaceport.

Brown hair and blondie were in heaven. It was like they were the team of blade-runners on the "Electric Sheep" show over the P Channel. There were some replicants to terminate and they were the ones on concourse level J to do it. It was their duty.

There were really only two locations the terrified FMs were trying to reach. One, anyplace there was a communications device they could use to try to summon help or let anyone else know their plight. Two, the Morgan-Fullmer gun store.

Brown hair and blondie loved it. It was like a dream come true. How many times had brown hair massacred FMs at the P-Shops? How often had blondie raped Napoleon twins at the pleasure palace? Countless times. But this was real. Much better than the recreations.

Ever since the two officials had met the experimental pair, they had become obsessed by them. Their lives seemed to revolve around the *Black Hole*'s escglobes, and the destined outcome of their taunting was the duo's destruction at the hands of the TM pair's goading.

Neither would admit his latent hatred or envy (hatred that the cat was free and envy that the FM warranted her company). But now all that was different. The NAO order had gone out and even the *Black Hole* pilots weren't immune. And if they ever got their hands on the two, they'd show them. And by all means, they intended to.

"She's a fugitive, right?" asked blondie as another FM charged into Morgan-Fullmer's store.

"Right," said brown hair. FMs had been charging into the gun store for several minutes. There were no gates or locks on the place. The first FM had pushed the clear glass doors all the way back upon running in. From that moment on the place had been wide open.

"So what is she going to do?"

"Run to her little freak friend?"

The FM ducked, pivoted, looked wildly around, and spotted a display case of crinklers. He ran toward it.

"No," said blondie. "He can't offer her any protection."

The FM swung his fists at the glass between him and the weapons. As soon as his flesh touched the surface, two red shafts of crinkler ray shot out from the wall and smashed across the FM's head and torso. He slammed back, spread-eagled onto the red carpet, everything from the waist up—crinkled.

"Hide somewhere?" asked brown hair as another FM went for the store and his partner charged the officials as diversion. The TMs stood in the storefront opposite the gun shop. Brown hair raised his shafter and sent the attacking FM back into a display window with a crushed sternum. As the window broke under the FM's weight, purple bars shot down from the ceiling, caught him in the back, and impaled him on the glass shards.

"Not for long," said blondie. "The military will find her." The nondiversion FM looked in horror at the other, mangled FMs. He looked around until he caught sight of the single Maghawk Strepper on display.

Brown hair frowned. "Then what?"

The FM reached for the strepper, which seemingly hung in midair, held up by three intersecting shafts of light.

"She'll come back here."

"Why?"

The FM touched the strepper. Instantly a thinner band of blue light streaked down and went through the FM's reaching arm, from his middle finger out his shoulder.

"Her escape pod is here, right? Her ship is in orbit, right? The only way to escape is up and out, right?"

The FM, in noncomprehending, terrible pain, reached for the strepper with his good arm. Another blue beam went through that. The FM stumbled back, screaming.

"Yeah," said brown hair. "So?"

"So this, jerk. If you were a desperate fugitive, would you go through this mess?" The FM ran forward again, screaming. A blue beam went through his head and out between his legs. "Or around it?"

"Oh, I get it. She'll try to take off without preparations."

Blondie smiled broadly. "Right."

"So what are we waiting around here for?" brown hair exclaimed. "Let's get to the takeoff bay!"

The salvage vehicle came right through the spaceport entrance. Glass broke and metal bent as Napoleon whirled the driving column around, crushing already dead FMs under the wheels.

"By the Earth Father, Nap!" Larry shouted, his head bouncing off the cab's ceiling. "Can't you watch it?"

"They're already dead, Larry," she hissed, fighting the steering as the wheels slid on the slick floor. "Concentrate on us, will you?"

Larry scowled. He didn't like the way death dealing came to him so easily. Before, it was his disgust of things not unlike the P Channel that separated him from his masters. Now he was bouncing around in a stolen salvage vehicle and shooting FMs like a drafted Sam Stone.

Was it worth all this? He looked at Napoleon. Her head was lowered, deep in concentration. He looked around. The spaceport was practically empty save for the bodies of FMs and SMs everywhere. He no longer felt nausea, just hate. He decided yes, it was worth it. Or else why did he deserve to survive, to escape? If he did survive, then his life would have meaning. If he did not, he would be beyond caring. It wasn't much, but it was all there was.

Napoleon didn't slow. She raced through the main hall of the spaceport, heading directly for the entry bay. "Get ready to jump out. We can't have the retaining light wall stop us," she shouted.

"No!" Larry yelled back. "Go through! Go through to the repair area! We have to get that OD!" Napoleon didn't question him. She sped past their usual entry area. "Once inside we have to find an engine and a ground vehicle to get it into our esc-globe. Then we get in and take off."

"Easy," said Napoleon sarcastically.

"Look," he snapped, "this is hard enough as it is."

She quickly pushed her shoulder against his. "Sorry. I'm just loosening my tail."

Larry nodded. The sooner they got out of here, the sooner they could come to grips with the monstrosity they had unleashed. It wasn't guilt. They didn't owe Earth anything. It was confusion. Mass murder seemed so unearthly, but they both accepted it so readily. What did that make them—FM or TM?

"Get ready," said Napoleon, speeding toward the

wall to the repair area. "We're going through!"

"No we're not!" yelled Larry, throwing open his door. "Brake! Brake!" He pushed Napoleon and, jumping out his side, his feet hit the floor and he cartwheeled three times, sat down, and slid into the side wall. Napoleon braked, jumped out the driver's side, landed on all fours, and slid into the opposite wall. The truck smashed into the far wall.

Larry was right. The dividing wall between the spaceport entry hall and the repair area was too thick. The vehicle broke through, but the cab was totally crushed. The wall held the vehicle like a cement hand. Thankfully, the truck wasn't going too fast when they jumped. Both got to their feet without injury and raced toward the newly crumbled vehicle.

There was no smoke from the engine; it was an OD variation. But there was mist from the wall components. It was through it that the two EXs moved. Night had been on their side, but now it was close to morning. A whole new shift of robots would be treading in. With any luck they would only be programmed for prime functioning, not to fry trespassers.

Already Larry could see three thread robots moving on the other side of the area and another one lying on its side near the vehicle snout, unaware that it had been knocked over. Larry could see no people, dead or alive, real or manufactured.

There was a central section cleared of everything except repair tables, with repair machinery hanging above them. To the right were shelves and shelves of spare parts (none, unfortunately, neatly labeled). There were no ships or sections of ships inside. All faulty parts were either repaired on board by the crew or hauled in here for work by spaceport staff.

At an unspoken signal both raced the length of the area, looking for a spacecraft OD. They met at the other end where a large hangar door separated it from the main field. They moved back, the way they had come, slower this time. Larry heard the feline's hiss and joined her at a table upon which a four-foot-by-three-foot roughly circular machine rested, looking a lot like the thing Larry had dismantled back at the lab. Napoleon glanced around nervously, her spitter at her chest, as Larry checked it over.

"It looks like an engine," he finally whispered. "It has parts I recognize. And the core could be an O'Neil Drive."

"You mean you're not sure?" Napoleon asked incredulously. After all, the FM had built his own ship. Larry shook his head forlornly. "Let's take it anyway and get out," said the still-wary feline.

"We should look around some more. To make sure."

"We have no time!" Napoleon hissed harshly.

"We have no choice!" Larry said back. "We won't have a second chance up there."

Napoleon opened her mouth, but she did not retort. She just took off. Larry did the same in the opposite direction. The sun began to rise, sending reddish-yellow shadows across the area that had previously been bathed in bright blue. The combined might of the satellite and the duex ciel kept the evenings well illuminated.

It was eerie. Here in the expansive repair shop the horrors of the spaceport seemed like a bad dream that could be woken from. The rising sun enhanced that peaceful effect, but it didn't make their search any easier. Instead, it hid many items in shadow and added a greater note of panic to the proceedings. The blanket of night was being pulled back to reveal them running around the sheets.

The two finally found each other back at the same table.

"I still say it's this thing," Napoleon maintained.

"I reluctantly agree with you," replied Larry. "I think I found a transport vehicle over on the other side there. Come on."

They ran to where a small rectangular affair on six wheels sat. On either end was a small cubicle, one of which was outfitted with a seat, two levers, and two pedals. The other end had what looked like wiring coming out of three tubes on the floor.

"I think this can either be driven by people from this side or machines from the other," said Napoleon.

"But not feline," decided Larry. "Get in the machine end. I'll get this thing started."

Napoleon opened her mouth again, but again said nothing. She decided she'd have plenty to say when and if they ever got onto the *Black Hole* again. She turned, marched back to the machine end, and then stepped aboard just as a yellow beam hit the vehicle entrance just above her head, vibrating the metal and numbing her left paw.

She whirled around to see the two spaceport officials walking toward her with two weapons aimed and two smug grins on their two faces. She smiled back at them, showing her teeth, and brought up her spitter.

Their smiles froze and they dove aside as Napoleon did her best to separate their torsos from their hips. It wasn't good enough. They leaped for cover as the feline's weapon tore up the floor and wall behind them. Larry jerked around at the sound.

"Get us outa here!" she yelled. Larry swung his head back and yanked on both levers.

Nothing happened.

Napoleon filled the room with deadly tubes of high-intensity light, drilling perfect holes in machinery and the floor. Brown hair sat behind one case of parts that was beginning to look like Swiss cheese. Blondie lay behind a huge metal tube. Neither stayed there long. Both had to keep moving or risk letting Napoleon get a bead on them. They ran around, still not believing that an EX-A had a weapon and was firing at them.

Larry pushed down both pedals with his feet. Nothing happened.

"Get back!" blondie shouted to his partner while running toward the entrance and blindly firing behind him. Napoleon had to jump out of the vehicle as beams smashed the visor glass, dotted the seat she had been leaning on, and went right through the vehicle. Larry stiffened as the bolts shot out next to his head and through the crook of both arms.

He moved the right lever and the left pedal. Nothing happened.

Napoleon appeared in the vehicle's opposite doorway. "The two Stoners escaped! They'll be dropping every TM within miles on us any second! Will you get us the Earth Father out of here?"

Larry pulled the left lever and the right pedal. The vehicle swung right over Napoleon.

She had fallen onto her back the second she felt the vehicle vibrate under her paws. The steel body went over her, the ball-like wheels just missing her. She catapulted to her feet as soon as her legs had room and dove into a pile of tires as the vehicle swung around and around.

Larry kept his foot on the right pedal and pulled back on the left lever. The vehicle moved straight to the left toward the table with the engine. Napoleon raced alongside and hopped in the cab.

"I won't be able to defend myself while I collect the thing," Larry warned.

"Why should anything change?" said Napoleon through gritted teeth as the vehicle sped toward the table. "Can you brake?"

Larry hadn't even finished saying, "I don't know yet," when Napoleon leaped out of the cab, hit a parallel table on her stomach, slid all the way down, and dropped off the far end. Larry violently returned all the levers and pedals to their original positions. The vehicle screeched to a halt, slamming the FM against the hole-riddled windshield. It cracked but didn't break.

Napoleon stood up behind the engine. "I'm having a great time," she said. "Are you?"

Larry pushed himself up and grabbed his spitter just as blondie and brown hair reappeared in the doorway. One carried the Maghawk Strepper. The other, the complete Cremor Adjusthunk. Around their legs came a swarm of at least a dozen foozles.

Larry threw his weapon at Napoleon and hopped into the driver's seat. Napoleon caught the second gun, spitting in frustration. She howled as she opened up with both weapons, one in each paw. The TMs jumped from the entrance to a shelf wall that rose from the floor to the ceiling. They could fire from many levels along its entire length.

Larry pushed down the right pedal and the vehicle lurched forward as the air was filled with stun beams. They all flew overhead and Napoleon angrily returned the fire, having to swing her weapons in wide arcs to keep the foozles at bay. Larry jerked the vehicle closer toward the table, pulling at the left lever until he was parallel to it.

"Get in, get in!" he shouted, looking out at her. When he turned back, a foozle was at the other door, its teeth bared. Larry screamed and hit it on the snout with all his might. The tiny creature dropped out of the vehicle. Napoleon fell to her back and fired under the truck upside down, killing the prone foozle.

The others charged her, thinking she would need time to rise, but before they had taken a step, she had already hurled her legs up and her body followed. She was firing all the while. Two other foozles flew back, their hides perforated.

Larry poked his head out again to see that the table was even with the bed of the vehicle—a bed that lay between the two cubicle cabs. The truck was stopped directly alongside the engine. All they had to do now was to get it on the truck bed somehow. Larry leaped out. So did brown hair. He was standing beside blondie on the third level of the shelving. He had the Maghawk. He aimed it. He pulled the trigger. Larry and Napoleon dropped.

The cubicle for machine driving exploded. The Maghawk Strepper was like the most powerful shotgun ever invented, only it had no kickback and was the size and shape of a beamer.

The foozles tried charging again, but the exploding cubicle rubble hit them like shrapnel. Napoleon looked under the vehicle and saw Larry in shock. Then the top three levels of the shelf wall spun outward and disappeared. Three bands of bright yellow light grew to fill the entire top portion of the repair area and ripped out the top section of the opposite wall a half foot deep. The rubble cascaded onto the floor next to the vehicle like a concrete waterfall.

"That was the Cremor Adjusthunk," Napoleon said, stunned.

"Get in!" Larry demanded.

She scrambled for the cab, firing with one spitter. He tore the other from her paw while climbing in as well.

"Let's go!" she cried.

"We need that engine!" he shouted back.

Larry whirled about, shot a leaping foozle full in the face, then sliced across the table legs. The legs nearest the vehicle splintered and broke. The table fell in that direction, dumping everything on it, including the engine, onto the bed of the vehicle.

A foozle tried going beneath the truck at that moment. The weight of the machinery pushed the vehicle down, crushing the attacker. Napoleon leaned out her side and shot at the others. She looked up. Blondie and brown hair showed themselves. Brown hair aimed the strepper. Napoleon just missed him with her spitter blast, but sent him reeling. She got him lined up in her sights and pulled the trigger with satisfaction.

It clicked empty. Her last sight as she whirled toward Larry was of blondie readjusting the Cremor directly at them.

"Go!" she screamed.

"Hold on!" Larry yelled, dropping his spitter and hauling the levers to the side. Napoleon gripped the roof of the vehicle with one paw and anchored her legs as Larry shoved the levers forward and jammed down the right pedal.

The vehicle rushed backward, running over another foozle. Larry pulled the right lever. The vehicle swirled right. Suddenly the two were facing the ECG men, but moving away quickly. Napoleon saw just the hint of a smile as blondie aimed the Cremor at them before she scooped up Larry's spitter and shot through the windshield.

The glass shattered and whirled away. The beam tore up the remaining shelves and struck the Adjusthunk just as its barrel went yellow. Blondie and brown hair were consumed in a ball of broiling fire and white smoke, their screams swallowed up as the shelves were ripped down the middle and sent spinning in all directions.

The tiny vehicle sped backward as wood shards littered the ground where their tires had just been. Larry loosened his foot pressure and pulled the levers back. The vehicle spun forward and charged at a closed door. He said no words. He simply screamed. Napoleon leaned out the cab and shot from the ceiling the ropes and chains that were holding the large door down. The opening started sliding up.

The little vehicle sped out, the bottom of the rising door scraping the roof of the truck just before the Adjusthunk's reserve power pack let go. The door was sliced in three equal yellow sections as the energy bands dissipated and winked out just over the truck.

Larry tore his eyes from the spectacle and tried to locate their pod. As they sped out into the sunlight, he spied it near the edge of the takeoff area. He pushed the levers forward again. The vehicle spun and raced at the pod backward.

"Will you stop doing that!" Napoleon yelled angrily.

"The hatch!" he yelled back at her. "The hatch! Open the hatch!"

She looked to where he was frantically pointing. She dropped the spitter and jumped out onto the paved ground and sped toward the esc-globe on all fours. The flatbed vehicle wasn't that speedy and she outdistanced it, arriving at the pod flushed, tail high, several seconds before it. Rising quickly, she opened the hatch outward and threw the door wide.

At that moment Larry slammed both feet onto the left pedal, locking all the wheels. The vehicle skidded, turned—Larry feverishly working the levers to line it up right—and then stopped. The payload did not.

The smaller parts sailed through the air like bullets. Napoleon spun away and hit the deck. The engine slid, rolled, then bounced right onto one of the chairs, crushing it, before hitting the far wall of the esc-globe.

"By CHESHIRE!" Napoleon shrieked, both at Larry and two remaining foozles that ran at them.

Larry reached for the spitter. Napoleon beat him to it, his fingers closed on air as she snatched it from beneath the passenger seat. The feline raced to protect the globe and Larry came out of the cab swinging. He slammed the pry bar he had kept hooked in his belt onto a foozle head as Napoleon shot the other down. They both jumped into the esc-globe, nearly tripping over three dead FM soldiers.

They were the men Wolf-Hoover had sent to guard the pod, but Larry and Napoleon didn't know that. All they knew was that three dead men were littering their esc-globe. Larry collapsed into his pilot seat while Napoleon hurled the corpses out of the pod with explosions of enraged strength. The bodies flew through the air and crashed into the flatbed truck.

She sealed the hatch as Larry contacted Mess.

"What took you so long?" it said, and instigated lift-off. Napoleon was slammed onto the floor as the *Black Hole*'s escape pod blasted into the sky.

Larry tried to laugh, but the g-force pushed the sound back into his face. He had made it. The decision Napoleon had made for him only a short while ago was now an unavoidable fact of his future. He would survive rather than passively be terminated. Suddenly he had a chance. A destiny, if you will.

Like it or not, come what might, he was free. He decided again, this time without haste, that the only way Earth would claim him again would be in death.

An uncharacteristic Harlan was waiting for them as they pulled themselves out of the tunnel into the passageway of the *Black Hole*.

"Did you get it? Do you know where my sister is? What happened?"

Larry ignored him, pulling off his shirt in triumph and shouting, "Mess! Status!"

"Status?" the compubot retorted. "What is status? What do you mean by status?"

So much for heroic swaggering. "The ship! Is it ready?"

"Of course it is! What do you think, I've been playing with myself up here?"

"Any approaching craft?"

"None. If any do appear, do I have permission to fire?" Larry wasn't sure whether Mess' voice held fear or anticipation.

"Let me know if anything does show up, then ask again."

"Right," said Mess. It was anticipation.

"Did you get the engine?" Trigor pressed.

"Mess," Larry said in way of reply. "Find the hunk of machinery where the co-pilot's seat used to be in the esc-globe and get it over to our engine area."

By the time the trio reached the engineering section, the floor was littered with metal debris from inside the esc-globe. Napoleon picked up the spitter. Larry picked up the pry bar. In the middle of the rubble sat the ball of machinery they had risked their hides for.

Harlan spun to Larry, beaming. "You have it," he said. "I recognize the design."

Larry and Napoleon relaxed visibly. The feline curled herself into a ball on the floor and Larry's chest swelled with pride. He twirled the pry bar in his fingers.

"Great." said Larry, pointing over Harlan's shoulder at the engine. "How soon can you install that thing?"

Harlan glanced around. "How soon can I install what thing?" he asked in confusion.

"That!" Larry said, jabbing his finger at the glob of machinery. Napoleon stopped purring and looked up sharply. "That thing!"

Harlan turned again. "That thing?" he echoed. "I can't install that thing. That isn't an O'Neil Drive."

"What?" Larry exploded. "Then...if not that, then..."

"That," said Harlan, pointing at the pry bar, the pry bar Larry had killed an FM, a foozle, and his own creator with, "that is an O'Neil Drive."

NINE

"Ship approaching. Permission to fire."

Larry glanced at Harlan, who worked in the pit obliviously. "Not yet," the FM said. "What kind of ship?"

"An Earth ship."

Napoleon paced, her tail lashing the air while Larry stood beside the bulkhead, breathing shallowly.

He'd take a few large breaths every time he got woozy, then breathe shallowly again. The whole idea that he was at the mercy of a foot-long piece of closed metal that he'd used as a pry bar and club was annoying. The annoyance was compounded by the fact that Trigor was uncertain whether he could make a complete transference to the O'Neil Drive.

"What kind of Earth ship?"

"Executioner class."

Larry felt a little better. At least it would be a one-on-one fight. The Executioners were basically just patrol ships. A Destroyer, on the other hand, had the capability of an armada of Executioners.

"Followed by a Destroyer," Mess finished.

"What? What? You said ship, singular!" Larry shouted.

"Sorry, it appeared on my sensors as I was talking," Mess said defensively. "Permission to fire?"

"On a Destroyer? Are you joking? Of course not!"

Napoleon stopped pacing near Larry. "Should I move to the weapons area?"

"What for?" Larry said, exasperated. "Mess, what are they doing?"

"Near as I can tell, they're stopping in formation. Executioner before, Destroyer behind. Permission to fire."

"No. Stopping? Why are they stopping?"

"Are you asking me?" Mess inquired.

Larry ignored it, thinking. Napoleon remained at his side. Harlan kept working. "Wait a minute!" Larry exclaimed. "Guilt. I heard guilt in your voice, Mess! Are they sending a message?"

"Well," it said. "Yes."

"Why didn't you say so!" Larry exploded.

"I knew you had a lot on your mind," Mess answered.

"You wanted to fire."

"No, really..."

"Listen to me, Mess," snarled Napoleon. "Firing on a Destroyer is suicide. You don't want to die, do you?"

"No!"

"Then put through the message!"

Mess did not reply. Instead, a voice that could best be described as "civilized" filled the engine area.

"Earth Ship *Black Hole*, come in, please. Answer, *Black Hole*, if you will."

Larry and Napoleon looked at each other in amazement. Larry thought fast but came up with nothing. He looked back at Napoleon. She shrugged.

"Stall," whispered Harlan, not slowing his work. "I can patch in the OD for partial use."

Larry looked up helplessly. To be destroyed at the cusp of freedom was torturous. To die after having killed to preserve one's life was a terrible thought. "Mess," Larry instructed, "pick up Napoleon's voice only."

"Me?" she mewed. "What'll I say?"

"You want me to transmit that?" Mess asked politely.

"No. Wait until I tell you." He turned to his copilot. "I can't talk to him. I'm an FM. All the FMs are being killed."

"But I killed Grossman-Smith!"

"Maybe he doesn't know that. Why should he? He's a Destroyer commander."

"But maybe he does!"

"One of you talk to him!" Trigor bellowed.

"Give him a story," Larry urged, backing away. "Make something up. Just keep him going for a while."

"Wonderful," snarled the feline. "You've been a great help. All right, I'll think of something."

"Now?" said Mess.

Napoleon nodded. "Now," said Larry.

"Hello, hello," she cried in a mewling, panicky voice. "This is the *Black Hole*. Who is this?"

"This is the Earth Destroyer *Murphy-Williams*, young lady," returned the cultured voice. "We have been informed that a female feline and a Weinstein-Hubbell experimental false male have been responsible for the deaths of five real Humans: one military, one scientific, and three Governmental. What say you to these grave charges?"

Larry looked at Napoleon in utter amazement. She looked back in total confusion. Larry threw up his hands. It was anyone's move.

"He made me do it!" Napoleon screeched. "I didn't want to. He just went crazy!"

"Is this the creation you are referring to?" returned the voice.

"Yes, yes. He just started killing!"

"My dear," soothed the voice. "A creation cannot go insane."

Napoleon grimaced and continued, "This one did. He's different. He wasn't drugged. He wasn't indoctrinated. He's evil, I tell you!" She lowered her voice and gave the inflection of a sob at the end.

What a masterful performance, Larry decided. But then again, she had been giving performances to humans all her life. There was a pause from the *Murphy-Williams*, then the voice resumed.

"Are you referring to the Larry individual?"

"Yes, yes!"

"I have been informed that what you say has some bearing." Pause. "But unless he has managed to find another young female or altered his compubot's voice, you would be the Experimental Alien Napoleon, would you not?"

"He forced me, I tell you!"

"I shall assume that is an affirmative?"

"They don't want us dead yet!" Larry blurted out, then slapped his hands over his mouth as Napoleon glared at him.

"Yes," she answered the Destroyer. "Please, please help me!"

"We shall do our level best," said the refined voice.

Harlan continued to work feverishly, but he couldn't resist smiling. The feline was doing it up well.

"However," came the voice, "I have been advised there may not be complete truth in what you say. According to my information, you appeared to be firing an—two—illegal weapons quite independently. And quite well too, I have been informed."

Napoleon bit her lip in frustration. "Fucking foozle," she muttered. "He forced me to! I couldn't help it!"

"Don't worry," said Mess' voice. "I'm on the job. They're not picking up anything but Napoleon's voice. And not all of that either," it said accusingly.

"Fucking, fucking foozle," Napoleon spit at Larry.

"Keep it up!" he pleaded. "They want to take us alive! We've got a chance. I don't know why yet, but we've got a chance!"

"Excuse me, young...lady," said the Destroyer commander, "but I have a...gentleman here who says, and I quote, 'That is a lot of Mantas meat,' unquote."

Napoleon turned to Larry, her arms out. He mirrored the movement. "You're going to believe a *foozle?*" Napoleon asked incredulously.

The commander cleared his throat. "I'm afraid the evidence is against you, my dear. I'm afraid I must deliver an ultimatum."

"Stall," Larry heard Harlan grunt. "More time." Larry made a circular motion with his hand. Napoleon raised her paws, shaking her head. She had mindlock.

"You must surrender immediately," said the voice. "Or we will be forced to annihilate you."

"They're bluffing," Harlan stood to say.

"Are you sure?" Larry's voice nearly cracked.

Harlan was already bent down, back to work. "Of course."

"I tell you I *want* to give up!" cried an inspired Napoleon. "I can explain, but not now! Not here! He won't let me. He has the weapons now and he's completely insane. Can't you understand? I'm in fear for my life!"

"My heart goes out to you," said the voice. "It truly does. But I have no choice in the matter. Surrender."

Harlan pushed his hand out once, twice, three times. Larry opened his palms upward, shrugging. "All right. We surrender," she said.

"A wise decision," said the voice. "We will dock and board. I look forward to meeting you, my dear. I am told you are quite extraordinary. Destroyer *Murphy-Williams*, AU out."

Napoleon swung a paw at the empty air. "What are you doing?" she snarled.

"Well, what *am* I doing?" Larry asked Harlan.

"We may have just enough time," he replied, not stopping. "Get to the bridge. Give me until the last moment, then hit the engines full."

Larry was already striding toward his pilot seat. Napoleon caught up to him. "What is going on here?"

"Only one thing makes any kind of sense," he said tightly, maintaining his stride. "They're killing all the FMs on Earth because you and I killed one of theirs."

"Revenge?" she wondered.

"Self-preservation. If we can do it, any other FM or SM could do it as well. They're getting rid of the danger."

"But what about us?"

"Don't you see?" Larry said, sitting down at his console. "They don't want to make the same mistake twice. There are too few RHs. They can't afford to. They want to know where we went wrong. Nap," he said, turning to her, "they still want us for our ATs."

The four ports, stretching from the pilot's to co-pilot's area, were filled with the expanse of the Executioner. Like four walls closing in on them. Before moving to her seat, Napoleon stood next to Harlan's space bullet suit and looked around. Before her spun the Earth. Behind her was the blazing sun. And on either side was the rest of the galaxy. She moved forward.

"Mess, approximate time of docking," Larry asked.

"What about it?"

Larry ground his teeth. "When will it occur?" Napoleon said.

"Approximately," the compubot drawled, "thirty-six—no, thirty—yes, thirty-six seconds from right—now."

"Start a countdown," Larry ordered.

"From right now," Napoleon added.

"Thirty-four, thirty-three, thirty-two..."

"Have you included an area of risk?" Larry asked, hands beside the console's engine switch.

"Of course—thirty—but wouldn't—twenty-nine—it be easier—twenty-seven—to simply blast—twenty-five—"

"Never mind," said Larry. He watched the ports, thinking, or rather hoping, that the compubot was just blowing off steam. The view of space was now totally blotted out by the Executioner ship. Just beyond it lay the Destroyer, hanging in space like a mother hawk waiting for baby to bring home dinner in all its perfect irony.

The Executioner's approach was slow, slower than expected. It was not the triumphant swoop he had anticipated. Larry suddenly realized it was because they had killed five TMs with deliberate speed. If he had been told of any FM doing that, he wouldn't have believed it. It was unbelievable insanity. Then if he had been told that he was the one responsible for the murderer's capture, his approach would be equally as cautious. Why, an FM capable of killing a TM was capable of anything.

"Twenty-five, twenty-four, twenty-three, twenty-two..."

Larry engaged the controls. The engine switch sat like a coiled snake by his left hand, waiting to strike. He wrapped his fingers around the metal viper. Ignition a second too soon would give the Destroyer a chance to blast them. Ignition a second too late would catch the Executioner docked. The SOD (Spacecraft O'Neil Drive) would probably rip off a weak section of the *Black Hole*'s hull and implode them all into the cold vacuum of outer space.

"Nineteen, eighteen, seventeen..."

Larry could almost feel the slimy scales of the serpent beneath his palms. Sweat slid down the slick switch. His fingers tightened as the Executioner grew larger and larger out the portholes. He glanced aside. Napoleon stood by her chair.

"Better sit down," he said quickly. "We don't know how this drive'll work."

"*If* it works," she corrected, nimbly moving into her seat.

"Fourteen, thirteen, twelve..."

The Executioner was only feet away, moving in for the final docking. Well, what do you know, Larry thought. Mess' math was right this time.

"Seven, six, five..."

Harlan worked intently in the pit. The pry bar/OD was free hanging. Mess' voice boomed in the engine area.

"Four—you-should've-let-me-fire—two..."

Harlan jumped back. Larry's hand tightened. Napoleon gripped her console.

"One. Zero."

Larry's arm moved back.

Nothing happened.

Three men in the Executioner docking bay pulled the manual switch to adhere the patrol ship to the *Black Hole*.

Harlan bellowed like a wounded animal and hit the OD with his fist.

Larry and Napoleon looked at each other and the ship took off.

Larry blinked and the *Black Hole* was somewhere else. No thrust, no g-force, not even a queasy stomach. There wasn't even a vibration.

Napoleon did not blink. She was watching the screens when it happened. One second the Executioner filled her view. She could see the "PENDL" and "BOLA" of their call letters through the screens. They flashed white for a split second and then no Executioner, no Destroyer, no Earth, no moon, and no Doomstar. They were somewhere else and motionless.

Harlan hit the OD again. They moved again. He hit it with his right fist a third time. The *Black Hole* jumped a third time. He hit it with his right twice more. The ship rocketed forward twice more. He hit it with his left fist. The ship shot forward and kept going.

Napoleon was somersaulted out of her seat backward, landing on her feet. Larry was pushed back in his chair. Now they were moving.

"Mess?" Larry called.

"Wow!" it said. "This is great!"

"What is it?"

"Just below light speed. Or maybe light speed, I don't know. But it isn't faster than light, that I can tell you."

"Can you handle it?" Larry demanded.

"Scientific impossibility is not something you 'handle,'" said the machine. "How am I supposed to handle something that can't be?"

"What is it saying?" Napoleon asked Larry in fear. Her hair stood on end as she crouched behind her seat.

"I told you scientists know nothing about life," he smiled. "They've always said breaking the speed of light was impossible. Hey, they said breaking the speed of sound wasn't possible. Taplinger-Jones, they said a bumblebee flying was impossible!"

"What I am saying," Mess cried, "is that it's a rush!"

"A rush?" she mewed. "What's a rush?"

"A drug term," said Larry with a grin. "Palsy-Drake was a drug addict near the end."

"He wasn't an addict!" Mess shouted. "He could stop any time he wanted!"

The cacophony was interrupted by Trigor, who ran in shouting, "I've been calling you for several seconds!"

"Mess," Larry said accusingly. "Why didn't you put him through?"

"Never mind!" Harlan barked. "This isn't even half the power. We caught the other ships by surprise, but they might catch up."

"How?" Larry wailed.

"They can accelerate, we can't," Harlan said, marching back toward the engine area. "Yet."

"Mess, how soon will they catch up?" Larry asked.

"I'll try to calibrate the new speeds," it promised. "Let's see; follow the six, carry the nine...."

Napoleon laughed in spite of herself, with just a touch of hysteria. Then she stood straight and reprimanded herself. "Go ahead, laugh. But in a few minutes we'll be back to where we started. Only at faster speeds."

"Seventeen minutes, sixteen seconds, to be more exact," deliberated Mess.

Larry said, "Can you connect the OD in time?"

"No," said Harlan.

Larry sat back, stunned. What was it all for—the

killing, the slaughter, the escape? He couldn't bring himself to look at Napoleon. He stared out into space. Through the porthole was shining black with bands of unnatural waving colors, colors that danced across spectrums. It was the source. The giver of hope and the bringer of death. -

And the trap was snapping shut again. The star Sol kept its prisoner Earth alive. Larry was beginning to think that this was his personal hell. To be forever on the edge of the Doomstar's snare.

"That's it, then," Larry sighed.

"That's what?" said Harlan.

Larry couldn't believe the man's obtuseness. "The end," he spelled out.

"Not at all. I am here."

"But you just said you couldn't connect the OD in time!"

"That is true, but I am not beaten."

"What do you expect us to do?" Napoleon flared. "Slip into an esc-globe and sneak out the back?"

"Don't waste time. You do not need your escape vehicles. Only my suit."

"It seems to me you could've been a little clearer," reprimanded Mess.

Napoleon giggled, then threw up her paws and walked away.

"Fight a Destroyer in that thing?" Larry said, pointing at the rock.

Harlan walked into the bridge area. "I can be ready," he said, hefting his exoskeleton. "I will defeat both ships, return to connect the drive, and then we'll be on our way."

"In *that* thing?" Larry repeated, his voice rising.

"I am not asking your permission," Harlan interrupted briskly, "but I am requesting your help. Here is the situation. I will fight irregardless. Whether you are destroyed in the process is up to you."

"Help the man, will you, Larry?" Mess wailed. "I can drive the ship."

"Talk," said the FM.

"It will take me longer to test my repairs than we have. The two ships must be kept at bay until I am ready."

"You don't have a chance," Larry said sadly.

"*He* doesn't have a chance," Napoleon piped in stridently, hitting Larry behind the ear with the back of her paw. "*We* don't have a chance. If he wants to commit suicide, the least we can do is join him."

Larry retreated from the feline, hands before his face. "What do you want me to do? Ram the ships?"

"No, no," said Mess. "He fixed us while you were Earthside. We have weapons now."

Larry looked at Harlan. He nodded. The FM looked at his co-pilot, mouth agape. "Here we go again," he said. Then he turned back to Harlan. "Well? What are you waiting for?"

The man with the civilized voice sat in his control chair amid the largest array of destructive weapons in the fleet. By his side was an astonishingly beautiful woman. In his role as commander on one of Earth's three Destroyer-class ships, he was privileged to be in one of the highest positions of the ECG hierarchy. In addition, he was privileged to live above the degradation that was Earth. And he looked it. It was a very secure position.

Black, curly hair, artificial both in color and composition, swept back from his forehead. Molded features, the best the landbound scientists could chisel, sat across his visage. A supple body, as much the work of a tailor as of exercise, sat on the individually contoured seat.

The only evidence of his original nature lay in his hands. They appeared rugged, but it was from flesh-painting—utilizing natural flesh tones to highlight soft, pulpy skin. Hair had been added to the backs and behind the knuckles to further the deception. He never shook hands or even used them unless he absolutely had to. Among the military they had a joke: if Commander LeClair-Becker was in a room with only a doorknob on the exit, he would never be seen again.

This jape never reached his ears, however. He was a commander of a Destroyer (*the* Destroyer, if the truth be known). He cared little for the prattling of others. He cared even less for the prattling that was reaching his ears presently.

"This is entirely unnecessary," came the coarse sounds. "It's foolish, dangerous, and unfair."

LeClair-Becker listened, picturing the speaker: thin, with sparse sandy hair standing out in tufts on a pale, speckled head.

"We will be in visual contact in moments," the gravelly voice continued. "I respectfully request to drop back and let the *Murphy-Williams* handle the destruction procedures."

The commander digested the request, then leaned forward and spoke, his voice resonant. "Stuck-Mark, be reasonable. You are not in any danger. It is a small vessel—"

"With two murderers on board!" the quavering bass interrupted.

"But this is our territory now," LeClair-Becker continued sweetly. "We rule space. No other can match us."

"Did you see how they took off? I was in the space

lock! If we had concluded the docking procedure, it would have been disaster!"

"For them, only for them," lulled the Destroyer commander. "My dear Stuck-Mark, did you *see* their vessel? A patchwork affair, a paltry example of inferior craftsmanship."

"They have the light drive," Stuck-Mark reminded him. "Who knows what else they have on board."

"They stole the O'Neil Drive from the Earth lab," soothed the commander. "Badly installed. Even so, we will catch and destroy—execute them."

"Why won't you lead?" Stuck-Mark demanded. "Why must our inferior craft face them first? It is endangering the lives of Real Humans!"

"Captain Stuck-Mark, you are the leader of an Earth Ship Executioner!" LeClair-Becker snapped. "Act like one!"

"Save it for your SM," the other man snapped back. "I'm issuing a formal memo." Then he broke the connection.

"Corman-Heath!" the commander said angrily. A short, curly-haired young man appeared by his side.

"Yes, sir."

"Please handle the Stuck-Mark situation when we sight the FM ship."

"Yes, sir." The curly-haired man disappeared.

"Thomas," said the woman, leaning toward him, "then there is a chance their ship is dangerous?"

LeClair-Becker took her hand in his and kissed it absentmindedly. His eyes were still on the forescreen. "Yes, my dear, I'm afraid there is that possibility."

"And you wish to see what weapons they do have before you engage them?"

"Very wise, my love. Yes, that is why Stuck-Mark goes first to see whatever that flying junkyard dishes out. Then we'll know what we're dealing with."

"But surely the ship is not capable of harming an Executioner?"

LeClair-Becker shrugged. "We shall see, my dear," he said, kissing her hand again.

The woman remained silent for a few moments. "And if the captain retreats or refuses to battle the *Black Hole?*"

"Corman-Heath will see to it."

"Thomas." She had given him this name. She hoped it was one his dead parents would have approved of. "If they do fire upon the Executioner, if it is damaged or even destroyed, what will you do?"

The commander turned to his love, his one true love, and looked deep into her eyes. "Andrea, my beloved. So that is what is troubling you." He sighed. "First we received word that the U.W. lab wanted both subjects alive for test purposes. Then I received a priority call from ECGC Linn-Bok, who instructs us to eradicate the pair and the ship completely."

The woman gasped.

"Yes, my dear, it seems that this murder spree and the O'Neil Drive robbery are just the tip of the iceberg. I have to assume that these two represent a far greater danger than we had originally anticipated. As you well know, Linn-Bok rarely acts out of vengeance."

"Oh, darling," she cried, "can't we let them go? What is a single Fake Man? A single Experimental Alien? Can't we just let the poor things go?"

"Andrea. They have killed five True Men. Try to understand that. I know you are young and the murder of Real Humans is incredible to you, but it has been done. *They* did it. And their actions have unleashed a terrible massacre of others. And remember, you are but a single Sex..." He couldn't bring himself to say it. "...artificial woman. But you are my one love."

The woman started to soundlessly, motionlessly cry. LeClair-Becker wiped away her tears tenderly.

"And if I didn't destroy them," he said. "If I let them escape, they would discredit me, dishonor me, and worst of all, take you away. They would take you away and kill you."

"There they are!" shouted Mess.

Larry was off and running. He passed Harlan, whose head stuck out of the space bullet suit, facing forward, facial muscles flickering as he tested the suit. Larry moved out of the bridge, sped down the hallway, took a right, a quick left, then another right, came to a circular hatch, slammed his hand on a red button, ground a gear around until it stopped, then spun open the door and stepped into a square room.

Directly before him was a small, slatted window above a tiny escape hatch. To his right was a six-by-two-and-a-half-foot slatted window facing the front of the ship. Yes, there was a front to the *Black Hole*. Lying across the right side of the enclosure was a console table with no chair. Right next to the entryway was a large stick switch.

To the left was a wall on which a spacesuit was attached in a standing position. Larry leaned over the console and pulled down a tiny switch below a box speaker.

"I'm here," he said into it. "What's the situation?"

"They're not in firing range yet," Napoleon replied, sounding as if she were at the bottom of a well. "Mess's calculated when they will be. It's on the console up here. You getting it?"

"No. This room was installed because it was there. I thought it looked good on the hull. The only connection I've got to the bridge is this. You'll have to keep me informed. I can only see forward and to the left."

"You mean out the port side?" Napoleon asked quietly.

"Is that port? Left?"

"Actually, I'm not sure. I'd thought you'd know. I'm getting tense."

"So am I," said Larry. "Keep talking. How much time left?"

"Less than three minutes."

"How is Harlan doing?"

"Still quivering. No sign of aggressive movement."

"I'm going to have to do this, aren't I?" asked Larry.

"Yes, you are," said Napoleon.

"All right. Have Mess prepare whatever defenses we have and give him permission to fire...." Larry heard the compubot's "Yippee!" in the background. "Damper down. Only at the first sign of attack. Their orders may still be for capture only."

"Wishful thinking," Napoleon said miserably.

Both fell silent. Larry looked out at the majesty of space, wishing Napoleon were with him. Wishing he were with Napoleon. Anywhere but in a closet ledge overhanging infinity. "How much time now?"

"A little over two minutes."

"Listen, I only have limited sensing capabilities in here. I need the Executioner's coordinates on a projected course. Can Mess get that?" Larry listened to the feline informing the compubot.

"It says it could if it knew what the Taplinger-Jones you were talking about."

One thing about Mess. It got Larry's adrenaline pumping. "Once the Executioner gets in range, I'll need to know what course it's most likely to take!" he spat. "I have to shoot where he's going to be. Once

Mess projects his direction I'll have to lock it into the aiming machinery. The firing switch is four feet away."

Again the feline translated for the compubot. "It'll do what it can. More than a minute left. Can you see them?"

Larry looked out the slatted window beside him. These slats would slam down automatically in the event the room was blasted off the hull into space. Given that it was a "clean" hit, Larry would have less than a minute to get into the spacesuit and out the hatch before the relatively flimsy space would be crushed. Naturally, the equipment couldn't be worked in a spacesuit and the spacesuit gloves couldn't be removed from the arms.

"I think I see one," Larry said. A small dot of glistening metal. Like a shooting star with no tail. That had to be the Destroyer. "What's the formation?"

"Same as before. Executioner leading."

"Start evasive action," he said, then muttered, "for all the good it'll do," as his hands swept across the console.

"A minute to firing range," Napoleon warned.

"Course projections?"

"Not yet, not yet," Mess said.

Larry hastily prepared the board. Everything worked, thank the Earth Fath—thank Destiny. All that was left to do was lock in the enemy's projected course coordinates. Larry had to stand there and wait for them.

"Larry," came Napoleon's tight voice. "Message coming in."

"*Black Hole*," Larry heard dimly over the speaker. "This is the Destroyer *Murphy-Williams*, as you might well imagine. You have forty-five seconds before we will be in firing range of your craft. You have absolutely no hope of survival if you engage us. I would very much like to talk with you personally, but if you persist in your escape or attack, you will be destroyed utterly. Please respond."

There were twenty-five seconds left. Larry could see the Destroyer clearly. A more nebulous spot preceded it: the Executioner. Both were bright spanking-new ships kept in peak condition, since they had never been called upon to do anything offensive before.

"This is the *Black Hole*," he heard Napoleon say. "We're really sorry, but this engine went crazy. We couldn't stop it. It just suddenly went on."

"Ah, my dear, it's you again!" LeClair-Becker announced. "How nice. First the FM goes crazy, then the O'Neil Drive. Is that it?"

"Yes, that's it all right," Napoleon replied without pretense.

"Well, it is a pity. We are now in firing range, and since you cannot stop we will have to eliminate you."

"Wait!" Napoleon yelled. "I think . . . we might just be able to . . . uh, disconnect it." She looked up at Harlan. He was completely engrossed in his checks.

"Very well," said LeClair-Becker. "You have ten seconds."

"Don't slow down!" Larry shouted. "Maintain evasive maneuvers. Is Harlan ready yet?"

Napoleon turned around. Magically, the stonelike helmet had completely covered Trigor's head. "I can't tell."

"Taplinger-Jones, I *am* going to have to do this. Mess, on my word."

"Permission to fire?" Mess asked gleefully.

"You got it, you paranoid pile. On my word."

"One second left, Larry!" Napoleon warned.

Larry watched them come in. They got larger and larger through the slats. "Permission," he said, "to," he said, "fire!"

A corkscrew of light spun out toward the Executioner, hurling some metal skin off the *Black Hole*. The Executioner slipped to the left and down, but the corkscrew ripped at its left side.

"Hit!" Napoleon shrieked. "It's still moving, picking up speed."

"Keep firing!" Larry boomed. "I don't care if you hit them or not. Just keep them dazzled and get me those coordinates!"

"The Destroyer is hanging back. They're letting the Exec take the worst of it. It's behind us, it's coming around!"

They were both shouting at the top of their lungs. Behind the feline's back, the space bullet soundlessly floated off the floor and moved toward the rear of the bridge.

Larry saw flashes of light reflecting off the side of the hull, his hands dripping sweat onto the navigational equipment. "What is going on? I can't see! Tell me what is happening!"

Both Napoleon's and Mess' voices filled his little room. "Incredible! Lights are blasting all over the area, every color! Exec moving down, probably for a bank run! I can't tell if I'm hitting it, too bright! It'll fire under us and move back for a run on the opposite cross! It's getting faster, faster! No damage! No damage! They're underneath! I can't see them anymore! I can! They're coming right up under us! They're coming to smash us in half! Larry, coordinates!"

He didn't know whether it was the compubot or the feline who told him. He just heard the letters and numbers and slapped them into the machine. Suddenly he was thrown backward off his feet. He was in midair when the ship was thrown in the opposite direction. His back hit the floor as it was moving toward him. He was thrown forward, his middle smacking the console.

"We're hit!" Mess screamed.

Looking out the front with bloodshot eyes, Larry clearly saw the Executioner streak off to the left, banking up. It was a W stuck on an upside-down V brightly edged and loaded with sleek equipment. At the tips of the W were weapons, at the central crown were ports banked by more weapons, and at the tips of the upside-down V were the engine exhausts.

"Damages!" he cried. "Napoleon, report! Mess, get me coordinates!"

"Damage to our right side. Lower observation bubble gone. Area sealed off. Bottom hatch secure. Area sealed off."

"The coordinates!" Larry repeated hysterically. The Executioner was coming back. Right at him.

"Same pattern in the opposite direction," said Mess.

"Numbers!"

He got them. His hands flew across the console. He moved dials, he stabbed buttons. Move, stab, move, stab, move, stab. Everything was up full. No second chances. As the last dial was locked into place, Larry reached for the stick switch and yanked. It wouldn't budge.

He stared in amazement at a countdown appearing at the top of the console. Eight seconds. The thing had to warm up!

Larry hit his chin on the speaker. "Don't let it hit us!" he cried. "The ship has to remain steady! Shoot at it, but don't knock it off course!"

"What?" Mess screamed incredulously. "How am I supposed . . . !"

"Five seconds! Five miserable, lousy . . ."

The sky began to crackle. Larry saw the rainbow

streak, arc, zigzag, and snap toward the oncoming Executioner. It made dazzling fireworks around the ship, doing as much damage as a waterfall off a boulder's back.

Larry saw it bearing down on him. Three seconds. If it fired, he'd be gone. The room would tear off the hull and shatter like glass.

Two seconds, one...

Larry's mind caught the beat. At zero his arm moved down, pulling the released switch. Even though he was using all his strength, the stick descended like a branch in rubber.

Larry slammed it to the floor. He was lying on top of it when the room began to shake. The floor rippled. Larry stood as if spring-loaded. Before his eyes one tube of solid beige smashed the Executioner in mid-flight. It broke like twigs.

The Executioner seemed to ingest the beige tube and then spin away in all directions. Larry heard a roaring in his ears. He stood motionless, his hands clenched into fists, his knuckles skeleton white. He suddenly noticed the cheers coming from the speaker.

"You did it!" Napoleon gushed. "I can't believe it! Did you see that?"

He saw it all right. The Executioner was gone. The Destroyer was moving in.

TEN

"Unbelievable. Incredible."

"Thank you, Corman-Heath, for that enlightening critique," the commander said dryly. "Still, it has happened, and our dear friend and colleague Stuck-Mark had to pay for underestimating the enemy."

"What—what was the weapon that was employed, sir?"

"Hardly time for an armaments lesson."

"What shall we do now, sir?"

"Let them go, Thomas!" Andrea pleaded. "They are too dangerous. You can tell Linn-Bok they destroyed the Executioner and got away on an O'Neil Drive."

"She's talking treason, Commander," Corman-Heath immediately stated.

"Silence!" LeClair-Becker raged at the young man. He struggled to regain his composure while towering over his assistant. "You are becoming annoying," he finally said, each word controlled. "You are eager to learn, so I will ignore your statement. But never address my woman again. Do you understand?"

"Yes, sir."

The commander sat down stiffly. He looked to his love. She was as white as a sheet, staring straight ahead.

"I love you more than anything," he told her. "But I could tire of you one day. Please remember that." He looked back at Corman-Heath. "To the Earth Father with murderers and liars, I say. I am going to engage this ship in battle and wipe it from the sky."

Larry watched the huge turtle-shaped ship move toward them. The turtle's head and legs were inside its shell and no holes were visible, but Larry knew that death could come from anywhere on its smooth surface.

"It's taunting us," said Napoleon. "It's moving in close, daring us to hit it with all we've got. It knows it can beat us now."

"Any suggestions?" Larry asked.

"This is it," said Mess. "It's all over. I never really thought it would come to this. Sure, I knew you two were unorthodox, but I never thought...It's too much, I tell you, too much!"

"Damper down," Larry said tiredly.

"Don't go to pieces," said the feline irritably.

"That's it." Mess spoke quickly, quietly, and intently. "Pieces!" The compubot's console rolled back and a shape sped out, clanking. It had two arms, but instead of hands it had gobs of equipment. A drill, a clamp, a wrench, a hammer. It had a head but there were grids and indentations where eyes and ears should have been. "I'm out of here," said the Mess-man. Napoleon spun in her chair to see a noisily retreating robot.

She spun back to her console speaker. "Trigor's gone!"

Larry hastily scanned the space outside. There was nothing. Nothing but the Destroyer. "He has to be inside the ship! He isn't out there!"

"He couldn't get to the back hatch. It's sealed off."

"Larry and Napoleon," said the commander over their AUs. "Good-bye."

The commander leaned back in his chair, smiling. Over Corman-Heath's AU came Harlan's mournful voice.

"How do I get out of here?"

Napoleon did it as Larry screamed it.

"Blow the seal!"

Exhilaration blasted Harlan's consciousness as his long-dormant instincts took over. The suit responded! He was alive again! The space bullet was sucked out as the feline blasted the seal on the bottom hatch.

"Look!" Napoleon said, pointing out the port. "There he is!"

Larry looked forward and saw a tiny thing zip up and course toward the Destroyer. His head shook from side to side, his mouth opened, but the FM couldn't say anything.

The dot charged the monstrosity.

"Sir," said Corman-Heath, "two items have left the ship. One moving away, one moving toward us."

"Another secret weapon, eh?" the commander gloated. "Analyze it."

"It's a mixture of ores, elements, and other material we cannot identify, sir."

A finger like ice touched the back of LeClair-Becker's neck. He spun toward Andrea. She had not moved. He pivoted back toward Corman-Heath. "Destroy it. Immediately. Completely."

"Yes, sir. Energy bolts aimed." The young man pressed a button. "And fired, sir."

They all watched as the broiling ball of white rolled

toward the oncoming projectile. The distance between the two diminished until the bolt blotted the tiny thing from their sight. Corman-Heath smiled but the commander leaned forward.

The bolt moved on into deep space and dissipated. The rock torpedo went through it.

The commander was on his feet, shouting, "Destroy that thing! Now! Our most powerful bolts!"

"We can't, sir," stammered Corman-Heath. "It's too close."

"Do it now! All energy diverted to bolts! Concentrate the beams!" The commander was practically babbling in his haste.

"Sir! We'll sustain damage."

"Damage or die, idiot! Now! Do it now!"

Corman-Heath lurched forward, his hands doing the commander's bidding. Andrea leaned forward and placed her hand on Thomas' arm. He fell to the floor, hugging her knees. "There are legends," he said. "Legends about..."

He never finished.

The second, intense lightning bolt of energy streaked out from the *Murphy-Williams*. The space bullet went after it, moving up to meet it squarely. The bolt hit the rock. It bounced directly back. Harlan was already gone, up and over, behind and under the *Black Hole*.

The turtle shell erupted out the top, the bottom, and the sides. It erupted silently. Larry watched as the gaping holes quivered and then sparkling pieces of iridescence, like tinsel, poured out. The holes widened until the ship was almost torn in two. Everything inside shot out, almost instantly frozen, facets reflecting the Doomstar's light.

Napoleon saw a man on the screen, his face four black dots. He flew upward, then disintegrated, flecks of skin winking in the eternal night. She watched intently, fascinated, not horrified in the slightest.

Suddenly the space bullet stood before his handiwork. Green bolts came from the rock, dancing over the Destroyer hulk. It tore the once great ship into nothingness. Light swallowed the *Murphy-Williams* and then swallowed itself, winking out.

Larry shielded his eyes and blinked rapidly. When he looked again there was only space. Only small flecks of metal gave any evidence that the Destroyer *Murphy-Williams* had ever existed at all. Now he knew what silent thunder sounded like.

It was too fast, Larry thought. Too fast. An entire Destroyer torn up like a cardboard box by a piece of rock only three feet taller than him. There should have been more conflict. There should have been more—something.

Inside the space bullet suit Harlan was reveling in his strength. It had been easy. These Earth ships were nothing compared to those he had faced over Destiny. His on-suit system had flashed the Destroyer's structural weaknesses seemingly into his brain seemingly instantly. It wasn't that his weapons were so powerful. It was that the Earthen ship was so badly made. Hardly better than the hand-built *Black Hole*.

Larry carefully opened the room's reentry hatch. He walked toward the bridge. He had to stop several times to wait for his tremors to subside. He had to stop three times to get over the shakes. He turned right just before he reached the bridge, stepped into the head, placed his hands on the opposite wall, looked down, opened his mouth, and threw up everything that was in his stomach.

Harlan returned with the freeze-dried Mess manifestation in tow. His suit expertly arranged reentry to the *Black Hole* and resealed the bottom hatch. Mess returned to its console and the space bullet floated into the bridge horizontally, parallel to the floor. It rose to its vertical position and the head began to unscrew.

"Do you think they'll send another ship after us?" Napoleon asked Larry. They were sitting in their pilot seats across from one another. Napoleon had her elbows on her knees. Larry was slumped in his chair.

"I doubt it," he said. "When they realize it was us and not space that did in both ships, they'll let space have us. Our price tag has already been too high. They don't have the ships or the RHs to spare." He looked out the front port and said quietly, "Now they'll probably kill all the Duex Ciel FMs too. Good-bye, Julius."

"It's fixed!" Harlan trumpeted as the headpiece fell back. "It works perfectly!"

"I noticed," said Napoleon, turning toward him, smiling.

"If this were Destiny," said the space bullet to Larry as he climbed out of his suit, "we would not rest until all the enemy were dead."

"Well, this is *not* Destiny," Larry retorted with vehemence, spinning around. "Earth is no garden planet; it has almost nothing to protect. But they won't forget. The message has probably already gone out to whoever they laughingly call their allies. Earth doesn't forget. Someday they'll collect."

Harlan snorted. "Postbattle paranoia. Forty-four enemies died today. I have many more on my conscience. But none have come back to collect, as you call it."

"Thank you very much," said Larry wearily. "But I don't feel like making up death tallies right now."

"Don't let it bother you, Larry," Napoleon said with

slight surprise. "Why should it? We're free now. Really free!"

"They were people!" Larry exploded. "FMs, TMs, EMs, SMs, what does it matter? Good, bad, right, wrong, what's the difference? They existed. They lived, damn it! Just like me. All right, we were put in a position where it was either them or us, but that's nothing to celebrate. They died, we lived, that's it, all right? What do you want to do, have a party? The whole thing is sickening."

He sat down on the floor. Harlan looked at Napoleon. Napoleon looked at Harlan. Harlan frowned and raised his eyebrows. Napoleon shrugged.

"Never mind, never mind," said Larry. "Let's get out of here."

"Now you're talking," said Mess. "Even though there's no 'here' in space. Where to?"

"Anywhere," said Larry, closing his eyes. "Anywhere, for now. Harlan, would you please finish connecting the OD?"

"On one condition."

Larry's eyes snapped open. "What did you say?"

Harlan didn't repeat himself, just stood implacably, arms crossed.

"What is it?" Napoleon asked warily.

"You tell me where my sister is."

Larry was up. "We owe you our lives, but you're asking the impossible in return. I don't know where your sister is. I wish I did."

Harlan remained immobile. "Then I cannot connect the drive."

Larry couldn't believe it. It was happening again. The Doomstar opens, then closes, then opens, then closes, then opens, then closes again. He would never get away.

"I don't know where your sister is! Why would I lie? Why should I hold back? I don't know where she is, I tell you!"

"Then we stay here until we find out," Harlan said flatly.

"She could be anywhere! We should go to Destiny! Somebody there has to know!"

"We cannot return to my planet until we find Hana."

Larry began to walk in circles, his arms chopping the air. "I don't know, I don't know, I don't know!"

"I do," said Napoleon.

JACKPOT

ELEVEN

If Destiny was a jewel and Earth a stone, then Jackpot was paste. Jackpot was a fake diamond, cut glass; flashy, faceted, sharp, and transparent. From a distance it looked bright, expensive, and enticing. Up close was another story. One could get badly cut on the edges.

"There it is," Larry had said, looking in the ECG Planet Directory, published by the famed Intercouncil of Brotherhood (IOB) "'Jackpot: Planet of Vice.'" Larry looked over his shoulder at Napoleon and Harlan before reading on. "A world of entertainment, dedicated to the creatures it serves. The biggest and most extensive spaceport in the system. The largest playground in the galaxy.

"All the mental and physical needs of every species known are seen to within the walls of hundreds, nay, thousands of establishments—all incorporating the sciences of countless planets. Drugs: liquid, powdered, gaseous, and solid. Games for the hands, for the eyes, for the body, for the mind. Endless variety in the never-ending night. Action all the way."

"Sounds like fun," Mess had said.

"For a price," Napoleon had added.

The commercials battled for space on the esc-globe's radio, overlapping each other, scrambling each other's signals. A message that was strong in the upper atmosphere would be shouldered out as they dropped. What was worse, there was no direct English-speaking incoming pattern. The Jackpot Lot Jockeys fit you in where they could. At least there were no gun or SM ads—that was strictly Earthen. Not many Earthens at all up here—R, F, S, or otherwise.

Once the pod neared touchdown, the incoming ads were a screech of jumbled music, words, and feedback. Larry's space-suited hand switched it off. He had spent part of the three-month trip to Jackpot finding new, non-FM clothes for himself and modifying the esc-globe for their deception.

They had all decided that they couldn't just drop in and say, "Hi, we're fugitive murderers from Earth with a traitor from Destiny here to abscond with his kidnapped sister." So Mess had been programmed, not to lie, but with a separate truth incorporating false flight information.

Now they were a ship from Luster, a thick-atmosphered planet with mutlilegged creatures who otherwise seemed to be all nose. The Jackpot Spaceport, commonly known as JacPort, was sectioned off, naturally enough, and if incoming landing requests were phrased in Lusterian, then the Lot Jockeys would assume it was a Luster ship and reserve a space in the TA (Thick Atmosphere) area.

Larry turned to Napoleon, also in a spacesuit, with her tail wrapped around her waist. He touched her shoulder and she returned the signal. Now all they had to do was wait until the ground crew pulled them into the entry chamber and hooked the spaceport compubot to theirs.

They were aided in the subterfuge by a totally automated ground crew. Lusterian words came over the AU. "Welcome to Jackpot," said the translator at Larry's waist. "Please have your monetary exchange ready." Napoleon had spent most of the trip here salvaging material from the ravaged sections of the ship to be traded for JaC: Jackpot Credit. The entire transaction would be taken over by the compubots.

"Monetary transferral complete," said the AU by way of the translator. "Credit has been entered to the sum of two thousand, minus five hundred for craft care and handling. Total, fifteen hundred. Have a good time."

"Five hundred?" Napoleon sputtered. "For parking? That's larceny!"

"It *is* the biggest parking lot in the system," said Larry. It covered most of the planet. "Save your energy. Remember we have about fifty feet to cross before we reach the emergency lock. Once there, it'll take some three minutes to open. Then there'll be another ten feet to the credit box, then another twenty to the outside."

Harlan had done ample reconnaissance with his space bullet (it, of course, was outfitted with some very impressive sensory equipment). As much as Napoleon and Larry distrusted scientists—and, in their cases, with good reason—they had to admit that the Destinian kind certainly came up with some handy stuff.

They both started taking off their spacesuits. It wouldn't do to drag them around. Napoleon eyed the interior of the esc-globe for her pile of equipment. They only had a limited amount of air in the globe so the Lot Jockeys wouldn't get wise to the scam. They had to let the gray goo in as soon as possible. For the next few minutes, curling on the floor, Napoleon took off the suit, buckled a small oxygen tank on her back, and slipped the face mask on.

Larry nearly tripped over her legs. He was dressed in basic black, and also had a tank on. He pointed to her otherwise naked body. She nodded and pulled a tiny wad of material out of a spacesuit pocket. It stretched into a purple body suit that covered her. Larry reacted as if sarcastically saying, "Great, now no one'll notice us." Around her waist she cinched a thin green belt with a red buckle. On her feet went socboos.

They emerged from the esc-globe into condensed cream of mushroom soup, which filled their craft. Ignoring the machines around them, they marched in the direction of the nearest hatch. After three minutes of pushing against the gunk, they found the hatch. They worked it open and walked down a goop-filled hall until they got to the JaC slot. Larry pulled three disks from it and they struggled on their way.

After two more slow, exhausting minutes they were at the hatch out. Larry pushed, his feet sliding back. The door swung open and they tumbled out in a pile of gray gunk. Larry quickly slammed the door on the torrent, allowing only a few gallons of gray atmosphere through. It slid off them and quickly disappeared in the air, illumination, and dark ground of the LA (Light Atmosphere) section.

Larry and Napoleon turned around to see miles and miles and miles of more parking lot.

"Oh, my," said Napoleon, taking off her tank and dropping it. "Which way is Jackpot?"

All the vehicles seemed to point north. "That direction, I guess," said Larry.

They started walking, leaving their deplenished air

supplies behind. Several times vehicles passed over-head, but for all the shouting and waving they did, nothing happened. Finally Larry tracked down a ro-bot and asked for assistance. It asked things in dif-ferent languages, ignoring Larry's translator, until it reached English.

"What race are you?"

"Human," said Larry.

"You'll want the humanoid section, then. Go to any rainbow-circle point and wait for the next JacBus to arrive."

"Where are the rainbow-circle points?"

"You can find the rainbow-circle points anywhere near the humanoid lot." The robot tooled away.

"This disguise?" said Napoleon, walking by him toward a bunch of vehicles that looked Earthen in origin. "A real good idea."

They reached Jackpot an hour after they landed. The drop-off point was a low, narrow building lined with booths for monetary exchange, translators, tours, insurance, and safe-deposit boxes. Speakers were blaring commercials for different establishments and little hoverz™ whizzed by, handing out leaflets.

Napoleon smiled at the energetic machines, looked toward the exit, and stopped.

"Guards," she said.

It was Larry's turn to walk by her. "JacGuards," he said. Sure enough, the staff security men only checked them for weapons.

"Do you agree to in no way hold Jackpot respon-sible for anything?" the guards asked.

"I do, I mean I don't. I mean, I agree," said Larry. Napoleon rolled her eyes and did the same.

Finally they were through. They walked outside into Jackpot.

Before them was a picture from out of their wildest

dreams. Creatures of every sort walked, rolled, slithered, oozed, floated, and flew alone and in groups. Creatures of baffling complexity as well as protoplasmic gobs shared space on a single walkway.

"Lawrence," whispered Napoleon, "what kind of place have you brought me to?" She was being sarcastic. This trip was her idea.

Larry was in absolute awe. He took two halting steps forward and then stopped as if he were still in Lusterian air. Earth was never like this. Four, maybe five alien types interacted there. Here they seemed countless. Most were air breathers but some carried adapters with them.

Napoleon looked at Larry. His face was frozen, his eyes wide, his mouth open. She giggled. He turned toward her. "What's the matter?" she asked innocently.

He grinned sheepishly. "Nothing. Nothing at all." It was just the country bumpkin and his cat on their first night in the big city.

The two looked around as they walked. Buildings of all sizes surrounded them, each with large signs declaring the wonders to be found within, often in so many languages the legends covered an entire wall. "I wonder if all those stories we've heard are true," Napoleon thought aloud.

Stories about endless vendettas that went undisturbed unless an innocent bystander was hurt or killed. Stories about the elite corps of PCs, Peace Containers—specially created creatures who literally contained peace, who had the ability to deal out death at a mere thought from a crystal embedded in the corner of their foreheads. Stories about fugitives who settled here, no questions asked.

And stories of the IOB, the intergalactic executives who controlled this world. "Don't hurt business," was their motto. Their creed was, "Betray your friends, sell your soul, lose all your JaC, but don't hurt business." And even with all the different races and all the different customs, it worked for them. Gambling seemed to be a universal language.

It didn't seem to make much difference that the mortality rate was high here. Many creatures came to Jackpot to die happy. For behind the slogans and stories was one of the greatest economic systems ever. The JacBank was the galaxy's strongest and most influential. The most brilliant economists worked here, controlling wealth and power that affected billions on many planets. Jackpot was a chillingly pitiless masterwork, cloaked by shrill laughter and the clatter of small change.

"The stories are true," Larry guessed, almost in awe.

It was JacDusk, so the surrounding diversions consisted of simple gambling and games of lightly strenuous thrill. Lovers of the more difficult, dangerous, and dirty waited for JacNight. "I'm hungry," Napoleon decided. "All we've had for three months is foodstuf. Let's get something to eat."

Curiously, although the air was filled with sounds and sights, it was nearly free of smells. With so many races shoulder to something, one creature's meat could literally be another's poison, so the odors were held in severe check.

They walked into a small bistro squeezed between two parlors and were immediately led to the back. As they sat down at a tiny round table, they were again reminded how unimportant man was in the universe. The other sections outnumbered the human area four to one.

As soon as their backsides touched the seats, the table glowed. "Please place your JaC on the table," it said. Larry raised his eyebrows and did so. Once the disks were on the surface, the table started displaying pictures of foodstufs. It was strictly Earth-import, dull and doughy.

"Do you have anything else besides Earthen food not poisonous to Earthens?" Larry asked.

"Any Mandarin recipes?" Napoleon suddenly suggested hopefully.

"Offworld, yes," said the table. "Mandarin, no."

More pictures appeared of far more appetizing goods. Napoleon looked disappointed. Larry looked famished.

"What is this stuff?" she wondered.

"I don't care as long as it doesn't kill me," he answered. "Is this real or fabricated food?" he asked the table.

"Our meals are made from the finest ingredients available and under the strictest nutritional supervision, in order to give you the most delicious..."

"Fabricated," interrupted Napoleon. "I'll have that."

She chose a bowl of chunky something in a dark sauce of some sort. He had a colorful plate of meatlike material covered with a thin, semisweet, crunchy coating. She drank a golden concoction; he drank a beige liquid with streams of red.

Although the food was artificial, the two ate with eager abandon. It was the first real meal they had had in a long time. As each wrapped up the sup, the table glowed again. "We hope you have enjoyed your meal. Can we get you anything else?" Larry looked at Napoleon, who shook her head. "Thank you," said the table. "The cost has been automatically deducted from your JaC disk—your total, fourteen hundred. Have a good time."

"A hundred for a meal?" Napoleon said, springing up.

Larry ignored her, looking at the seat instead as he rose. "Great sensors," he admired. It could tell they didn't want dessert without Larry having to say anything. He took Napoléon by the arm and led her out. The place had filled up while they were eating, and though everyone seemed to be eating, Larry could see no employees, machine or otherwise.

The two went out the door. A blinding blast of sight and sound pushed them back against the restaurant wall. The street had changed completely. The handbook had tried to warn them about this. This was "JacNight: where things really happen." If the pair thought it had been dreamlike before, now it was a tornado dipped in hell.

The pure mass of undulating matter was breathtaking. The sounds were excruciatingly magnified and the colors crowded on top of one another as they assailed their neural centers. The restaurant had been windowless and soundproof. Larry tried to get his senses organized. Napoleon was too busy trying to slink away with her tail between her legs to consider such a thing.

The incredible garishness of it all was compounded by catering to many races, not just human. It was a powerful mixture, intoxicating to the uninitiated. In a minute Larry's eyes were able to uncross and Napoleon was able to straighten up. He turned to her and said that they should get inside somewhere. All she saw was his mouth move. She screamed, "What?" back at him, but all he heard was the roar of the crowd.

Larry wrapped his arm around her neck and she held him around the waist. Together they moved slowly to the left, hoping the living maelstrom didn't sweep them away or separate them. Larry edged toward a barely open yellow door. He pulled at it and slipped in, Napoleon still clinging to him. When they stopped gulping and the ringing left their ears, they heard a friendly voice.

"First time, eh?" Larry looked over to see a snout with an apostrophe-shaped nostril and a small, smiling mouth. "It can be a shock until you get used to it."

Larry moved his head back. Now he could see the snout was attached to a small, tubular head with three eyes on it. In an unusual display of verbosity Larry said, "Huh?"

"A bit of a shock," said the snout. "The whole thing. I said the whole thing can be a bit of a shock."

"A *bit*?" Larry snorted.

"What?" said the snout. "I can't hear you."

"I said, not just a bit!" Larry shouted.

"Ah, yes, quite right," said the snout, seemingly in a moderate voice. But actually, Larry realized, his volume was extraordinary. He also realized that Napoleon was no longer at his side. He looked beyond the snout. He was at the top of a small ramp with banisters on either side. At its base was a room filled with bright, flashing boxes, rectangles, triangles, and balls. Around all the machines were creatures who swayed back, forth, right, left, up, down, and all variations thereof.

"Where's the feline I came in with?" Larry shouted. "Eh?"

"The feline I came in with!" Larry screamed in the snout's snout. "Where is she?"

Napoleon tapped him on the shoulder. He jumped.

"Right behind you," said the snout, laughing. His laughter was slightly braying but not unpleasant. Larry turned to see Napoleon smiling, her eyes slits, her paws over her ears. Larry turned back to the snout.

"Thank you."

"What?"

172

"Thank you!"

"Certainly." The snout exhaled sharply, turning toward the throng. It had ears on either side of its tubular head, with dark hair surrounding them. Its body was a backward J shape wearing a furry, sleeveless shirt. It supported itself on four one-jointed legs. One short, rubbery, seemingly jointless arm was in front of its torso, another on the back. "Not to worry," it continued. "You'll adjust. I never thought I would, but look at me, the old pro."

Larry did indeed look at it. It returned his glare evenly with its leftmost eye, then held up a dark, three-fingered hand. "Until then, however, you might want to try these." On his palm were four dark earplugs. The pair gratefully took them.

"Thank you!" said Napoleon with relief.

The snout didn't say anything, so Larry shouted, "She said—!"

"I can hear her quite well," the snout smiled. "The plugs amplify words while eliminating much static. I was just appreciating her, that's all. She's quite a fine-looking cat. Your mate?"

Larry turned, expecting to see Napoleon's negative reaction. She just kept smiling. "Yes," said Larry, consciously lopping off the "uh" that was going to proceed his affirmative. "I'm...uh..." He couldn't avoid it this time. "...Lawrence-Harlan and this is...Trigor-Mess."

Napoleon turned toward Larry, glaring. The snout seemed to ignore the awkward names. "I am Palend, owner of this establishment. May I show you around?" Larry nodded, his throat getting sore. Palend started to move down into the room proper. The duo followed.

"This is an establishment of innocent delight," Palend said as a creature behind him smacked the side

173

of a machine. "A place for games of limited skill but limitless enjoyment. It is a place of constant entertainment where the rewards are not only for one's credit disk but also for one's soul. Oh, yes, the concept of the soul is not limited to human planets. Here we sell joy, thrills, and finally contentment."

The trio passed one boxlike machine with another snouted creature playing it. They watched as a series of square light beams shot out of a panel toward the ceiling. It put out its arm to block one. A silver ball shot out across the table, leaving a trail of fading blue orbs in its wake. The ball sped to the edge and seemed to bounce off it. The blue orbs turned green, then faded out to be replaced by a golden stream as the ball picked up speed.

The ball was about to disappear under the panel of light, but the smaller snout interrupted another beam and the ball went to the right, vibrating through floating circular shapes as if they were made of mercury. Then, bouncing off the edge again, the ball split into three. As they sped off, the board changed. A veritable roller coaster of paths appeared, growing toward the ceiling. The three balls took separate paths, moving up, then down, then all around. The snout's fingers started dancing among the light shafts, chuckling with genuine glee.

Larry noticed its other arm. The player had a single finger in a hole on the game's side. "What's that?" he asked Palend.

"Shh," Palend whispered, snout right by Larry's ear. "Don't distract the player. That's JacSlot."

Larry hated to show his ignorance, but what the hey. "What's that?"

Palend looked at Larry with narrowing eyes and genuine surprise. "The payment and prize," the creature said. Larry's expression remained vacuous. "As

174

long as he plays he is rewarded with knowledge."

Larry looked at the creature's face. As the balls moved, it too seemed to light up. "And if he makes a mistake?"

"A minute is taken from his life expectancy." Palend again read Larry's look. "Please. It is merely a minute. Other establishments take away hours, days, weeks, months, years! At least I do not gamble with a player's genetics like...others I could name."

The balls created a rainbow-tinged ballet before Larry's eyes. Finally all three balls settled into a red mound in the middle of the board. The creature pulled his hand from the light. Napoleon started to move away, thinking the game over.

"Wait," Palend suggested.

The roller coaster sank into the board. The board changed again, revealing a maze of grooves, holes, and circular posts. The three balls split again, making a half dozen orbs, which shot off in all directions, jockeying for position. The snout's fingers were in the lights again, following the balls jump, change lanes, ricochet, and disappear, each leaving the multi-colored, ever-changing wake. At times the board seemed to be obscured in silver and blue, but then colors would seem to splash up and against the table sides, creating an ocean of wonder. Larry had to turn away. He was getting dizzy.

"A delight; agreed?" Palend exhorted, a smile widening across the bottom of his snout.

"Agreed," exhaled Larry.

"What?" said Palend.

Larry nodded vigorously.

"Bottomless Pit," said Palend. "There are an infinite number of playing surfaces. Although it may seem haphazard and happenstance, I can assure you that every move of the ball has meaning, and that little ace knows them all. Care to try it?" Larry shook his head. "For free?" the affable creature offered.

"I'm afraid we have a most pressing engagement," Napoleon said.

"Do not be afraid. Even business can be a pleasure on this planet. If I can be of any further assistance, please inquire and do not worry." He looked at Napoleon and wagged his finger at Larry. "I see the gleam in the human's eye. If you can you will be back to play."

"Perhaps you can help," Larry said weakly.

"Perhaps," Palend agreed. "I have many machines at other establishments as well."

"We need to find the offices of Bishop-Fortune," Napoleon said. "Can you give us directions?"

Palend's eyes were suddenly bracketed by lids coming from both directions and above. "It cannot be," he said, taken aback. "My judgment has never been wrong before...." His cloven hand settled with urgency just above Larry's elbow. "I shall take my life in my hands. I must inquire. You do not actually intend to patronize his establishment, do you?"

The room raged around Larry. There was no reason to reply to the horse-headed creature, but his expression was so intensely concerned that he could not help it. "Well, not exactly."

Palend turned toward Napoleon. "Please come with me," he begged. "Do not fear me. Please. It concerns your very lives." Palend turned and walked between a row of wall-sized, standing machines. Behind it was an opening. Larry preceded Napoleon, passing a humanoid on his right who had a finger in a hole, an eye glued to a peephole, and was giggling like a child. Napoleon saw the game's name: "Libido."

Once they were inside, he saw that the room was small, bright, and sparsely furnished. It was a clean beige but with strips of colors circling the walls near the ceiling. Palend's desk was a large console with a stool, like a carpenter's horse, on a track on the floor. He moved there, touching a section of the desk's surface, which closed the door.

The sound of the games remained, coming from invisible speakers behind the fugitives. Palend pressed another section. The noise disappeared. Another section pressed, a wall-sized view of the game area appeared behind them.

"In case of trouble," Palend explained. "Please, sit."

Three other seats were cushioned squares. The pair shared a glance before settling onto the soft plush, enjoying the quiet, listening to their ears buzz. Napoleon slipped off the seat to curl up on the floor. Palend pressed a fourth section.

"Refreshments?"

Larry declined for the two of them.

A tube appeared between Palend's fingers as he raised his hand to his mouth. He put the opening in his snout, inhaled, and swallowed.

"We don't have much time," said Larry.

"I apologize deeply, with sincerity," Palend gasped. "This is the only thing I've had all day. You must understand how hard this is for me. I am putting myself in a terrible position."

"You seem concerned with our safety," said Napoleon from the floor. "Please speak freely."

"Very well, then." Palend rose and addressed Larry. "I could see you were novices here. Not just in my establishment but in the ways of this world. Do you know what will happen if she enters Bishop-Fortune's?"

"No," said Larry honestly.

"I thought not," Palend said gravely. "Do you love her?"

Larry looked at the feline in surprise and then back at the snout. "Yes." She looked up at him.

"Then you must be warned. She would never leave. Your cat would disappear and you would be paid or killed, depending upon your demands."

Napoleon sat up. "Not here too!"

"Felines are unheard of throughout this galaxy," Palend told her gently. "You are safe as long as everyone assumes you are an artificial. But I knew better. And if I can tell, then Bishop-Fortune can too."

"Uh-oh," said Larry.

Palend nodded bitterly. "I would not be surprised if you have been 'scouted' already. Perhaps a good many shops have been made aware of your presence. Even now they may be making plans to acquire you."

"Is there no place safe?" Napoleon snarled.

"You are a feline," Palend stressed. "Creals, Moffats, Farzaks, Methsons, Lidenboks, Pankies, even Domnackizins we have, some in abundance. There are only two things we don't have. Women and felines."

"Why are you telling us all this?" Larry asked.

"I don't know, really," the snout said. "If Bishop-Fortune knew I interceded and could prove it to the Intercouncil..."

"I just cannot understand this," Napoleon seethed, standing. "Why me? What is so Taplinger-Jones marvelous about me? I don't comb my fur, I don't trim my whiskers, I don't buff my paws. Why must I be hunted and possessed?"

"Nap," said Larry quietly. She snarled and threw herself to the floor. "You're in danger, that much is obvious. We have to do what we came to do, then get out real fast. Let's just hope the P-Shop procurers don't try anything in these crowds."

"No, they'll be able to silence, drug, and spirit her

away before you notice she's missing," Palend warned.

"This is incredible," Napoleon moaned.

"Palend," Larry pleaded, on the figurative and literal edge of his chair. "You've done us a great service. You've also exposed yourself to great danger. But I have to ask you to expose yourself to more."

"I considered that before warning you," he said earnestly. "Pray continue." The snout leaned on his console and folded his arms across his side. "And please. You must call me 'Pal.'"

TWELVE

Bishop-Fortune's Treasures was a magnificent structure designed to fill patrons with awe while keeping them in their place. All of the other establishments were built with the customer in mind, but here the visitors were incidental. Bishop-Fortune was doing them a favor by letting them even enter.

The cavernous interior made Larry feel small. The delicate-looking, frizzy-haired Creal with a three-inch scar across her face greeted him haughtily and reacted to his request with twisted amusement.

"The Destiny Princess?" she sneered. "You sure about that, Earthen?"

"Yes, I'm sure," replied Larry hastily. "I have credit. I can pay."

"You had better, Earthen," she answered wickedly. "It's still early yet. Maybe she can squeeze you in." She laughed shrilly three times, making her scar turn red, then white. Her face settled back to a sneer and her hand came up, curling. Her fingernails were six inches long. "Let's see the size of your JaC."

Larry pulled out the three credit disks they had started with. The girl snatched them and threw them on a stand beside her. It shone yellow, then red. She pushed him back, one hand on his chest.

"Not nearly enough, Earthen," she laughed. "Where do you think you are? We don't cost dirt here, Earthen. We're respectable females. We don't come cheap." Her raucous laughter filled the sumptuous foyer again. "If you want to taste the one and only sweetness of Destiny," she snarled sarcastically, "you'll have to cough up more JaC."

Larry reluctantly pulled out the JaC Palend had given him. He held it out to the girl, but when she reached for it, he slipped it onto the stand himself. One didn't live on the chauvinistic Earth for all one's life without learning a few tricks.

The stand glowed yellow and stayed that way. "Just made it," she announced sullenly. "You can go through, Earthen, but don't dawdle. You hardly have enough time to sneeze. Have a good time." She turned away as if he didn't exist.

Larry hesitated but then retrieved the now empty disks. He moved up a ramp toward a glowing opening. This was the final test. If the sensor picked up anything untoward, be it a weapon, communicator, or anything, his visit would be over, his trip would be over, his quest would be over, his escape would be over, and his life would be at its end.

Larry did not hesitate. He went up and through a wash of yellow and a curtain of black and then a hallway of dark green, where there stood a man in dark clothing. In the dimness it was impossible to see his features, but what the FM could see was the jewel shining white on the side of his forehead.

It was all just as Palend had said it would be. Different entrances for different races, the insulting hostess fleecing every credit, the sensing portal, and the Peace Container—each PC individually posted at the section of his race. A human PC for a humanoid section.

That was as far as Palend had been informationally able to take him. He could give Napoleon weapons and a ship, he could give Larry a nonworld communicator secreted in his hand that wouldn't set off the alarms, but from here on it was Larry's game. He moved past the PC.

He moved down the hallway. Although it was lined with doors, none had opening devices except the one facing him at the end. He approached it and touched his hand to a plate in the middle. The door swung back, both sides sweeping outward. The hall shone with soft white light.

Before Larry was a small, carpeted balcony overlooking a deep brown, wood-hued room with a high ceiling. Before him was a pillow-strewn floor and high bookcases filled with ancient volumes. Before him were tall windows interspersed with the bookcases, framed with delicate curtains that ruffled from an unseen wind. Before him was an eight-foot, framed mirror reflecting his image over a fireplace filled with softly burning wood, adding a further glow.

And before him was a girl. She held a book in her hand and was leaning over a servo-robot. She wore a white gown tied from her waist to her neck with small, thin bows of material. It rippled across her body from the wind. Her eyes were large and dark, her hair black as space, shining with the gleam of the fire.

Larry held on to the balcony's banister to remain upright. He tried to swallow, a buzzing filling his head, one having nothing to do with the roar of Jackpot's night. She turned toward him.

"Close the door, will you?" she said in lyrical tones, pulling the book to her chest and shooing away the little robot on wheels. It was all Larry could do to keep from falling over. He felt his face flush and he nearly tripped over his own feet, turning. As he pulled the door shut he found his mouth hanging open. He shut that as well. He returned to the balcony's edge to find her smiling, almost impatiently.

"Come here," she said.

Larry nearly vaulted over, but he managed to locate the stairway leading down to the right. He quickly stumbled down, at one point grabbing the wall to keep his balance. He angrily told himself to calm down.

An instruction that did no good once he had walked up to her. Before he could think further she stepped forward and kissed him. Slowly, her hands still holding the book to her chest, and softly, a flesh caress.

Larry's mind was suddenly awash in a sea of smoke. He had to close his eyes. His hands, not knowing what to do, shook. The rest of his body acted accordingly. He felt himself tipping over. Automatically his arms sought the nearest thing to right himself. It was the girl. He felt the softness of her dress. Then he was rolling beside her on the floor.

She was laughing. "A grand start," she said. "Shall we continue?" The book was thrown across the floor. The beautiful young girl was on her knees, her hands reaching for his pants.

Larry suddenly remembered who she was and what he was doing there. He realized that they didn't have much time before the planned rendezvous.

"Hana Trigor?" he said. She stiffened. Her eyes sought his, a hard edge to them.

"What...who are you? What do you want?"

"You are she, aren't you?" he queried from his back on the floor.

"How did you get here? What is all this about?" She was whispering roughly into his face.

"We came with your brother. We're here to rescue you," Larry said quickly, wondering how it would sound to her.

"Really," said Hana with no anticipation in her voice. "So you found me. You'll never get me out of here." She rose and began moving quickly toward the stairway, picking up her book as she went.

This was not the reaction Larry had expected to get. He wasn't sure what he was expecting, but this wasn't it. He was on his feet, ran, and grabbed her by the arm as she made the first step.

"Don't worry," he said sincerely. "We have a ship coming at any moment. We *can* get you out of here."

She looked him in the face, shifting her gaze from eye to eye. All she saw was eager integrity. She said nothing, merely swung the spine of the book in a vicious arc. The binding caught Larry on the side of the head, pushing him down to the floor.

A numbing sensation moved over him, but it wasn't until he reached his knees that the pain sped like lightning to his brain. The wavy haze that had clouded his mind turned to a red and black storm.

He heard Hana's voice through the thunder, crying for help. Thoughts of survival suddenly replaced his rescue operation. Even through the violent clouds he instructed his legs to get him up and away. They replied sluggishly but still got him shakily to his feet. From there he pulled himself over to a window.

The room moved in and out of focus, shifting like a holographic image, as he stumbled toward the opening. As the blackness beyond beckoned him and the wind ruffled his hair he heard her urging someone to hurry. His knees touched the edge of the windowsill. But instead of pushing him forward, it turned him around. His eyes saw her on the balcony, by the door, standing back as the Peace Container, his face dark, strode in. The man's glowing forehead jewel was the last thing he saw before falling back.

The ceiling moved and black swept over him again, but his eyes did not close. He thought he saw a red bolt streak overhead before light burst around him, but he couldn't be sure.

Suddenly his mind was clear. The pain had receded to a throb and he could think again. He knew he was on his back among six-foot-high pillows. He realized he had fallen through a set of black curtains that separated the library from the rest of the dream factory.

Larry found his feet and stuck his head above the rim of the pillows. Around him dozens of alien creatures undulated, quivered, and shook. He had stumbled on a communal orgy. The jellylike Umwards gave off energy that other Umwards could receive. When engaged in sexual pursuits the pleasure was heightened in company.

The floor was completely covered in the tall padding, so running was impossible. Larry began to bounce toward an exit on the other side of the room.

As he neared the door he saw the Peace Container drop through the hole he had made in the curtained ceiling. He rolled through the opening and down a ramp, barely missing another Umward couple who squished in surprise.

Larry rolled as long as he could, rising to his feet only to jump around a corner as another red lightning bolt struck the wall behind him. He somersaulted and was on his feet, running down another hallway. He pressed his right thumb to his forefinger twice, then spoke.

"Nap! I'm in trouble."

His fingernail replied scratchily, "Where are you?"

Larry saved his breath until he leaped through a porthole and fell down a slide meant for Moffats.

"I just left an Umward section. I'm at the bottom of a Moffat ramp. How do I get out of here?"

The slide had been coated with a dark beige ointment with which Larry was now covered. He heard mumbles from his fingernail as he sought refuge. The Peace Container would be there any second.

"Palend says that you should go for the Farzak section to the far left. There'll be enough creatures there for you to be protected until we get there," Napoleon said from his fingernail. "But don't go to the near left. That's the Methsons' section. You wouldn't last half a minute in there."

Larry didn't need to be told twice. The human Peace Container appeared at the top of the ramp with an Umward associate. Two bolts melded into one, striking out at him as he sped around the corner to the far left. He ran to a door at the end and hurled his body through.

He smashed up against a huge boulder and fell back onto the dusty ground, winded. When he could breathe again, a moment later, he saw that he was in an excellent recreation of an ancient village, with rooms etched out of rock. It was a veritable community of caves, with bones littered about and a painted wall depicting an eternal sunset.

Larry scrambled to his feet to see that the room stretched out for some length, interrupted by campfires and boulders. Before he was able to do anything more, a huge figure moved into view from a cave opening before him. As it came out into the permanently dying light, he saw it was an eight-toothed, one-eyed creature.

He didn't need a translator to tell him what it was growling now. With a bellow the cyclops ran forward, his massive right fist moving down. Larry stepped over to the left and stuck his leg out. The clumsy giant tripped and fell, roaring with anger. Immediately the cave entrances were filled with huge, hulking brutes and their mates.

The females seemed upset at the interruption, but the males moved forward eagerly. Larry realized he could not move back and he could not move forward. The Peace Containers would arrive any second and he was facing a mob of angry, one-eyed monsters.

Then one monster got too close to another while moving in. The one on the left dug an elbow into the other's ribs, urging him to move aside. The one on the left got a fist in his face for his trouble. He rocked back and delivered a resounding blow to the other's head in return. The one on the right stumbled into another beside him and received a kick in the stomach as balance. He dropped to the ground cringing.

But the one on the left wasn't going to let the third get away with that. He buried his fist in the third's face, knocking him, and two others, to the ground. All three were up and on top of the nearest to them in a flash.

Suddenly the whole group turned in on itself. Fists were flying in every direction as dust started making a natural curtain. One Farzak closest to Larry almost had its huge, gnarled hands around the human's throat when another caught him in the back with both knees. The two Farzaks dropped to the ground, pummeling each other with great abandon.

Larry heard the Peace Containers enter. He jumped into the whirling cloud of gold. The red bolts could not be loosed for fear of harming an innocent patron.

But Larry was far from safe. One errant punch would probably rearrange his face or permanently damage an important internal organ.

He tried to keep near pairs of struggling white-skinned fighters. He jumped over one team of wrestling creatures, dodged another who were bashing at each other's faces with little effect, and ducked as another flew through the air in the midst of a tackle. It was like moving through a particularly bustling dance floor at a slaughterhouse.

Larry turned to check on the progress of the Peace Containers. He couldn't make them out through the dust of the writhing figures. But he knew that if any Farzak tried to include them in the battle the group would stop being "innocent" and the deadly lightning would strike.

Larry turned forward just as a glaring red eye came leaping out of the cloud preceded by two massive gripping hands. Larry had just enough time to fall to the side before the hurtling Farzak crashed into his shoulder. The cyclops fell on his head and Larry went spinning atop another two kicking fighters. His left arm was numb, a pain forgotten when one of the two he had interrupted swatted the back of his head.

Larry actually flew forward five feet and rolled across the rocky ground for several more yards. He desperately struggled to regain consciousness. He thought he saw a red jewel among the dusty haze, but he could not be sure it wasn't a side effect of the pain. He could detect more fighters all around him and felt the vibrations of their violence under him. The jarring energy didn't revitalize him.

His sight was colored dark green with a curling cloud of black moving in. He felt fingers curling around his ankle. He was being dragged into the thick of the battle. Just before losing consciousness he figured that was it. The Peace Containers would find only a mangled hunk of battered flesh.

A beam of bright orange filled his vision and he realized he was awake and alive. A howl of pain louder than the grunts and scuffling went up and suddenly the fighting stopped. As the golden cloud began to settle, Larry saw Napoleon standing beside him, a beamer in one hand, a spitter in the other. Before this vision even had time to collect in his brain, the feline fired both weapons, howling.

"Get up! Let's go!"

Larry ignored the pain that ripped at his shoulder and neck. He rose quickly to his feet and circled his co-pilot as the Farzaks ran screaming. The Peace Containers were forced to take cover behind a rock. She was moving back as Larry noticed she was wearing a holster over her slit body suit. He reached around her waist and pulled out his own beamer.

"Up," she cried, leading the way. They ran through a hidden doorway, laying down a veritable floor of fire.

"Every Peace Container will be converging on us in a moment!"

They ran up a ramp and turned right. Larry saw one of the hallway doors with a gaping hole.

"Through here," said Napoleon. They jumped through into a billowing black curtain. The feline snarled, pulling it off them. Larry was back in the library, running beside Napoleon for the stairs.

"The girl! Was she here?" he shouted.

"Not when I showed up," she replied, streaking up to the balcony. Larry saw a rope dangling down from a hole in the ceiling.

"Go," she said, "I'll cover you."

Larry didn't argue. He pushed his beamer into his

belt and scurried up the line as three Peace Containers appeared. Napoleon fired madly, keeping them from getting a clear shot with their glowing jewels.

Larry pulled himself up and over onto the roof. He swung the rope over to where Napoleon stood and pulled out his weapon, switching it to its widest, deadliest position.

"All right," he yelled, firing through the opening, slicing great hunks out of the room. A tail end of one beam ripped open the fireplace, sending burning logs rolling onto the floor.

Napoleon was outside as the rug, curtains, and pillows caught fire. Across the roof Larry saw the bullet-shaped ship Palend had supplied and ran for it. The noise of the Jackpot night roared them on, covering the chaos with Bishop-Fortune's establishment.

As the two jumped into the vehicle, red bolts started ripping through the ceiling toward them. Larry initiated lift-off just as two bolts arced by each other, creating a blood-red X streaking off on opposite sides of the ship as it leaped into the sky.

THIRTEEN

"I don't believe it!" Harlan roared.

"I don't care!" Larry yelled back. "If you hadn't refused to part company with that precious suit of yours for a while, you would have seen. She tried to kill me at the thought of rescue."

"Larry," said Napoleon, "could she have been an artificial?"

"Yes!" Harlan boomed. "A recreation of my sister!"

"It would be against IOB rules," Larry said. "Even Bishop-Fortune wouldn't cross them."

"It is impossible," Harlan contended. "She was ripped from her home, our parents viciously murdered, she is marketed like food, subject to the slavery of the vilest man in the galaxy, and you tell me she wants to stay?"

"I'm telling you she hit me on the head and called a Peace Container to do me in," Larry explained. "Whether she wants to stay or not is a moot point."

"Maybe she didn't trust you," Harlan mused. "Thought it was a trap...."

"I used her name!" Larry cried. "I told her about you. What more could she want?"

"I still don't see—" Harlan began.

"All right, all right," Napoleon interrupted. "This isn't getting us anywhere. What do we do now? is the question."

They all stood on the bridge of the *Black Hole* as it sat behind a speeding asteroid. The space rock moved in such a way that, before it rocketed back into outer space, it stayed along the *Black Hole's* orbital path around Jackpot, shielding the Earth ship from discovery. A pocket of safety but only for a limited time.

"Do what you wish," Harlan answered her question. "I am not leaving this planet without her."

"Well, that's that," said Napoleon easily.

"No, wait a minute," interrupted Mess. "Maybe something can be arranged along those lines...."

"Damper," Napoleon warned the machine before continuing to Harlan, "How do you propose to get her out?"

"I will simply go and collect her myself," said Harlan. "In my suit. It was what I should have done initially."

"I see," said Napoleon. "Do you also propose to have her suffocate and burn up in the atmosphere or do you think the Peace Containers will give her time to dress up in a spacesuit after you bash through a wall?"

"I don't feel that that is any—" Harlan blustered.

"Do you even know where she is?" Napoleon pressed. "The Bishop-Fortune place is in a shambles, thanks to us. They will have moved her and everyone else to different headquarters until they can find and deal with us. Do you intend to blast every place you suspect?"

"I can't say how...." Harlan attempted.

"Last time it was a surprise," Napoleon rolled over him. "This time they'll be ready for an attack. They won't expect it, but they'll be ready for it. They won't wait while you land and search."

"They cannot harm my suit, no matter what they do," Harlan said forcefully.

"No, but they can harm your sister with no trouble at all," Napoleon reminded him.

"All right, you have made your points," Harlan conceded. "I am sorry, but this is my sister. You have described a person I do not know." Harlan's normally calm, rock-hard face had become misty, confused, and sad.

"It has been more than a year, her time," Napoleon said gently. "A lot has happened to her body and mind, none of it good. Jackpot has a way of making you give up hope sooner than you might anywhere else."

"All right, all right, all right," Harlan said quickly, straightening up and waving his hands. "What can we do?"

"Palend is following through with his duplicity," Larry took up the dialogue. "He supplies Bishop-Fortune with machines for the personal use of both him and his patrons, but fortunately hates the man's guts. It is incidental that if the dream factory suffers a loss he stands to recoup his losses twelvefold."

"How's that?" Harlan inquired.

"He wouldn't explain completely," Napoleon said. "But we think there's some kind of political rivalry going on. Palend has been too small a concern to do any real bad damage up until now. But he sees us as a powerful and profitable wedge. He'll arrange suitable camouflaged transport, both to there and back."

"But they know you two," Harlan complained. "They have your descriptions. How can you hope to infiltrate?"

"Your sister was alone in the library when I found her," said Larry. "Except for one small thing. A servobot. A machine that serves her like a maid or a butler."

"A servobot?" Harlan repeated. "Where are we going to get a ..."

He stopped and the three heads turned as one toward Mess' console.

"What did you stop squabbling for?" asked the machine. "It's fun to watch."

"Mess?" Larry said sweetly. "You know those spare parts of yours?"

"I'm sorry, sir," Mess replied. "I don't understand."

"Mess," said Napoleon. "Your manifestations."

"I'm sorry, it does not compute."

"You want to be disconnected and I'll put it together myself?" Larry asked.

"I'll blast you!" Mess suddenly replied.

"Not without my permission," said Larry. "Mess ...?"

"No, I won't do it! It's too dangerous! I might get fried! No, no, NO, I won't! You can't make me!"

A table on wheels buzzed around the small ship's bridge as the ship streaked toward Jackpot. All around its circular middle was the legend—Palend: For The Thrill Of Your Lifetime ... At Your Fingertips—in dozens of languages. From the bottom of the craft, two converging tubes bore the engines' power. Four small nozzles at the front were its only weaponry and two triangular windows were its only portholes. But it was fast and capable of great agility. It was perfect for their needs.

Larry sat in one chair, Napoleon in another. Behind them Mess moved about before a bed outfitted with straps. Above its four wheels was a solid square of machinery—his brain, speech, and hearing console. One flashing light on three sides gave it 360-degree sensors, while one side bore six more sensors, a row of switches interspaced with dials, and a speaker grid.

Above the block was a rimmed table with plate and cup holders. Mess spun to and fro, testing its new ability, occasionally squealing, "Whee, whee!"

"As usual, we don't have much time," Larry was saying above the machine's playground noises. "The *Black Hole* pocket will only stay viable for a few more hours. Then the ship will be open to attack. Harlan will be outside in his suit to cover our return in case of a chase. As long as we get back in time and the ship stays beside the asteroid, we'll be all right."

"Not to worry, not to worry," said the moving table. "I left enough of me back there to take care of the ship."

"We're coming in," said Napoleon. "Get ready."

The ship swept down over the main city of Jackpot, automatically taking care of the pressure and coordination situation. Without assistance it hovered above Palend's establishment, then slowly lowered into the plaza. The plaza roof covered them and the console lights turned off. The door opened and Palend entered quickly, his snout smiling but both lids nearly covering his eyes.

"My friends, my friends," he intoned, arms out, "You take great risks and do me great service."

"And you us," said Larry, rising. Palend took him by the shoulders, at which Larry winced. The creature immediately released him.

"I am sorry. I had forgotten about your recent wounds."

"I wish my body would forget," said Larry.

"It will, it will," said Palend. "If you would wait a moment my land vehicle will come alongside and we can get on our way. The fewer who see you the better."

"Agreed," said Napoleon, strapping on her weapons.

The table moved over to where the three stood. "You sure this is going to work?" it asked.

Palend turned. "This must be Mess, then."

"You told it my name!" Mess cried accusingly. "Why did you tell it my name? It knows too much! Permission to fire!"

Palend moved back quickly as Larry moved forward.

"Don't worry," he soothed the snout-faced creature. "He gets a little overwrought in times of crisis." He kneeled down next to the shaking machine. "Mess, we're not on board ship now. You can't blast this fellow. He is our friend."

"Not when they start sticking needles in him!" Mess said. "Permission to fire."

"No, now damper down."

"The vehicle is here," said Palend tentatively. "We had better get on board." He quickly moved out, keeping away from Mess' front.

The Earth pair followed him, guiding a reluctant Mess. The land rover was a boxlike affair, large enough to hold six or eight of Palend's floor machines but still thin enough to maneuver through the narrow roadways of Jackpot.

The piloting cubicle was connected to the rear storage area by a band that allowed both parts to be ninety degrees to each other on tight turns. There were openings on all four sides that made for easy loading and unloading. There were no wheels. The bottom of the vehicle was several inches off the ground and humming. It could be directed both by manual or transport-band control.

Napoleon and Larry hopped in. Mess needed a ramp set up. In seconds they were ready. The interior was windowless and held only four rectangular machines used in front of each entrance. The rest of the area was empty except for one chair sealed to the floor and outfitted with straps on the legs, arms, and back. They all knew what it and the bed-in-the-air vehicle might be used for.

As the vehicle began to move forward, Palend pointed to two small piles of black clothing on the floor.

"Better put these on," he suggested. Larry and Napoleon took up the one-piece coveralls and began to pull them over their legs. With the movement of travel to contend with, they wound up on the floor. As Larry got both his legs in, Mess moved up to him.

"In...in case anything...you know...happens," said the machine, "I just wanted to say that my consciousness is on a little red plate. I made sure all the other parts weren't red, so...in case I get...I get... well, you know...scattered...you'll know which piece is important."

Larry smiled. "Don't worry, Mess. I won't let them scatter you."

"Thank you," said Mess. "Do I really have to do this?"

"I'm afraid so," Larry replied. "Our demise would be certain if we didn't."

"Wouldn't it be easier just to blast Harlan and go?"

"We need someplace to go," Larry explained. "Right now Destiny is the only place we'll be safe."

"I won't argue the point," Mess sighed. "Just don't forget about the red plate, will you?"

"I won't," promised Larry.

Napoleon had pulled the black garment all the way on. It effectively covered her from the chin to her feet, obscuring her size. Even though her weapons were on the inside, the black sheath had no telltale bumps.

"How does it feel?" Palend asked.

"I can move, but just barely," the feline answered. "How do you expect me to fight?"

"I hope that will not be necessary," said Palend. "But if you need mobility just squeeze the shiny area by your left wrist. The outfit will peel off around you."

Larry pulled his head through the neck opening and rose, clasping the chest opening together. "How long before we get there?"

"My informants tell me that this Destiny woman has been placed apart from the others in a Bishop-Fortune habitat by the edge of the main city. She can keep her schedule of appointments in even greater splendor than before, I'm told.

"Naturally her security has been magnified. However, with the delay, many patrons had to be rescheduled, creating a waiting period. My machines were ordered to keep the customers happy during the delay."

"Very interesting," said Larry. "But how long until we arrive?"

"Oh, I'm sorry," the creature sputtered. "I suppose I must be nervous. In several minutes. We are taking the fastest transport band."

"Let's go over the plan one more time," Larry suggested.

"Fine," said Palend. "We enter the establishment from the back and beneath."

"While you keep the guards busy, we start unloading the machinery and Mess moves upstairs," Larry continued.

"We give it a few minutes to do what is necessary," Napoleon took up the narrative. "Then deal with the guards and get the girl."

"My ship, meanwhile, automatically comes over and lands."

"We take off and you set up the cover story," Larry finished.

"Cover story?" Mess said. "What cover story?"

"Leave that to me," said Palend. "It will look as if I, too, was a victim of an offworld attack. They may be suspicious but they will be unable to prove anything."

The vehicle began to slow. "It is changing bands," Palend said. "We must be drawing near."

The four waited nervously as the vehicle slowed even more. "Quick. Put on your masks," Palend instructed.

Beneath the chair sat two large, solid headpieces, flat white except for two opaque eye slits. With a press on the side, each popped open. Larry and Napoleon fit them on their heads and sealed them closed. With the coveralls and helmets they looked almost like robots. Their black boots and gloves completed the effect. There could be almost any humanoid form encased within.

"It is going to be hard for me to take this," Larry heard Napoleon say in his mask's receiver. When he turned toward her, all he saw was the white mask and gray eye slits.

"Try to hold on," he said. "But if you feel like mewing, go ahead. Only I can hear you."

"We are inside," the two heard Palend report. "We're moving down a long tunnel, down into their receiving area. Get ready."

The truck stopped and the doors moved open. Four guards stuck their heads inside. Then they were gone and Palend hopped out.

"Wait until he instructs us to move," Larry said. Mess remained motionless, his lights out. Larry waited, looking out the left door.

They were hovering in what appeared to be an ancient high-ceilinged dining room. A long table lay before an empty, closed-off fireplace. The walls were pasty-white while the furniture was dark brown. One couldn't see a Farzak in there unless he smiled.

"Start unloading," came Palend's voice from somewhere outside the vehicle.

"That's it," said Larry. "Let's go, Nap. Once we get the ramp set up, Mess, you get upstairs. You'll have three minutes. All right?"

Mess remained motionless. "Mess?" Larry repeated.

"Couldn't I just blast her and say she got caught in a crossfire?" came the machine's strident voice inside Larry's helmet.

"No! Come on, Mess, get ready."

Napoleon had hopped out, pulling the installed ramp from the edge of the vehicle rim.

"We can tell Harlan that she was executed for treachery," Mess suggested.

"No."

"That she wandered into the line of fire."

"No."

"That she fell down a flight of stairs."

"No!"

"That she asked me to put her out of her misery."

"No, by the Earth Father! Mess, you nervous network of cowardly cirquids! Get moving!"

"Will you keep it down?" came Napoleon's voice in a harsh whisper. "The guards might hear you, even outside the helmets. They're not reinforced steel, you know." She had the ramp in place.

"Mess, move it or we're all as good as dead. There'll be no one to pick up your red plate then. You'll never get back to the ship," Larry said cruelly.

Mess' lights turned on and it sped down the ramp. To his left was another ramp, leading up with a bronze-colored band lying in the center of the incline. Mess silently rolled up to it, and as soon as its two front wheels were on either side, it shot up as if pulled.

Larry stuck his masked head out of the truck to see Palend talking animatedly to the guards. All their backs were toward the vehicle. They had not seen or heard Mess' exit. Larry started counting the seconds as he pulled the machines out of the truck.

Less than two minutes later the large rectangular games were on the floor. They had been outfitted with a system of bearing that made for easy movement. As soon as the unloading was complete, the four guards accompanied Palend back into the room proper. Larry and Napoleon retreated back into the vehicle.

"These are new, eh?" said one of the guards.

"Only my best, which is *the* best anywhere, for the Bishop," said Palend. "Specifically built for this fine establishment."

The guard who spoke moved over to the four machines. All he saw were sloping shiny smooth rectangles of blue metal.

"They look like sculptures. How do they work? Where is the power supply?"

"Where is the power supply for anything?" Palend said easily. "Can you find the energy for our countless restaurants, transport bands, and houses? They are everywhere and nowhere. But you shall go forward and touch the machine."

That was what the guard was waiting for. He moved even closer to the nearest cuboid and placed his hands on its rounded rim. Suddenly the seemingly solid surface became clear and a vast panorama appeared, depicting a forest as seen from the sky. The guard actually gasped.

"I designed this to give the customer a taste of Destiny," Palend explained. "Based on its mythical legends, the player becomes a god. The object: control the weather. If you run the planet smoothly you keep playing, visualizing countless wonders, experiencing the greatest power ever known—creation.

"If not, you witness great disaster, floods, earthquakes, storms, untold devastation, and tragedy."

The guard was smiling broadly. The other three's expressions were of rapt attention. One of the trio said, "But if one isn't a good player, isn't the game very short?"

"Nature's fury isn't spent in seconds," Palend smiled. "Even if the player is the dullest of men, the game will automatically continue for three minutes, come what may."

The words "three minutes" were the signal. Napoleon pulled off her gloves. She neared the open door to the left.

Palend suddenly cried, "What is this? Oh no, don't!"

The four guards whirled to where Palend was looking, turning their backs on the vehicle. Napoleon pointed a gold-covered claw. A bright yellow field of energy blanketed the room. All four guards and Palend toppled over. Only the vehicle was untouched. According to the snout-faced creature, all that he and the guards had seen was a yellow flash obscuring all else. They would be unconscious for more than an hour.

Larry and Napoleon leaped out and ran toward the bronze-banded ramp. The feline pounced upon it with all fours. She streaked up and away. Larry jumped on in a hunched position, knees bent. He, too, shot up. They moved around corners and spun up and up until each had counted three floors.

Then they both stepped to the right. Without any discomfort or dizziness they were standing before a black curtain. Without hesitation, Larry pressed his left sleeve and moved through the curtain, Napoleon right behind him. Their masks sprang open and dissolved before they hit the floor. Their black outfits ripped off and spun into nothingness as if they had been sucked into a cosmic hole.

Napoleon's paws pulled out her spitter. Larry's hand had settled on his beamer in its holster as his other hand whirled the curtain aside.

Before the two stood Hana Trigor, daintily undoing her gown, standing before a figure lying with his back to them, propped up with pillows, sipping a drink. Beside them was a blinking Mess.

Her dark eyes moved up and locked on Larry's light ones. Then confusion. Napoleon was flying through the air toward the girl. The man on the floor was turning as Larry pulled out his beamer while running forward.

Larry saw Napoleon's spitter drop soundlessly to a pillow and her paws hit Hana's stomach as she opened her mouth to scream. He fired his weapon as the two females fell back, the human's cry turning to a gasp of escaping air. The beamer's ray bathed the man in yellow and his head dropped, his eyes closed.

Larry didn't stop, however. He also dropped his weapon onto a pillow and leaped toward the mass of flesh and fur on the floor. He fell on top of them, and for a moment the three scrambled, half on the rich carpeting, half on a slick, shiny, tilelike covering. Larry's hand fell across Hana's mouth just as she was getting up wind for another scream.

Napoleon wiggled out from under them. Larry pulled the girl back, arching her body. He slammed her head against his own chest as he sat on the floor, trying to keep her disoriented. His other hand sought one of her arms. He failed on both counts. Her head did more damage to his chest than vice versa and her breath had returned, so she was twisting her limb away from his further grasp.

Larry pressed his hand against her mouth, tightening his grip, still searching along the cloth-covered body for her arms. She bit his hand. He clamped back his own yell and pulled his arm up under her chin to keep her mouth shut. Her own hands finally appeared, fingernails digging into his forearm.

Larry pushed his body down to the floor, keeping hers underneath. Her arms automatically went out to break her fall. He grabbed one with his free hand and wrenched it up her back. Her muffled cries turned into a gasp of pain. He released it a bit and she started to buck. He pushed it higher again and applied as much body pressure as he could. She arched and spat under him. Napoleon grabbed her spitter, surveying the room.

"Do something," Larry whispered through clenched teeth.

"I can't," Napoleon whispered back. "My beamer would knock you out too."

"Then use the device Palend gave you."

"That blankets the entire area."

"Mess, Mess," Larry continued whispering. "What happened?"

The table moved over to where the girl struggled beneath Larry.

"I couldn't do it," it said quietly. "You didn't tell me about the customer. I couldn't deal with the customer too."

"I didn't know about a customer," seethed Larry.

"You do now," complained the machine. "I couldn't do it. If you hadn't arrived they would have known I did it and destroyed me."

"We're here now," Larry spat. "Do it!"

"I can't, I can't. We'll never escape. They'll disconnect me!"

"Mess," said Napoleon. "Do it or I'll destroy you now."

"You wouldn't," whispered the machine.

"My hand is slipping," said Larry. "Do it, Nap."

Hana's face was red and sweating, her long black hair a pool on the floor. A small part of her upper lip could be seen above Larry's clasped hand and her complaints were getting increasingly loud.

Suddenly a cloud of smoke wafted over from Mess' speaker. Larry held his breath. Hana must have gasped when it happened because she immediately went limp. Napoleon moved in and held a beamer against her temple, just in case. Larry rolled off. His hand was a mass of wet mucus and blood. Another wound to add to his collection. He wiped his hand unceremoniously against his pants leg.

"You cross me again, machine," he directed at Mess, "and I'll wipe your brain. Understand?"

"I'm sorry. Really, really, really."

"How do we stand?" he whispered to Napoleon, who kneeled by Hana, still aiming her beamer.

"We've lost time. There's no room for error now."

"Let's go, then," said Larry, moving to Hana's side. Her hair spread around her face like the rays of a black sun. The muscles of her face were relaxed but not lax. Her mouth was open but not drooping. She lay against the floor as if it were a dear friend.

Her unconscious face appeared angelic. There were no forced looks of lasciviousness. No knowing quirks of the lip. No winks or arched eyebrows. No amount of makeup could hide her innate innocence. As Larry pulled her onto her back, her legs peeked out from under the slit evening gown, creamy white, long, and unblemished. Her round, high breasts moved freely beneath the gauzy, clinging white.

What was the big deal? Larry wondered. He had seen dozens of SMs more beautiful. But his body was telling him it *was* a big deal.

Larry pushed his arms under her shoulders and legs. He pulled her to him and rose slowly. She was light but solid and warm against his torso. One arm was across her lap, the other hanging down. Napoleon moved over and placed it atop her waist. She nodded quizzically at Larry. He breathed deeply and nodded back. They began to leave the room, Mess rolling along behind.

The ramp was still clear since the patron Hana had been seeing to had a few more minutes left. They moved down without incident, but when they returned to the original level they began to hear weapons fire from outside. The trio froze.

"What is that?" Larry asked.

"Our doom, our doom," Mess crackled.

"Don't get excited," he reprimanded. "It could be another vendetta, or a fight between customers."

"It's the ship!" Napoleon said with certainty. "Palend said the security had been tightened. We were delayed so now they're shooting at our escape ship!"

"I knew it," Mess continued. "We are doomed."

"Damper down. We don't have time for this," Larry instructed, the girl still in his arms. "Get inside the vehicle. With this alarm, guards will be streaming into all areas of the building. Mess, you try to close three of these doors with electronic signals. Nap, you cover the fourth. I'll strap the girl in."

The three ran up the ramp into the cargo area of the transport. Larry lowered Hana into the chair as Mess started blinking furiously. Napoleon stood by the door, tense, waiting. Larry held the beautiful girl's shoulder as he strapped a belt across her waist to hold her in the chair.

The band pulled her dress even closer to her waist, accenting her chest and hips. Larry began to breathe deeply to control his feelings. Ever since he had first seen her he had been excited even by the thought of her. The feel of her in his arms, even writhing below him on the floor, had made him aware of instincts he had only heard or read about.

He attached the waist strap, but he couldn't leave her like that; she would fall forward. He pulled another belt around that encircled her body just below her breasts. The constriction there did amazing things to his mind. He was getting angry with himself. Years with a naked feline had done nothing physically to him, but a few moments with this Destiny woman in a torn frock and he was about to bang his head against the nearest wall.

The chest strap held her upright, her head lolling down. Larry's hand was reaching for her chin when he heard Napoleon's sharp hiss.

"Here they come."

Larry turned to see two men turning the far corner, holding large, riflelike weapons. They were both humanoid and extremely ugly. All four doors of the transport vehicle were still open and Mess looked ready to explode.

A hysterically quick series of lights switched in different combinations across its board, trying to find the correct electrical signal. As soon as it saw the guards, though, every light on its console went on in surprise. Three of the doors closed with a resounding clang.

At the same moment Napoleon tore the men down with her spitter. Mess spun around.

"I was going to try all of them last," it said happily.

"Can you drive this thing?" Larry asked.

"Find me the motor," Mess replied.

"Cover me," Larry said to Napoleon, hopping out the door. As she pulled off the golden hand-covering Palend had supplied and pulled up her spitter again, Larry ducked his head under the bottom rim.

"This place is going to be a death trap soon," said Napoleon, listening to the sounds of battle outside. "As soon as they find the girl gone, they'll put two and two together and get the Peace Containers."

Larry didn't reply, just hopped back into the cargo area, walked over to a spot near the back, pulled his beamer out, and fired at the floor. A gaping rip appeared. Behind it hung a thin slice of machinery.

"There," he said to the animate table. "Hurry."

Mess rolled over to the hole for a moment, then a few of its lights blinked. The vehicle vibrated and jerked to the side. Napoleon fell out the door and Larry hit the wall, his beamer clattering on the floor.

"Sorry," said Mess.

Just then three more guards appeared at the ramp. Napoleon had dropped her spitter in order to land on all fours, and Larry's weapon still spun on the ground. The feline looked up in shock, and Larry grappled with his spitter in its holster as the three men started raising their weapons to annihilate the furry female on the floor.

Mess ran them over with the vehicle. Their bodies were crushed against the wall and were made sausage beneath the turning bulk of machinery. Napoleon grabbed her spitter and ran to the moving doorway. She leaped inside as the sounds of powdered bones, ripped limbs, and burst skin died out. The men didn't even have time to scream.

"Where to?" asked Mess merrily.

"Out the way we came," said Larry numbly, grabbing his own fallen weapon, trying to ignore what had just happened. Mess had been able to destroy the three without direct permission, since Larry had already instructed it to drive the vehicle. It was a maneuver which had saved their lives but was still disquieting. What else was the machine capable of doing beyond its programming? What other tricks did it have up its cirquids?

The vehicle moved quickly through a sloping gray tunnel, the wall zipping past the one opening. Larry turned and saw Hana's arms shaking by her side from the vibrations as well as some quivering movement beneath the dress. He quickly averted his gaze. He had other things to worry about.

Napoleon's tail was lashing to and fro and Larry realized that it would be extremely difficult for both of them to shoot from the same opening.

"Mess, can you open the door on the other side?"

"Mess, can you drive?" the machine mimicked. "Can you open doors? Can you gas people? Can you shine the ship? Must I do everything?"

"Just answer the question. Can you?"

"I can try."

Larry held on to the wall as the vehicle slowed slightly and a variety of lights winked in groups across Mess' console. Suddenly an opening appeared in front of the truck. For a moment Larry saw a group of armed guards, Peace Containers, and others of all alien types bunched before the end of the ramp to the outside. Most were facing in the opposite direction, but the ones who weren't saw a hurtling vehicle with a human, feline, and bound woman inside.

"Wrong door, Mess!" cried Larry. "Close it! The other one, open the side one!"

The guards' weapons were firing as the front sealed off. There was a searing crackle, red light appearing between the wall and the side opening, then the trio saw the gray wall turn black in a spot as they sped by. The initial blast was followed by others.

The Bishop-Fortune group were now fully aware of their approach and were trying to destroy them as they raced for freedom. Thankfully, Palend had outfitted both the truck and the ship with protective force shields or else they would already have been ash.

The area across from Napoleon opened up. Larry moved over to it, expecting the vehicle to speed up again. Instead, it slowed even more.

"Mess, what's the matter?" he shouted. "Why are we slowing down still?"

"Not now," said the table. "I'm busy."

Its lights flared momentarily and the truck picked up speed.

Larry turned toward Napoleon. "As soon as we hit daylight, fire everything you've got and keep firing. Mess, you go right for the ship, no matter what condition it's in. As soon as we're close, seal off these doors and open the front one, facing the ship, so we can make a fast transfer."

The front wall was being bombarded even more heavily. The vehicle began to buck and vibrate from the force of the onslaught.

"We're getting closer," said Larry.

"They're getting stronger," said Napoleon.

"And it's getting harder to control this thing," said Mess.

Sparks and bolts reflected off its metal surface from the gash in the floor. Suddenly the whole front wall bent in. Both Larry and Napoleon jumped to the back. Mess shut down in fear for a second, all its light winking off. The vehicle started to slow again.

Mess blasted back on, stunning Larry with the brightness of its lights, but it was too late. The floor began to peel back. The wall began to bubble and boil from the top. The vehicle rolled to a stop.

The wall separated from the roof and the floor completely fell off. Before the stunned trio and unconscious captive was a line of Peace Containers stretched across the tunnel, each of a different alien type but all with brightly glowing jewels of destruction. They had banded together to create a bolt even stronger than the protective force shield.

Behind them lay the entrance to the outside and the scorched escape vehicle beyond. Very close, but it might as well have been infinity. A black Mantas, whose deep red jewel still glowed with power, moved forward.

"I am Isenraid," it hissed. "Throw down your weapons before you. Stay exactly where you are."

Larry and Napoleon saw no recourse. Mess had no weaponry to ask permission to fire with. Hana Trigor was still beyond caring. Larry and Napoleon unclipped their belts after throwing down their hand weapons. They didn't even consider trying to make a break. Behind the Peace Containers were armed guards. All in all, it was a veritable army.

They knew that even if they tried to use the Destiny girl as cover the red bolts would slice off anything in sight. The holsters dropped upon the weapons. Isenraid and three others looked at the pile. Four bolts shot out their foreheads, then disappeared. The hunk of metal and material crumbled into a puddle of burning-hot liquid and flaking ash.

"Undo the Destiny child and bring her forward," bid Isenraid.

The two did as they were told. Napoleon pulled out a ramp as Larry undid the straps, pulling Hana onto her feet. Napoleon moved back and took one arm. Larry held the other. They got under her shoulders and carried her to the floor of the tunnel. Mess was motionless back in the vehicle, all its lights out. If it could convince the massed enforcers that it was a harmless machine, it would wait until they left to escape. But by then it would be too late for Napoleon and Larry.

"Lay her down," said Isenraid. "Carefully."

Larry lowered her himself on bended knee. She looked none the worse for wear, still completely unconscious and at peace, stretched across the floor.

"Move over to the wall," Isenraid instructed. Larry's heart sank. If they were to be detained for questioning, they would have been taken away. It was shaping up to be an immediate execution. The pair stood by the wall. The line of Peace Containers began to move over.

Napoleon's left leg began to quiver. "I will not die standing still," she hissed.

"Do what you want," Larry whispered back, his mind dull. "It will hardly make a difference."

She looked at him with fire in her eyes. The catlike pupils said that he could not be more wrong. To her it made *all* the difference. If she had wanted to stand still for death, she would have remained on Earth.

But Larry thought it meaningless. To attack, to fight, to kill when death was inevitable seemed futile. He had tried his best; they had had incredible luck and they had succeeded. Up until now.

The Peace Containers stood before them. Mantas,

human, Farzak; glop, tentacled, and stalked. Each faced them and the jewels glowed even brighter. Larry felt Napoleon's muscles bunching for the final attack. His own adrenaline started pumping through his body. His eyes found Hana lying before a kneeling guard whose hand moved toward her chest.

That opened Larry's mind up again. He realized that death was *always* inevitable and not to fight for life when there was the slimmest chance was a waste of your whole life. He was set to join Napoleon when it happened.

The opposite wall, ten feet down from them, exploded.

Napoleon and Larry hurtled forward as great chunks of stone and metal flew in a wide half circle, a huge cloud of dust and dirt covering the area. The force of the concussion cut a swath through the guards. A rock the size of a fist bashed into the kneeling guard's head. His hand never reached its lush target.

Hana herself rolled over to the wall. The Peace Containers dropped like dominoes except for the two Larry and Napoleon collided with. The feline tore at the human while Larry smashed the Farzak in the eye. The falling debris forced both to roll off their executioners and scurry under the vehicle for protection. They watched as from out of the gaping hole in the wall came a huge, nine-by-five-foot rock.

Through the gray haze a bunch of multicolored lights blinked on in the cargo area of the vehicle.

"What an entrance!" whistled Mess. "What timing!"

The space bullet was different this time. Its limbs were detached from the main body proper, hanging from the shoulder area like two arms.

Before their amazed eyes one arm rose. Not slowly, not quickly, but faster than the eye could see. One moment it was a crooked hunk hanging from the

shoulder area, the next it was straight, aimed at scurrying guards and stunned Peace Containers. The next
second four stone fingers were discernible, and from
those fingers came a wash of green.

The moving bodies contorted and fell. The globs
of matter rippled and spread. The stalks curled and
collapsed. The tentacles quivered and dropped. And
most incredible of all, the jewels of the Peace Containers nearest the ray turned opaque.

Mess rolled out of the vehicle to call to its associates.
"He was talking to me!" it cried. "Get the girl and
get inside the craft. He'll take care of things here."

They didn't have to be told twice. Larry crawled
out and ran to the prone Hana. Napoleon scurried
after a rolling Mess, bouncing over the rocky terrain.
Without ceremony Larry pulled the girl up and
dropped her onto his back. He trotted as quickly as
possible by the space bullet.

Harlan's sensors picked up one guard and one
Mantas moving back into the house. No one was
outside. But he did note that there were two guards
in upper stories, waiting to pick off the feline and
humans as they entered the craft. That would not
do.

Larry stumbled outside, seeing Napoleon nearing
the escape vehicle. Mess was already putting the automatic entrance into effect. Larry got ten yards farther when a section of the house was sliced off and
fell in on itself.

He fell forward from the force, Hana rolling over
him. Napoleon ran up as Larry looked behind. A
cloud of smoke was clearing, leaving the inside of the
house exposed. Patrons were running in all directions,
electrical wiring was cracking and spitting sparks.
Water, wine, and excrement was shooting off in all
directions. The ramp leading to the tunnel below was

all but obliterated, but from beneath came another sound.

Suddenly a hole burst open and the space bullet shot out into the sky.

"Come on," Larry heard Mess' voice. "He says he'll meet us. Hurry!"

Larry turned back to see Napoleon dragging Hana by her arms toward the ship. He found his legs and ran to help her. They pulled the unconscious girl inside. Larry dropped her on the bed and had just enough time to strap her legs and chest to the couch before it was his turn to hit the floor. Napoleon had hopped into the pilot's seat and initiated lift-off.

Outside, the space bullet matched its ascent for several seconds before peeling off and heading downward. Napoleon looked closely out the small porthole. As the land receded she couldn't spot Harlan anywhere. But as she was watching, Bishop-Fortune's establishment exploded, great gobs of yellow-orange-red fire billowing up and out.

By the time the ship left Jackpot's atmosphere, the house of vice was a hulk of flame, a black plume of smoke reaching for the sky.

FOURTEEN

"Let's burn them out of space!" yelled Bishop-Fortune.

"Hardly necessary," replied Isenraid. "Besides, you saw what the Destiny soldier did to your establishment. You should guess what I know. Killing a space bullet is no easy matter."

The two stood in a white room decorated in bright silver. Bishop-Fortune had a thing about bright silver. His hair was bright silver, he dressed in bright silver, many of his women were given silver eyes, all of his women wore silver, most of his credit was in silver, most of his star fleet was bright silver craft.

He sat in a chair built of bright silver slabs and cushioned with maroon pillows before a console of glinting silver switches—the control room of his personal space corps. He wore a vaguely military uniform, but it was dotted with bright silver spots.

"I don't care," he complained. "They deserve to be destroyed."

"And they will be," said Isenraid. "In good time."

The Mantas stood, a blue outfit draped across his body, several beige bandages lining his upper appendage, arms, and legs. Its foozle stood by its side.

"I have much to pay them back for—the same as you," the Mantas continued. "But I'm willing to wait to collect the complete vengeance."

"You are talking in riddles again," said Bishop-Fortune. "These weren't your establishments, these weren't your men. They were mine! I have been insulted by their escape. Twice!"

"And we have been insulted twice besides that," the Mantas replied smoothly. "Once, when the space bullet escaped from Destiny, and once when the Earth pair escaped from their own planet. We had all the evidence to assume they had come into contact with Trigor, but we did not act. We allowed others to deal with them. We were not sure."

"You are sure now!" Bishop-Fortune exploded. "Did you *see* what they did to my places? My two best places. I say destroy them, utterly, now."

"And I say that you should trust us as you have until now," Isenraid returned. "We have an arrangement as I am sure you will recall."

"It's hard, believe me," Bishop-Fortune reminded him. "It's been more than a year."

"You have not suffered," said the Mantas. "The Destiny girl has given you pleasure, and your customers even more. You have reveled in her beauty, you have celebrated inside her, and you have honored the credit she has brought in. That alone is worth more than both the destroyed establishments."

"Yeah," said Bishop-Fortune, remembering. "Yeah. She fought like a tigress the first few months. But I could tell she was enjoying it. They always do. The way she writhed. It was something. Strongest I ever had. I gave her to the people or else she would have gotten too sure of herself. Yeah, like a tigress. A real tigress."

"If you destroy the ship now," Isenraid interjected, "you will lose both your child of Destiny and an actual tigress."

"The cat!" Bishop-Fortune exclaimed. "That's right. That Mandarin female. Now there's a prize. With those two I'd be the biggest attraction in the galaxy, bar none. Destiny wouldn't try to find Trigor. They think she's dead. And Earth wouldn't care about an escaped murderess. They'd let me have her with blessings, figuring it was what she deserved. What an incredible conquest."

The foozle looked nauseated.

"If you destroy the ship with your fleet," Isenraid repeated, "you lose both."

Bishop-Fortune sat pulling at some loose skin on his lip. "All right," he finally said. "What do you want me to do?"

"Nothing," said Isenraid. "We shall handle all the problems."

"That's what you said last year," muttered Bishop-Fortune.

"But now our space bird is coming home to roost," said Isenraid. "I have been ... in contact with Ministic on Destiny. She feels that there is no reason why our postponed plan cannot take effect. The Trigor parents are still dead and disgraced, the children are still missing. The questions are still being asked. Their loyalty is still in serious doubt. There is no reason why Harlan cannot still kill the Queen."

"And then?"

"And then Ministic takes temporary control and dispatches the space bullets to find their treacherous brother. Ministic heroically manages to flush out and destroy an Earth accomplice. By then the weapon will be finished and the space bullets will be helpless."

"And then?" Bishop-Fortune was smiling.

"The planet will be defenseless," said Isenraid. "Your fleet will move in and take control, having all the advantage and reaping all the profit."

"Ah, yes, the profit," Bishop-Fortune mused.

"Yes, mineral and physical wealth. Ongoing supplies of food and clothing. The most beautiful females of the humanoid species. And the child of Destiny and the feline."

"Excellent," said the Jackpot denizen, rising. "Excellent. You sound assured of the plan's success."

"Of course," said Isenraid.

Bishop-Fortune moved toward the door. Before he reached it, he turned.

"Tell me something. You're not like the other Mantases. You are not so...fanatical, let's say. What are you doing this for? What's in it for you? A permanent home? Shared wealth? What?"

"You are not like other humans," Isenraid said dryly. "Do I ask you questions?"

"What happens afterward?" he pressed. "What will you do then?"

Isenraid moved up to where Bishop-Fortune stood.

"We will do as we always do," he said. "Advise those in power. We are rarely wrong. People listen to us. All the races listen to us. For instance, after the first attempt to take the Destiny child, did you listen to me when I advised implanting a device inside her?"

"Sure, it was a good idea. We know where she is now without having to follow her. We can pinpoint the Earth ship at any time."

"It will make the final destruction simple." Isenraid nodded. "And did you listen when I told you who the Earthen's associate on this planet was?"

"Of course. It had to be Palend. Why else would he outfit his vehicle with force shields?"

"And did you listen when I suggested the best way to achieve both your ends just now?"

"Yes. It sounds good. We not only get rid of the space bullet and the FM but I get Destiny's riches and the feline as well."

"Good, good," said Isenraid. "It is as it is on almost every planet. Now you tell me, Bishop-Fortune. Who is really in charge here?"

With that Isenraid left the room with the foozle. Bishop-Fortune was speechless. Then he began to laugh.

DESTINY

FIFTEEN

The *Black Hole* was no stage for a scene of happy reunion. There were no cries of delight, no tears of joy, no solid hugs of welcome, not even comfortable relaxation.

As soon as Hana awoke and was unstrapped, she ran right for her brother and tried to scratch his eyes out. When Harlan could not get her to stop, he slugged her across the face.

Larry brought her to a cabin where, when she came to, she sobbed for a few days. When the swelling of her jaw went down, she cried for two weeks.

At first Harlan thought he could talk her out of it, only to get screamed at. Occasionally she would attack him. That was always followed by her being hurled back onto her bed or another slap, followed by more crying.

Later, the only times Harlan would see her was when she was asleep. He would stand outside her cabin, tears collecting in his beard, sometimes for as long as eight hours.

Larry gave her her meals. The first few days she usually threw them back at him, followed by more crying. After almost a week she began to eat, but would constantly throw up and occasionally would beat at Larry as he tried to attend to the disorder.

Later she would be able to eat the full meal but would tell Larry what terrible things Bishop-Fortune would do to him, which almost always ended with her delivering a nonstop string of obscenities.

By the third week she ate in silence but tried to make serving and cleaning up as difficult as possible. Larry would walk around depressed and Harlan remained despondent.

By the end of the first month in light drive, she appeared on the bridge. She still wore her white gown, ripped and dirty and flecked with sickness. She stood at the back and said nothing. She moved away as Harlan attempted to approach her. That evening Larry asked him what size clothes she wore. He put a shirt, pants, and boots he had altered outside her door.

The next day he found them strewn across the passageway. He refolded them and put them by her door. He repeated this for a little more than two weeks when he found them thrown, kicked, or torn. When they were ripped, he sewed them up. When food was dropped on them, he'd clean them.

By the end of the second month in their three-month journey, she was visiting the bridge every day, wearing the boots, shirt, and pants. Larry thought they looked very good on her. He said nothing, however. By then Harlan and Hana were actively avoiding each other. Shortly thereafter Mess spoke up.

"She's in the cargo area trying to sabotage the ship. Can I blast her?"

"No," said Larry miserably. "Is she doing any damage?"

"No."

"Then leave her alone."

"I think I should blast her."

Larry did not reply. Napoleon agreed with the machine but had more understanding and sense than to say so.

In the days that followed Mess kept them abreast on her movements and her attempts to do them all in. Then her emphasis began to change. Her endeavors leaned more to self-destruction than mass destruction.

For hours she would sit in an escape pod trying to jettison it. Then she would try to jam open the escape hatch. Finally she would wander around the engine area trying to find an exposed area of power. Mess made sure nothing worked for her, under Larry's orders.

The ship sank into space like black depression. The passing planets and speeding stars held no more wonder. Space became cavernous and uncomfortable to Larry, who up until then always thought of the *Black Hole* as home. He couldn't understand his feelings. There were times when he just sat and stared at nothing for hours. He didn't talk to Napoleon or yell at Mess anymore, no matter how much they tried to reach him. The prospect of Destiny became an obsession.

Hana began to wear her disintegrating gown again. She would stare out the portholes, radiating beauty and hate. She was pale, her hair was matted and unwashed, she had gotten thinner, but her inner pain made her even more lovely to Larry. Her skin had become chapped, her pupils red and watery, her fingernails chipped, but she was still beautiful.

One day Destiny came into view. At first it was a speck. Later it grew into a dot. Soon it was a marble, a green-streaked marble. Then it was a jeweled ball, a sparkling space weight.

On that day Hana ran onto the bridge screaming. Larry sat in the pilot's chair looking at his thumb. Napoleon was tinkering near Mess' console trying to piece together a new weapon for herself. Harlan was wandering around the ship.

The Trigor girl ran to the port facing Destiny and looked. She then ran to Larry and started beating him in the face, her arms two thrashing windmills.

The first fist hit him on the bridge of the nose, the second in the eye. The pain was shocking enough to keep him stunned and helpless. Her small, hard fists continued to pummel him.

"Where are we going?" she screamed. "Where are we going?"

Napoleon was up and behind the girl. She wrapped her arms around her waist and pulled Hana off the pilot. Hana's legs kicked, shapely flashes of flesh streaking out under her torn dress. Her hands tried to push away the furry arms holding her. All she felt were tightly bunched muscles. When she got her feet on the ground, she leaned forward and spat.

"I'm not going back! I can't! I'll die first!"

Then she continued screaming. Long, wrenching cries of "No," drawn out and finished with wracking gasps. Harlan ran in and tried to take his sister in his arms, his face twisted in despair. She pulled away from both Napoleon and her brother, spitting at them. Then she ran out the hatch.

Harlan and Larry were on their feet to follow her. Napoleon cut them off and raised her paws.

"Neither of you move. You understand? I should have done this weeks ago." She turned to move out. Harlan took a step after her. She turned back. "I mean it," she assured him. "Follow me and I will maul you.

Either of you." Her tail beat at the air.

Larry moved forward and put a hand on Harlan's arm. He stopped. Larry nodded at Napoleon. She turned and ran out on all fours.

She caught up with Hana by the girl's cabin. She had tripped on her gown and was getting up, tearing at the cloth, screaming, and crying. Napoleon spun her around and hit her hard three times across the face. She then pushed the girl into her cabin. Napoleon entered and closed the door.

She turned to face the shocked Destinian.

"I am as beautiful as you. I am wanted as much, if not more, than you. I have been used worse than you. I have suffered more than you. Yet I do not try to destroy myself or the ones close to me. It means nothing and it accomplishes nothing. You will stop it. Now."

"You—you do not understand," sputtered the girl. "He'll kill me."

"He has no more control over you," said Napoleon. "I thought you would have realized that by now."

"He has ships. A fleet. He can destroy us anytime."

"Then you have nothing to fear. You will be free."

"No! No! He'll kill you all and take me back. He'll use me."

Napoleon moved in and took Hana firmly by the shoulders.

"He cannot take you back if you do not wish it."

"He has strength," the girl pleaded. "He has straps and drugs...."

"He cannot take you back. He would not take you back without trying to take me. I will not be taken, because I am not afraid."

"You don't...you don't understand! You don't know how I feel! You're, you're not human."

Napoleon hit the quaking girl once more across the face. The tears and sobs were cut off.

"I am female. I feel the same things you do. Must I show you? I am a woman. I am not afraid of it."

The Destinian would still not meet her eyes.

"You are not afraid of him," Napoleon said with certainty. "You are afraid of *yourself*."

"I ... I ... am afraid...."

"Of yourself. You are a woman. You are a female. You cannot ram into them. They can only ram into you. You are afraid of accepting that. You are afraid of liking that."

"I ... I do not like that."

"What can you do when a male you hate takes you? There is pain, but there are the other senses too. Hate is the only thing left you. But after months and months, even hate is dulled. You have no choice. You live with the pain, and the hate. It becomes your reality. But how can this be? you ask yourself. How can this be my life? How can I accept this?

"You tell yourself you cannot. But you have. You *have*."

Hana started to cry again. But they were not tears of shame or of horror or of hate. They were tears of release.

"Then you have a choice," Napoleon continued. "You can hate yourself and your sex for this acceptance. Or you can become what they want you to become. A thing. You can shape yourself in their image."

Napoleon waited until Hana's eyes found her own. They were two different kinds of eyes, one deep and dark and tearful, the other bright, slitted, and aware. But they were all living eyes. They were all eyes that attached to aware brains. They were the same.

"Or you can understand that you exist. That you are a woman. That this is your reality and you can be the best or worst woman you want to be."

Hana shook her head.

"No," said Napoleon. "Don't do that. You must accept yourself. You are yourself. You have been used. There is nothing wrong about not being able to fight that. There is nothing wrong about not dying or killing yourself. You were used and now it's over. You are still you. You have changed. That is all right too. You have been hurt. It is over now. Over. Understand that it is finished."

Hana rubbed her eyes with the palms of her hands. She stared at Napoleon, not seeing the fur or the whiskers or the eyes. She saw another woman. She nodded.

"I'll try," said Hana.

"You will," corrected Napoleon.

Hana looked away. She saw herself reflected in a porthole. Her dress was ripped, exposing most of her chest. Her face was streaked and dirty. Her eyes were puffy and bloodshot. But she could see the woman superimposed on the green planet of Destiny. She turned back to Napoleon.

"I will," she said.

The four sat on the bridge in a semicircle. Mess was kind enough to supply two more chairs. Destiny loomed large in all the windows, bathing the area in brightness tinged with color. Hana was once again dressed in the black tunic, gray pants, and boots. She had washed as well, making her look as fresh as a new morning. Her appearance and subsequent explanations had brightened the ship more than Destiny and its sun combined.

"It came down to Bishop-Fortune being my only savior after a while. You didn't come," she said to Harlan. "And he would tell me all these stories about what happened to you. That you were killed and your suit was a coffin in space, that you had tried to assassinate the Queen and were executed. That you went crazy and killed our parents.

"The one time I tried to think for myself he put me on the open market. That was where you found me," she told Larry. "When you first told me the truth, I thought it was another trick. To degrade me even more. Then I couldn't face that truth. I could never escape. He'd always find me."

"You have escaped," Larry reassured her.

"Classic brainwashing technique," explained Napoleon. "The starvation causes an imbalance in the brain fluids, where the subject is open to a far greater range of suggestion. Normally things you would never accept become all too possible, since you can't think straight."

"Incredible," said Harlan. "What kind of people are these? You mean you did not want to return to Destiny because you were different?"

"I can't explain it exactly," said Hana slowly. "I wasn't fit. I wasn't worthy or something like that. I just couldn't think and I was so used to not thinking I couldn't break it. You see, it's easier not to think. It's easier to be what they want you to be. It's easier not to look at yourself. It's easier to look at yourself through others."

"Heavy," said Mess.

Following the silences, she asked uncomfortably, "So what now?"

"I have to tell you what happened, really," said Harlan. "It is not much better than what you were told."

She looked from Napoleon to Larry. "I'm ready," she said to her brother, rising. Harlan got up and walked with his sister out of the bridge.

"Really incredible," said Larry, leaning back and sighing.

"And how are you feeling, pilot?" asked Napoleon, grinning.

"Better." He leaned forward and cocked an eye at his co-pilot, who sat back regally. "You know things like the back of your hand, don't you?"

"Paw, Larry, paw," the feline retorted. "I've spent a lot of time in Earth labs and in the observation of the way humans work."

"Then explain it to me, will you? I'm confused."

"You're in love," Napoleon corrected. "Or 'in like,' or 'infatuated.' You've experienced your first full woman and your poor, undernourished psyche can hardly handle it."

"Are you making fun of me?"

"Hardly. Most of the dried-up fossils back on Earth only feel lust. Their feelings for the opposite sex are put on a level of craving. Like an appetite for food. They think they can live without love, as if that made them 'real men.' You're more real than any of them. It was no mistake they didn't make more like you. A man who honestly feels is dangerous to the way things are going."

Larry shook his head, smiling. "This is too much. I'm no different from anyone else."

"Don't sell yourself short. What are you feeling for that girl? Passion? Desire? Not much, I'll warrant. You have strong feelings but more like tenderness, regard, and affection. Attraction. You need her, you want her, but you don't *have* to have her. You know what I mean."

"Yeah, I think I do," said Larry, rising. He walked around the bridge, looking out at Destiny when it came into view. "How about us, though? We've been together a long time. We feel things for each other."

"Must we define them?" Napoleon asked with a tinge of exasperation.

"You already have in your own mind," Larry replied. "It's harder for me. My experience is limited."

"Point taken and understood," Napoleon went on. "I suppose this kind of thing is all you can do on a three-month space trip without busywork."

"Well?"

"We have everything," said the feline, rising and approaching him. "Affection, respect, attachment, friendship. Everything but one. Attraction. For some reason we just don't excite each other. Thank Cheshire."

"What's so great about that?"

"Ah, love is a funny emotion, Larry. Could you imagine what it would have been like all these years if we *were* attracted? We'd have been eliminated long ago."

"I suppose so."

"On Earth? With Grossman-Smith wanting me? With every scientist waiting for you to make a wrong move? You *know* so."

They stood side by side in front of the port, Destiny making a spotlight around them.

"I know so," said Larry.

"We're talking like old friends about to die," said Napoleon.

"An interesting point," said Mess.

At the sound of its voice they both jumped.

"Does anyone know what we're going to do when we reach Destiny orbit?" the machine demanded.

"That's right!" cried Larry. "We're not in the clear yet."

"We're wanted by the Earth Government, the Jackpot Intercouncil, and the mightiest vice-lord in the galaxy; we're flying into an alien-spawned conspiracy and he says we're not in the clear yet," whined Mess. "We won't be in the clear, *ever.*"

"Damper, you glomerated mechanism. Why didn't you speak up before?"

"You people are so much fun to watch."

"Never mind. What's our situation now?"

"Mentally or physically?"

"Both."

"Mentally, you've just deciphered your place in the universe. Physically, we're a few hours from orbit and in a lot of trouble."

"What's the matter?"

"We've been tracked the last ten minutes. No radio message, no verbal transmission of any kind. No overt defensive actions. Just tracking."

"Are you sure?"

"Of course, I'm sure," Mess said defensively. "It took me awhile to be sure that's what it was, but when I speak up you can be sure I'm sure."

"That's odd," Larry said to Napoleon. "I'd imagine we're unlike any ship they've ever encountered, yet they don't contact us."

"According to Harlan, Destiny shoots first," Napoleon reminded him. "Perhaps we had better do the signaling."

"Mess, call Harlan in here," Larry instructed, moving over to his console. "We've been so wrapped up in ourselves we haven't thought out our approach at all."

"Slim," said Mess. "Very slim reasoning."

"I said damper down!" Larry shouted.

"Well, we're feeling much better now, aren't we?" Mess replied in a huff.

"Did you call Harlan?" Napoleon interrupted.

"Naturally. *I* haven't been wrapped up in myself."

"What is going on?" asked Harlan, moving quickly into the room, followed by Hana.

They all huddled around Larry's chair.

"Destiny has been tracking us for a while. They haven't done anything yet. We want to know what they're likely to do," Larry said from his seat.

"They can see we are not part of a fleet," Harlan mused. "They should have contacted us."

"We should have contacted them," reminded Napoleon fretfully. "We have no markings; Larry took them off on our way to Jackpot. They might be unsure as to how to handle us."

"What do you mean, Larry took them off?" Mess complained. "Larry told me to take them off. And Earth and Jackpot could have described our ship to Destiny."

"Destiny is not interested in outsiders' problems," said Hana.

"But we do monitor transmissions in case they prove any danger to our security," said Harlan.

"Some decision has to be made," Larry chipped in. "Harlan, what do you advise?"

"Contact them. Tell them the story of our escape from Earth. Leave me and Hana out. They still think we're traitors, probably."

"Mess," Larry instructed, "get in touch with the planet. Say we're the *Black Hole* escaped from Earth and in need of assistance."

The group waited a few seconds while Mess tried a wide range of transmission frequencies.

"Mess?"

"I've sent the message out every way possible. No reply. Not even evidence that they're receiving."

"Try again."

"I have already. Twice. Nothing. We had better turn back."

"We can't," Larry said. "Harlan, what now?"

The Destinian stood with his hands joined before his face. Slowly, they rocked back and forth. Suddenly he brought them down and spoke decisively.

"There's little choice. Keep sending your message. Give them the whole story if necessary, without mentioning us, with or without reply. And don't try to run their orbit or land. We have the best defense of any planet in the galaxy." He turned and walked toward the rear hatch.

"Where are you going?" asked Napoleon.

Harlan stopped by the exit. "I'm getting into my suit. Just in case. I advise you to do the same." Then he was out and gone.

"Mess, go ahead," said Larry. "Stick to the basic facts. Napoleon and I were being used. We escaped to Destiny. We come in peace with information vital to their safety and all that. Just keep repeating that and don't get strident. Tell me of any change in tracking." He turned to the two females on either side of his chair. "We had better suit up."

The hours moved by without incident. Mess kept sending the message. No reply. The tracking never ceased. They found a spacesuit that could fit Hana, and all three donned suits as Destiny began to take up three-fifths of their horizon. They returned to the bridge, clumping in their boots.

"Any change?" Larry radioed to Mess.

"None," the computer replied.

The three moved around the area like deflated balloons. The suits were gray and blue. Larry's had a gray top and bottom with blue gloves, belt, and boots, while Napoleon's was the opposite. Hana got a mixture of the two to fit her better, made of spare parts. A gray top, a blue bottom, a gray belt, gray gloves, blue boots.

The helmets were tubes that ended in a rounded top. A clear screen stretched across their visages, ending behind their ears, giving them a better than 180-degree view. The clear screen had the same attributes as the ship's port windows. They would gradate depending on the amount of light as well as protect the wearer from cosmic radiation. The bulbous belt was not only an oxygen holder, but a mixer of it as well.

"How much longer until final orbit?" Larry inquired.

"Four minutes, twelve seconds," Mess said tensely.

"Harlan, can you hear us?" Hana shouted into her suit.

Larry and Napoleon winced as her voice boomed through their receivers.

"No need to shout," said Napoleon. "The microphone and speakers are part of the screen. Even a whisper can be heard."

"I hear you all very well," came Harlan's voice. "As well as the computer with whom I've established a long-term communication. Now be prepared for anything. Absolutely anything. I do not like this feeling. Never in my experience have they waited this long to take action. This denotes no good. Look out for a collection of flashes from the following locations."

Harlan then rattled off sixteen coordinates before Mess interrupted him.

"But how about..." It too gave a different coordinate.

"That is another," Harlan said in surprise. "How did you know?"

"Because that's where the flash just came from,"

Mess said hysterically. "Unidentified craft sighted. Permission to fire!"

"Space bullets!" came Harlan's voice. "They're attacking. Quickly, get in your escape pod."

"Permission to fire, permission to fire!" Mess cried.

"Harlan," Larry shouted over the confusion, "can't we stall them? Talk to them?"

"You can't," Harlan replied, at which point Larry waved at Napoleon and Hana to get going. "But *I* can. Get in an escape vehicle and take off. I will cover you."

Larry moved as the head of the fleet of one hundred space bullets appeared on his screen. Napoleon and Hana were already out of the bridge area. He stopped by a rear panel and pulled out his beamer rifle.

"Hey, what about me?" cried Mess.

"Open the bottom hatch for Harlan, then come on!" shouted Larry as he moved out the rear. Sounds of frenzied vacuum packing assailed Larry's ears as he trotted toward the escape-pod area. Then the whole hallway rocked from side to side. The space bullets had begun their attack.

"Get out!" shouted Harlan's voice. "I deflected that shot or else it would have destroyed your ship. Get going!"

Larry galloped into the escape hallway to see Napoleon and Hana huddled before a hatch.

"Too many of us for one pod. We've got to use Palend's ship. Hurry!"

The ship started bouncing in rapid movements. The three bounced about the small tube like candy in a box. The jumps subsided to a vibration and the trio found their feet again.

"Mess," said Larry. "Close the bottom hatch and prepare the ship."

There was no reply. The three began to run toward

the bottom of the ship.

"Mess, Mess, where are you? Mess!"

The ship lurched to the right. The three hit the left wall. Napoleon howled in frustration as her suit diminished her natural balance and freedom of movement. Larry pulled himself erect and kept going, collecting a hunched-over Hana in the process.

The ship shook back and forth, but the trio kept going. They made it to the bottom hatch to find it closed and the ship atop it, its doors open.

"Mess did it," said Larry. "Get in quickly."

The three pulled themselves in, Larry shutting the door after him. As soon as they were sealed in, Larry saw the console lights flash. The bottom hatch opened again and they were streaking through space.

All three floated to the roof of the bullet-shaped ship. Through the small porthole in front, Larry saw an incredible display of light and galactic fire. Rocks spun at each other with unbelievable agility and in amazing patterns. Weaponry of all kinds burned, bristled, curved, and arced out of the shooting stones.

Larry pulled himself away and started to maneuver himself to one of the four seats near the tip of the craft.

"Strap yourselves in," he instructed the others. "We'll be hitting the atmosphere soon."

In one of the seats was a flat-topped metal tube lined with clear semicircles atop a smaller-necked tube atop a sloping cone that branched out into another thicker chest tube that ended in four quadruple-jointed metal legs, two ending in wheels, two ending in small, boxlike treads.

"In fifteen seconds, to be exact," said the metal creature. Larry ignored Mess' latest manifestation, pulling Hana into a seat and strapping her in instead.

Napoleon had maneuvered into her own. Larry pulled himself back to the seat beside Mess as Harlan's voice assailed them.

"They've got your ship; I couldn't cover it all. I'm pacing your escape craft now. I'm trying to keep them off all sides, but there are many of them. They've spotted me and your vehicle. How much time to re-entry? How much time left?"

Before Mess or Larry could answer, the escape ship spun as if struck by a giant palm. Incredible pressure pushed against Larry's head and body until the light went out.

SIXTEEN

"I feel terrible," said the voice.

Larry awoke to find himself under a blanket of green beneath a sheet of brown.

"What an awful feeling," said the voice.

The first thing Larry heard was a loud bonging, as if something were hitting a large bell with a soft mallet. Beyond that was a constant rustling.

"Careful. Careful, now," said the voice.

Against his face Larry felt moisture of two kinds. One was cool and the other was warm, dried in places. Beside him, against his torso was another type of warmth. Soft, pliant, comfortable.

"Wow, that's better," said the voice. "A little more."

Beneath his head was soft ground. He called on his muscles to raise him up. Complaining, they complied. Needles of ice attacked his neck, his shoulder, and his hand as he rose. All his old wounds were back to plague him. His vision clouded, but he managed to get up in a sitting position. He stayed there, looking down into his lap until he could see again.

"He's awake," said the voice.

Larry saw Mess' manifestation standing on its legs, the treads in back, the wheels in front with Napoleon in front of them, banging its chest area with a rock. The chest area was bent in several places and the feline was trying to right it. She herself looked none the worse for wear. She turned to him.

"Welcome to Destiny," she said flatly and went back to Mess' chest.

Larry sat in a daze for a moment, then turned his head, ignoring the renewed pain. Lying beside him was Hana. She seemed to be sleeping comfortably. Her breathing was regular and full and there were no signs of external injuries. He suddenly remembered he had strapped her in but neglected to do the same completely for himself. No wonder he felt so bad.

In a pile behind them were the spacesuits. Beyond that was the salvage craft, now salvage material itself. Its sides were crumbled and it was bent in half and sitting on a large rock.

"Mess kept aware the entire trip down," Napoleon filled him in. "We were damaged and floundering, but he managed to find a break in the trees and put us down." Napoleon had moved over and knelt down next to Larry, the rock still in her hand. "Or so he says."

"It wasn't easy," complained Mess. "At great physical damage to myself, I piloted the ship down and saved all your lives. Suffering great personal torture, I might add."

Its chest area was somewhat level again, though bumpy still. It maneuvered over to where the trio of living creatures huddled.

"Where are we, exactly?" asked Larry, the top of his mouth feeling like the inside of his nose.

"Don't I even get a thank you?" asked Mess.

"Thank you," said Larry, swallowing with difficulty. "Where are we, exactly?"

"I don't know," said Mess. "When we were hit the navigational equipment was damaged."

"That always seems to be the first to go," interjected Napoleon.

"I brought us down on my own imput with great anxiety and daring," the machine added proudly.

"All right, we said thank you," Larry retorted.

"He's feeling better," Napoleon told the machine as she rose.

Larry took a moment to look around. The blanket of green was leaves. The sheet of brown was tree trunks. They were at the base of a very high forest. But where, exactly? Destiny was covered in forests.

Hana sucked in a deep breath beside him, making a snoring sound. Her body curled and her eyes opened. All heads turned to her. Mess didn't have to, since its sensors covered its crown all the way around. The raven-haired girl sat up quickly.

"Destiny," she said. "The forest of Destiny. We're here."

"Yes, we're here," said Larry. "But where here? Which forest?"

She pulled her legs around, making two crooked v's beneath her torso. "I'm sorry. I was confused. Until I noticed you I thought I had awakened from a nightmare. As if I had never left."

The group fell silent, remembering what they had been through. And thinking about what might come.

Hana scrambled to her feet and looked about. "We must get out of here. All forests are the same on

Destiny. Wild beasts roam freely. We hunt them from our automatic stone factories."

"Automatically?" Mess echoed. "You mean involuntarily?"

"No, we have factories that line our cities," she explained, "that hunt down the forest creatures for food and clothing. The beasts are too dangerous and too numerous to be hunted by our people. They are pinpointed by sensors and killed by beams from a distance. We collect them later."

Larry and Napoleon looked quickly around, viewing the seemingly calm forest in a different light.

"But if they sense the creatures, they must know we're different from them," said Larry. "Maybe their equipment can't detect us at all."

"No," said Hana. "They must know we're here. We crashed the ship on the planet. No other attack has managed to do the same. I'm sure they're trying to locate us at this very second."

"How long have we been here?" Larry asked hurriedly.

"A few minutes," said Napoleon. "I haven't been counting."

"I have," said Mess. "Fourteen minutes, forty-two seconds."

Hana gasped.

"Let's go, let's get out of here," Larry declared. He saw that everyone had on his or her shipboard clothing, he and Hana the shirt, pants, and boots, and Napoleon wore sandals on her rear paws, special palm protectors on her forepaws, and a leotard with lacing up the front. The beamer rifle was strapped on her back.

"Anything else in the ship we need?"

"Nothing," said Napoleon. "No food, no water, no other weapons. Nothing."

"Come on, then," said Larry. He took Hana's hand without thinking and started walking away from the ship. Napoleon reached down and picked up a thick wooden staff as tall as herself that she had fashioned just after taking the suits off her companions and just before tending to Mess.

As she began to rise and Larry reached the top of a small knoll with Hana, a strong buzzing was heard in the distance, getting louder.

"Get down!" Hana cried.

She fell to the ground, pulling a surprised Larry down with her. Napoleon stretched her arms and legs out immediately, spread-eagled even before she hit the leafy surface. Mess pushed its own legs out until they were parallel to the ground. Then, turning one wheel to the side, it pushed itself over.

The buzzing filled the air now. Through the trees Larry saw flickering sparks. Suddenly loose chips of bark were flying all around him. Leaves started swirling from the forest floor. Hana cried out. Larry wrapped his arms around her protectively. Napoleon gritted her teeth and screwed her eyes shut.

It was as if their own section of forest were caught in the eye of a minute inferno. Everyone's hair stood on end and crackled. Heat singed their skin and small shocks touched every nerve. Even through closed eyelids, patterns of electrical force appeared. Then, just as quickly as it had come, it disappeared.

The buzzing receded and the wood was silent again. Larry was afraid that when he looked up his friends would be smoking carcasses, but when he raised his head he saw Hana and Napoleon doing the same. Mess was blinking on its side. They all looked around from their prone positions to see if they were all in one piece. It was discovered that they were. Suddenly all heads turned to the escape ship.

It was totally unrecognizable. The top half had melted down, covering the bottom with gobs of pulpy metal. The bottom area was lined with ragged tears and holes. It was half the height and twice the width it used to be. Smoke was curling from the holes as the remnants of electrical circuitry and furniture burned. It was a frightening example of devastation that wasn't lost on any of them.

Napoleon jumped to her feet and ran over to where Hana and Larry stood. Mess pushed itself erect with difficulty and rolled by the three, not stopping, blinking erratically. The flesh and blood followed without a word.

They ran for quite a distance without stopping, until their hearts thudded heavily in their chests and their legs felt like sacks of sand. The actual distance was not that far. Although they all were in fine physical shape, they had been in space too long. Larry stumbled before anyone else. Hana knelt down next to him.

Napoleon knocked on Mess' back with her staff to get him to stop. None of them had spoken as yet. The fear of omnipresent death had settled on them all. The thought that the buzzing could return and single out any or all of them created an undiluted paranoia. They each looked at the horizon differently.

The spaces between the trees held danger. Somewhere out there could be a cross hair or beam of energy that would transmit their image to the eyes of the hunter. Even Mess was not immune. Its own situation was especially acute. Without the protection of the *Black Hole* to call on, it felt extremely vulnerable. Even as the group rested, their eyes and ears were wary. And with good reason.

The buzzing started again. Napoleon was the first to hear it.

"Look out," she howled and ran in the other direction. Hana and Larry followed only to stumble to a halt as the way before them disintegrated into rubble. A wall made of flaming wind faced them, hurling up dirt, bark, leaves, and rocks.

They all turned and ran in the other direction, terror being their spur. They ran farther this time, ignoring their various aches and wounds. Each area they entered changed subtly, but it all looked the same to them. Trees, leaves, trees, leaves. Unending green and brown. Unending shadows and shade. The united hands of the foliage above kept the sun from their view. When next they stopped they unconsciously chose an area of light.

"This is useless," Napoleon gasped, sitting atop a rock, breathing deeply. Larry and Hana, bringing up the rear, sank to their knees as they neared her. Mess just kept right on rolling.

"We don't know where we are or where we're going," the feline continued. "These hunters, whoever they are, seem to love noise, but they aren't the best shots I've ever seen."

"It is surprising," admitted Hana, breathlessly. "They have a great reputation."

The buzzing started once more.

"Here it comes again!" Napoleon cried, leaping up.

Larry and Hana fell forward. The feline hopped over three large rocks and leaped between two huge trees as the crackling storm smashed down. The rocks she jumped over exploded and the trees she threw herself between were sliced halfway through. Hunks of stone thunked into tree trunks hundreds of feet around. Leaves rustled madly as other rocks rushed past them. Their dust settled atop great strips of bark ripped from the cut trees.

Larry pushed himself to his feet and ran unsteadily to the sagging opening the torn trees had made.

"Nap? Are you all right?" he yelled hoarsely. "Nap!"

In answer, the tree to his right began to crack above its wound. The huge arm of the forest began to topple. In its path lay Hana. The Trigor girl had risen to her knees with her back to him, her ears buzzing still, making her unaware of the situation. Larry ran to her as the falling tree picked up speed. The uncut trunk had begun to rip open, spitting wood and bark chips. Larry grabbed the girl under her arms and lifted her, still running. His shoulders popped and his head filled with pain. She flopped into his arms like a rag doll, her feet flying back into his.

His freedom of movement was cut, but not his momentum. As he felt himself falling he threw his weight to the side. The two hit the ground, which thankfully sloped downward, and rolled. Branches cracked under their weight and stones punched their moving bodies, but nothing stopped them. As Larry spun, a huge brown beam flew through his vision. The ground disappeared, leaving them floating in midair. Then a great, hollow thump smashed into their ears.

The ground came back like a fist, slapping their entire bodies, jarring their teeth. The two skidded to a stop. Not three feet away was a brown trunk as thick as Hana was tall.

Larry held on to the girl until she started hitting him with the flat of one hand. He let go then and rolled the other way. His head was aching with a steady throb and his shoulders felt as if they had been cooked over an open fire. His legs felt as if they were made of knife cuts and his neck felt braided. Napoleon had to call him five times before he heard through the pain.

He turned to see the cat standing on the fallen tree trunk, pointing off in the direction she had run originally. Larry tried to listen, but his ears were roaring. He tried to get to his feet, but he could only reach his knees. Hana came over and helped him. "You're good at saving me," she said.

"Thank you," he said as he began to move slowly around the base of the fallen tree. He walked out into sunlight. The forest had stopped momentarily to make way for the base of a mountain. Napoleon and Mess stood in the light as Hana and Larry approached.

"We were being guided," said Napoleon. "The whole thing doesn't make sense otherwise. Why should they destroy our craft completely, then miss us twice? Someone is leading us somewhere."

"Must have a great sense of humor, by the Earth Father," said Larry, pushing his thumb back toward the tree.

"You'll have to come up with a new curse," said Napoleon lightly. "We're not on Earth anymore."

"By the Destiny Father?" Larry suggested, squinting at her.

"The Destiny Mother," Hana corrected, looking up at the mountain.

While the three bantered, their spirits started to rise. They weren't just targets anymore, waiting for execution. They still had a chance. Maybe. They surveyed the incline. A band of rocks curved off into the distance in either direction, topped by a row of trees leveling off before another bank of rocks stretched in both directions. That covered their sight lines; what was beyond would have to wait until they mastered that.

"It's one of the string of mountains protecting the central city," Hana said excitedly. "I'm sure of it."

"That's incredible luck," said Larry. "What do you think? Were we guided to this particular area of forest too?"

"There is always that possibility," said Mess. "I was working diligently but quickly from any incoming information my sensors could gather. It might have come from Harlan or the cities below."

"You're beginning to sound more and more like a regular compubot all the time," Larry said.

"Extraordinary situations call for extraordinary measures," said Mess.

"More like the electronic storms have addled your brain," said Napoleon. "Can you make it?" she finished, gesturing to the mountain.

"I built myself to handle just such an eventuality. I can maneuver up to sixty degrees."

"Larry?" Napoleon next said. He had leaned forward against a rock and not moved.

"What?" he replied, still not moving.

"How are you?"

"If I'm not dead, I'm fine."

He pulled himself onto the incline, followed by the others.

They had made it three-quarters of the way up the initial rock face when the first spear hit. It was a crudely shaped projectile made from a branch and given a point by a diagonal break, but it was hurled with such force that it shattered when it struck.

Shards slapped against Hana's body. The pieces of wood stung and the attack surprised her, but she held on. Her hair was plastered against her neck and hung in damp beads across her back. Her face was bathed in sweat.

"Larry," she cried. "The monsters!"

Larry looked up to see several vaguely humanoid beasts by the next band of forest, shaking sticks and screaming through wide, brittle-toothed mouths. He was expecting four-footed animals with fur and fangs, so the sight stunned him. Their skins were dark brown, enabling them to blend in with the trees, and they had no necks. Their heads sloped into their shoulders and arms.

Their eyes were small and their noses, with two nostrils, were pushed up. Their hands, with no thumbs that Larry could see, were filled with rocks and branches, the things that they started to rain down on the climbing party.

Hana and Larry ducked behind some boulders while Napoleon and Mess anchored themselves in the open. The feline swung the beamer off her shoulder and aimed. Before Larry could call out, she fired. The orange beam sliced through the air and disappeared into the ground below the dancing creatures.

Suddenly the outcropping beneath the creatures' feet gave way and they tumbled down over the rocks, spinning and smashing as they went. Spurts of blood shot out as they fell, glinting red in the sunlight.

"They're warm-blooded," Larry spoke in a hush.

"So?" said Napoleon, her feline hearing picking up his whisper. "We've seen enough of that red stuff this trip."

Their conversation was cut short by the appearance of many more creatures, all along the lip of the upper forest, all dancing and screaming. They, too, began to hurl down pieces of stone and wood. Napoleon started her beam from the left and cut across, dumping some down onto the rocks and slicing others in pieces.

"Stun them," Larry shouted. "Switch to stun. We

can't just kill them all!"

"We can't just let them kill us either," Napoleon howled. "Now or later."

"Nap, they're warm-blooded," Larry pleaded. "They're using tools. They're not just dumb beasts."

"Larry, they're warm for *our* blood," Napoleon screamed back. "And they're using their tools on us." She continued firing as the line of creatures replenished itself. "We have one weapon. Who's going to cover me while I switch it to stun? I'm not interested in fairness. I'm interested in survival."

Two more beasts toppled over, their limbs spinning off their bodies as they crashed into the stone wall below them. The remaining survivors ran back into the wood. No one in the human party sustained injury. Mess moved upward without comment. Napoleon swung the beamer onto her back and continued climbing as well. Larry scrambled over to where Hana was hunched. Her face turned to his, pale and damp.

"I thought I had seen everything on Jackpot...." she started.

"Those were the forest creatures?" he asked.

"Yes."

"But those weren't animals. I was expecting some sort of savage beast, like, I don't know..."

"I...have eaten their meat and...worn their skin all my life." She swallowed. "I never saw one before."

"You said they were dangerous."

"They are. We were taught that they were ferocious and filled the forests. I..." She grew even paler.

"Kneel down. Put your head between your legs."

"Larry," Napoleon called. "Hana! Come on."

"Are you all right?" Larry asked the girl.

"Yes," she replied, head still down.

"We had better get going," he told her gently.

She got up without incident and the two began to climb again.

The four reconnoitered at the top of the rocks. They stood among the first level of trees. The two humans were sweating profusely; Hana's shirt was torn at the side and Larry had tied his around his waist. Napoleon was wary, eyeing the forest. Across the lip of the rocks, the alien beasts lay dead.

"There are more of them," the feline was saying. "That much is certain. From here on up we have to be even more careful."

Larry had not argued, but he had taken a moment to look over a fallen forest creature. Although his initial guess had been correct—they had no thumbs —he noticed that there was a small stub where the human thumb usually was. Were they developing or regressing?

Larry raised a rough-hewn eyelid. The eyes were smaller than what was considered normal, but with human parts, just the same. Pupil, iris, cornea. The body was covered with hair, but Larry could see that they had sexual organs. The feet had five toes each, but like their fingers they were longer, much longer, than what could be considered normal on Earth.

He returned to the group and they moved back into the darkness of the thick wood. Napoleon led the way, handing her staff to Hana and unslinging the beamer. Mess rolled its treaded way alongside Larry.

"Where do you think these creatures came from, Mess?" Larry asked quietly.

"From a sperm and an egg, probably," said the compubot.

"Thanks for your assistance," Larry muttered sarcastically.

"Well, if you think I'm getting into a long-winded discussion on the possibility of a higher force just to pass the time, forget it," Mess said testily.

"I don't care about a higher force. These creatures could be the original inhabitants of the planet, who evolved into these tree dwellers. Or they could even be the Destinians' human descendants, arriving eons before the O'Neils."

"Look, for as much as we know about faster-than-light travel, they could've arrived after the O'Neils," said Mess.

"Quiet," urged the compubot. "I think I sense something."

They were moving deeper into the wood now and the darkness was coming on fast. A green-brown dusk settled over the party as they pulled their tired bodies across the steep forest floor. The wood stayed quiet except for the rustle of the wind and the party's footsteps. When Mess failed to discern anything tangible, Hana slowed down so Larry could catch up with her.

"What happens when we reach the central city?" she asked.

"*If* we reach wherever whoever is guiding us wants us to go, we'll see when we get there," said Napoleon.

"We're at your planet's mercy," Larry elaborated. "I haven't really understood anything that's happened since we picked up your brother."

No one had to say that Harlan was now gone and that no one knew where he was or that they were now complete pawns in a situation that went way beyond their control. Each knew that they had changed, but no one knew where they now fit in.

"All right," said Napoleon. "I can see the light ahead. We're almost through the wood."

As the last word left her mouth, she heard a rushing above her. Before she could react, a large hunk of wood fell across her face, landing on the crook of her arms. She howled in pain and fell back, the beamer spinning off in front of her. The rest of the group stopped in shock as rushing wind assailed them.

From out of the trees dropped dozens of forest creatures, who bounced on the ground, rolled, and leaped upon the party. Two dark feet banged against Mess' head in the blind spot of its circle of sensors. As it began to topple over its forward wheels, it said, "I knew I should have put one on top."

It moved its wheels forward and kept erect but was now low enough to the ground for five more creatures to swarm over it, pulling it down. Its wheels spun frantically as they pounded it with sticks.

Napoleon somersaulted backward to land on her hind legs, holding her wounded forepaws close to her chest. As she dove forward to recover the fallen beamer, a large branch swung from behind a tree and caught her in the stomach.

She slid backward on her knees until another branch, wielded by another creature, smacked into the back of her head. She fell forward as if she had been pulled. She lay on the forest floor, still.

Two creatures leaped on Hana, wrapping their arms around her, spinning her to the ground. The stick she held dropped away from her. Its tip bounded it over in the air and it fell at Larry's feet.

One creature was on top of her, moving in an unmistakably sexual rhythm. Larry dropped to his knees and grabbed the branch. Two feet planted themselves before him. He looked up to see a screaming creature bringing its own stick down toward Larry's skull.

Without thinking, Larry brought his staff around in a fast arc near the ground. The creature missed by a good six inches as the wood connected with its ankles, toppling it over backward.

Larry jumped to his feet, hearing movement behind him. He turned, swinging the branch at the same time. It felled a charging tree creature in midleap. Larry spun again to see the creature he had tripped trying to rise on shattered leg bones and the creature still moving atop Hana beyond.

Larry ran forward, slammed the tip of his pole into the rising creature's chest and vaulted over to her, landing on top of the creature pinning her. They rolled off the girl, Larry losing his grip on the stick, but the creature was taken by surprise as well.

Larry was the first to his feet, noticing a third creature swinging a stick at his head from the side. As the creature who had been atop Hana rose, Larry fell on his back, the stick whistled above him and was stopped by the rising creature's face. Larry kicked the attacking creature in the crotch and grabbed its weapon.

Another creature moved toward Hana and Larry batted it in the head. Another came at Larry from behind. He swung the stick back, catching the creature in the throat with its tip. Another moved in from the side. Larry swung the stick back again, at waist level, knocking the creature rolling.

He stood above Hana, whirling the stick like a man deranged, ignoring his pain and exhaustion. He willed his muscles to move and they moved. The laboratory-created human being discovered his physical self. It was almost like handling a mathematical problem. Employing the proper muscles of eyes, legs, arms, and head, you could solve the problem. The stick whirled like three, weaving in and out, catching creatures on their heads, stomachs, and legs.

The creatures stopped charging. They began to circle the pair, thrusting their sticks at them, but not trying to connect. More and more joined the circle until the prone Mess and Napoleon were obscured from sight. A solid wall of brown-skinned creatures with sparkling eyes faced them.

Larry kept his stick raised, slowly circling, himself, as Hana rose to her knees, eyeing the veritable platoon of tree creatures.

"What are they going to do?" she whispered while rising.

"How should I know?" Larry said helplessly.

Suddenly a part of the circle began to separate. As Larry and she watched, a tree creature appeared through his fellows, holding the beamer rifle like a club. It walked over to where Larry stood and grunted, brandishing the weapon. Larry watched unmoving. The creature turned and motioned to the others, growling again. The circle moved back, leaving a large area clear.

Through the shuffling brown legs Hana could see a battered Mess and an unconscious Napoleon. The creature with the beamer turned back to Larry again, once more brandishing the weapon and grunting through a large twisted grin.

Larry remained watchful. The creature repeated his action. Larry watched. The creature frowned and moved back. He growled at the crowd. They began to move forward. Larry tensed and raised his stick. The crowd seemed to sigh collectively and moved back again.

At this, the first creature actually smiled. He put the beamer between his legs and rubbed his hands. Two other creatures ran forward suddenly and seized Hana. Larry spun as she was dragged away, but a loud growl from the first creature forced him to turn back. The creature had its hands at its sides. It slowly took the beamer by the barrel.

Larry suddenly knew what was going on. He was being challenged. He had shown ability, so now he was being challenged by the tree creatures' leader. Four other creatures were standing on each side of Hana, separated by the length of their sticks held at waist level before them, effectively making a cage. It was obvious she was the victor's prize. To the loser, defeat or death?

Larry had little choice but to find out. He slowly undid his shirt from his waist. The creature facing him was thin, but tall and well muscled. His ability at fighting and climbing must have been excellent and well developed. Larry figured the only way to get out of this in one piece was to play on the creature's supposed lack of subtle intelligence and human experience. Although they were rulers of the forest, according to what Hana had said they had yet been unable to deal with advanced technology.

Larry took off his shirt and hurled it in the air. All eyes followed the garment and an audible gasp went up as it unbunched and the sleeves rippled in the air.

Larry lifted his staff and swung. It seemed destined to become part of the creature's skull, but at the last second the beamer stock moved up and blocked. The creature stepped back out of the way of the twisting weapons and spun the beamer out from under Larry's stick and swung it backhand at Larry's head.

Luckily it was used to the longer sticks, so the butt of the weapon breezed by Larry's forehead, ruffling his eyebrows. Both fighters thought their strategy sure, so both were surprised at each's subsequent failure.

Larry then had an opening, but not enough leverage. He managed to poke the creature before it batted away his stick with the beamer, skipping to the left. Larry moved to the right as the creature pivoted. The beamer sped down to cleave Larry's skull. The stick came whistling across and knocked it out of the way.

But the strike was telling. The stick stung his hand with tight vibrations, and solid bands of pain moved up both arms. The beamer came right back, speeding in from where Larry had deflected it. He wasn't able to get his stick back up in time and the butt hit his left shoulder and sent him stumbling, Hana's white face passing through his view.

He sliced his stick back and forth through the air to keep the creature away while he tried to think straight. The creature began pivoting again. Left to right, right to left, left to right, right to left. His dark skin began to blend in with the cover of dead leaves on the ground.

The pain in Larry's arms began to throb. The creature's edges were beginning to blur. Larry held his staff up, his eyes moving with the creature's movements. The creature ran in semicircles, pivoting back and forth, turning, twisting, moving in and out. Larry just stood and moved his body, trying to face him at all times.

The creature began chattering in a singsong voice. He kept moving, right to left, left to right, right to left, the song coming in from one side when the creature was on another. Larry felt the energy rising in the crowd. He knew that the creature was going to attack any moment, and it would have to be just luck to guess which direction the blow would be coming from.

The movement intensified, the singsong getting louder and louder. It reached for its crescendo. The creature's left foot didn't pivot, it rooted itself. Larry swung left. The creature swung right. The weapons met in midair.

A sharp crack filled the clearing and echoed through the wood. Larry felt his arms shake in their sockets. His back was stung with a slicing pain, but his feet held. His staff didn't. It shattered with the force of the speeding beamer. He felt the slice move under his hands and separate.

The end of the stick was dust, the middle was a forest of broken edges, the grip was a split piece. The creature's back was to him for a split second as it followed through, but there was nothing for Larry to attack with. The creature spun toward him with beamer intact.

The creature smiled and moved in. Larry kept his eye on the beamer. He knew this creature was not going to congratulate him for a fine fight and invite him over to the tree for refreshments. He would split his skull and use Hana in any way he saw fit. They may have been more intelligent than they were given credit for, but they weren't civilized by any means. It was time to use that advanced technology against them.

The beamer began to curl in and out. The hard butt moved in semicircles. The creature came closer and closer. Larry stood his ground. The creature swung; Larry jumped. The beamer hit him in the solar plexus as his arms sought a hold. Larry's feet kicked out, catching the creature under the knee. Larry hit the ground on his back, holding on to the butt of the weapon.

The creature stood holding on to the barrel. It took a step in to wrench the beamer out of Larry's grip but fell from the wounded knee. Larry pushed his finger past the metal guard and depressed the trigger.

A beam of orange moved up the creature's arm and pounded him in the chest. He flew back, releasing the barrel and landed on top of his shoulders. He tumbled over onto his side and lay still.

Larry gripped the weapon tightly. He noticed the barrel had been turned to the stun position during the fight. Then Hana was tenderly touching the myraid scratches across his torso.

"Are you all right?" they asked each other at the same time.

Hana couldn't help but smile. And even after all he had been through, Larry felt his face flush. He turned to see a group of creatures prodding their prone fighter.

The rest of the group had accepted their leader's defeat, but they weren't happy about it. They broke the circle, growling and grumbling at each other. Two took the unconscious creature by the arms and pulled him away. The others moved as well, occasionally howling and leaping.

"I can't believe it," said Hana. "They're leaving us alone."

"Well, I won, didn't I?" said Larry. He got to his feet, beamer in hand. "They have rules. They have weapons. They have organization. They're not just animals to be killed."

He trotted over to where Napoleon lay, Hana at his side. A nasty bump appeared on the back of her head, blood already clotted and flaking. Larry shook her gently, ready to jump back if she tried to scratch him while asleep.

She mewed, then growled deep in the back of her throat, her eyelids fluttering open. "Ouch," she said, touching the back of her head. "Ouch, ouch, ouch. By Cheshire, that hurts. What happened?"

Larry quickly explained while the huge mass of tree creatures receded into the forest. The cover of the wood seemed to open for them, their bodies mysteriously fading as they walked.

"All right, so you passed the test and you're an honorary tree creature," she growled. "What now?"

Hana was about to reprimand the feline for her lack of feeling and Larry was about to explain that she was always testy after waking, but the forest roof ripped open, answering her question.

The trees above them tore, spilling branches everywhere, leaves aflutter. Lightning bolts of many colors reached down, plucking tree creatures up and hurling them away. Still other rays burned them where they stood. Animal howls were drowned out by an incredible burst of wind and noise.

Napoleon grabbed a tree, her paws ripping grooves in the bark as she was pushed back by the force. Larry and Hana grabbed each other and went rolling off along the swirling ground. The beamer rifle flew into the wood.

Through the trees broke a spaceship. Shaped like a great pair of frowning lips, it ripped open a landing space and settled down into it. As Larry and Hana stopped rolling they felt something hard poke their heads and bodies. They were weapons held by men in spacesuits. Silver spacesuits.

As Napoleon opened her eyes after the wind had died down, she saw a semicircle of weapons pointing at her. Other spacesuited men collected the carcasses of the dead tree creatures, dumping them on a large mesh tarp which they had laid out. She heard one of them say, "Destiny will eat well tonight!"

Larry and Hana were herded back to where Napoleon stood. Her skull injury was bleeding again and her fur was dirty, coarse, and tufted in bunches. Larry's hair was matted, as was Hana's, with his shoulders and neck a livid red and his arms and torso dotted with cuts. Hana's shirt was ripped along the sides and front, exposing her dirt-streaked frame. They all faced the bright silver ship, waiting to see what would happen next.

From out of the top of the ship, a man in a bright silver spacesuit beckoned. When he was sure all eyes were on him, his arms reached up and removed his bright silver opaque helmet. When he spoke, his words were meant only for Hana.

"My dear," said Bishop-Fortune. "What a pleasure it is seeing you again."

SEVENTEEN

Hana's face began to collapse into fragments of pain and defeat, until she felt Larry's hand at her elbow and heard Napoleon snarl. These two had existed up until now as slaves. Slaves of ignorance, of bigotry, of preconceptions. Their world had stuck them in neat classifications. They had fought their way out, declared themselves as free individuals capable of deep emotion and incredible physical feats in the face of ridiculous odds.

She was luckier. She was a slave for a little more than a year. A year that meant nothing. A year that could not be forgotten but could be used to make her own freedom all the more precious and her self-awareness all the more powerful.

Her face stopped its fall and, before all their eyes, put itself back together into the same look of defiance that glowed on Larry's and Napoleon's faces. Bishop-Fortune, his loose outfit swirling, looked disappointed.

"Most of my girls drop to their knees when I claim them, or at least burst into tears."

"I'm not one of your girls," she said evenly, the words almost catching in her throat.

"You are. You shall see when I return you to Jackpot," Bishop-Fortune assured her. "Whether you know it or not, you are. As is the cat beside you."

"Little chance, spawn of Earth feces," called Napoleon clearly. "I've faced the likes of you before."

Bishop-Fortune blanched visibly. No creature this side of the universe had ever said anything like that to his face.

"I shall be prepared, cat," he boomed, finding his voice. "You shall be brought before me."

Bishop-Fortune tried to deliver a withering stare, but even astride his great steel ship and draped in sparkling silver, Napoleon defeated him. His concentration broke and he turned, beckoning downward.

"Little matters, small, inconsequential matters," he said, turning back to them. "When I get you back to my establishment you will pay dearly for your actions. You are helpless, totally alone."

"If I'm alone then I'm never totally helpless," Hana heard the feline say clearly. Bishop-Fortune went on regardless.

"The coup is complete. Five of you." He ticked them off on a hand. "No more effective than a gust of wind." He dealt with each finger one by one. "Harlan is certainly destroyed. Hana is my prize again. The FM is as good as dead, his head destined for a pike in the central city square. Napoleon is another of my prizes and Palend has paid for his interference without the assistance of the Intercouncil." His hands curled into a fist.

A figure began to rise up beside him. It took shape slowly, growing from the ship-top entrance. The first thing Larry could discern clearly was the red jewel in its forehead.

"Isenraid," he breathed.

"Indeed," shouted Bishop-Fortune. "You pitiful creatures. You have no idea what you have been involved in. The control of a paradise planet. A world of incredible wealth. You entered the story after years of ground breaking. You only stumbled into the final phase."

"Explain!" Larry shouted. "You've known where we were all along. You circumvented Destiny security. How?"

"The Mantas race has been adding to the universe's might for centuries," hissed Isenraid, now standing atop the ship alongside the vice lord. "We lust for order. A common order, unfettered by race or boundaries. When none exists, we create it. Destiny was not part of the universal order. Steps were taken eons ago to correct that."

"Then you were not born here?" asked Hana. "You were not spawn of this planet?"

"No, my child," said the Mantas. "We were seeded. My race travels through the galaxy pinpointing worlds outside the Universal Rule. We strive to unite each under The Rule, the only true Rule. Once we establish ourselves on a world, we aide others until we acquire positions of power. Then we help the planet adjust."

"We made a deal," Bishop-Fortune translated. "I would supply the physical might while the Mantases infiltrated and paved the way for me. But I needed an assurance of their cooperation and good intentions. You," he pointed to Hana, "were that guarantee."

"Her?" Larry exploded. "A person? You gave a human being in payment?"

"You have the gall to say that to me?" Bishop-

Fortune said in disbelief. "You have the unmitigated, Taplinger-Jones balls to say something as stupid as that to me? Where are you from, jerk?"

Larry stared in equal disbelief at the Jackpot vice lord. His manner had completely changed. No longer was he a demigod. He was talking to Larry on the level. He was talking...the way Julius would talk to him. Or Oliver. Or Eugene. In fact, he even looked a lot like Julius.

"Remember Earth, idiot?" Bishop-Fortune taunted. "You know, like a half year ago? That place where they sell you like socboos?" Sudden awareness dawned across Larry's face.

"Wait a minute," he sputtered. "You..."

"Now you got it, fool. And a bigger one I've never met. Yeah, Larry. You had it made. You had freedom, you had the feline, you had the ship, but you were too much of a coward to do anything about it before the space bullet showed up. Not me, brother. I got out. I nearly got killed hundreds of times, but I made it. I made it without anything. I made it without any of the stuff you had."

Napoleon and Hana looked from the vice lord to Larry and back. The look on their friend's face told them something was going on backstage but the curtains hadn't completely opened yet.

"Yeah, *Larry*," the vice lord spat. "You know what they named me? Get a load of this now. They named me Shemp. The other guys got Stan or Lou or Jerry. I get Shemp. You better believe I'm going to take an RH in payment. And an Earth Mother at that."

"You're an FM!" Napoleon blurted, pointing. "You're a Taplinger-Jones FM!"

"Not anymore, pussycat," Bishop-Fortune said viciously. "I'm no FM or TM anymore, sweetie. I'm a JacBoss now."

"He required a human being, a woman, this woman," Isenraid interrupted impatiently. "It was for the best. Her family had been chosen to take the blame for our actions," the Mantas said simply.

"But when her brother got away," continued Bishop-Fortune. "Certain precautions had to be taken."

"We watched and waited," said the Mantas. "Knowing he would rescue her and return here."

"So we planted a homing device inside her one night. We've known where she's been every moment."

Hana looked in shock at Larry. If she were expecting disgust or accusation in his look back, she was disappointed. He looked to her in shared pain with rage and a growing shrewdness. He touched her arm, shrugging as if it weren't important.

Bishop-Fortune was now openly disappointed. He thought such a revelation would make at least one of them sick with remorse.

"Others have been seeing that all is in readiness," continued Isenraid. "The Queen has 'taken ill,' Ministic has closed down the factories and sent the space bullets to destroy your ship and the traitor Harlan Trigor."

"My fleet is on the other side of the planet," Bishop-Fortune gloated. "When the Queen is dead, we will attack."

"No!" screamed Hana, moving forward and pleading. "How can you? You have lived with us all these years," she cried to Isenraid. "You have grown side by side with us. You know the love our people feel for your race. Have we been meaningless ciphers to you all these years?"

"Order must be maintained," hissed Isenraid coldly. "The Rule must be obeyed."

"Don't you realize what you are doing?" Hana spoke out. "Have the years in this place not touched you?

Good cannot be taken to an extreme. Your wish for order will destroy this planet! You've settled your pact with scum."

"We will see that this world is used to its best advantage," spoke the Mantas. "One world's wealth is the solar system's wealth."

"Well, it has been fun," said Bishop-Fortune. "But I have a world to see to," He signaled and the line of space-suited guards began to move in.

"The space bullets will stop you!" Hana screamed.

"No, they won't," said Isenraid with certainty.

The line of guards continued to circle them.

"Prepare to sleep," said Bishop-Fortune. "When you awake you and Napoleon will be back where you belong. You, *Larry*, will join Palend. Your luck has been incredible. Absolutely. The five of you have been incredibly lucky. But now your luck has finally run out."

"Six," came a voice. It boomed out of the forest and echoed against the mountain. So grand was it that everyone stopped for a moment.

"Six," the voice repeated. Bishop-Fortune looked around wildly, shouting instructions to his men that they couldn't hear over the reverberation.

"The six of us have been incredibly lucky," continued the voice. Isenraid spotted the shaking branches and pointed off beyond. The guards lined up away from the human trio and the two atop the ship waited as the leaves parted.

And out rolled Mess. Its wheels were bent and wobbling. One of his treads was broken and the leg attached was twisted out of shape. His torso area was rutted and sliced in places. Three of his six sensors were cracked and dark. And he moved unsteadily, in fits and starts.

Around Larry and Napoleon the guards looked in

absolute wonder. Bishop-Fortune began to laugh. Hana placed her hands on Larry's shoulders for support, frowning.

"Another trick?" came Bishop-Fortune's voice. "Another secret weapon? Destroy that machine immediately," he instructed his guards, his voice dripping with mocking scorn.

Larry's brain was awhirl. What had the machine done this for? To overcome its programmed rule for self-preservation in order to buy them time was unbelievable. It was a machine; it wasn't capable of feeling or sacrifice.

Bishop-Fortune and Isenraid stood imperiously on the ship. A group of guards pulled their spinners over to aim at Mess. It made a ludicrous target. The machine stopped rolling before their weapons. Its remaining sensors blinked red and its head popped off its body.

Larry grabbed Hana and Napoleon and jumped to the side. The guards immediately opened fire. Larry rolled and watched helplessly as the spiraling projectiles bore into Mess' body. The head moved over, hovering eight feet in the air to avoid the fire. As Bishop-Fortune shouted and pointed at the head, Mess' wheels moved forward. The body arched down, the open neck pointing at the huge silver ship.

The spinners tore into the body as the machine fired. A huge flame was emitted from the neck hole, pointing up. The force of the weapon rocked the guards. The next second Bishop-Fortune disintegrated. The ashes of his body flew off in all directions, a cloud of atomized red and silver. He looked like a tiny sun glistening in the forest before his remains dotted the top of the ship and surrounding trees.

Isenraid was hurled off the top of the spacecraft by the concussion. He lay dazed, one leg broken, his head waving from side to side. Then his eyes and jewel cleared; he turned toward Mess and a red bolt struck out from his head. It connected with the center of Mess' "chest." The machine exploded with a force that killed several guards nearby. Metal parts reached high into the trees, then fell, spun, and floated down. Mess' sensors went dark and his hovering head dropped to the leaves.

Larry picked up a dropped spinner and drilled a hole in the middle of Isenraid's face as Napoleon leaped onto a tree. As the Mantas' face ripped back onto the silver ship, covering the area with a terrible stench, she scrambled up to a large branch overhanging the ship.

From there the feline leaped onto the silver craft and disappeared inside, howling with bloodthirsty glee. Hana, in the meantime, had also relieved a guard of his weapon by hurling a rock through his faceplate. She and Larry stood back to back, blasting away at the stumbling guards.

"We've got to get under cover," Larry shouted to her without turning his head. "Start moving behind those trees."

Out of this massacre appeared a walkway, seemingly materialized from the top of the ship to the forest floor. Napoleon appeared at the crown, Bishop-Fortune's weapon in paw.

"Come on!" she yelled to Larry. "I'll cover you."

The two began to run for the stairway when Larry stopped. Hana stopped automatically as well.

"You go ahead," Larry told her. "I'll be right there."

She didn't argue, cutting down a guard who was trying to shoot them instead. She then ran for the ship, knocking stumbling guards out of the way.

Larry ran in a wide semicircle, the center of which was the scorched piece of dirt where Mess had been destroyed. He found what he was looking for at the base of a thick tree fifty feet beyond. Larry reached down and put the red plate filled with microcirquidity in the waist of his pants. Then he turned and ran for the ship.

"This is a friend of mine," said Napoleon as she picked her way among the four slashed and cut corpses on the floor of the bridge. She motioned toward a pale, brown-haired foozle standing by a console fitted with six screens and advanced technological equipment.

"Hello," it said.

"Do you know how to run this thing?" Larry asked.

"He's alive, isn't he?" said Napoleon out of the side of her mouth. "Just do as we say and you won't get hurt."

Larry looked at Napoleon with angry disbelief. She shrugged. He returned his attentions to the pooch. "Take off," he instructed.

"I thought you wanted me to fly the ship?" the foozle said.

"I mean lift-off, get going, let's get out of here!"

The foozle hopped into the pilot's chair.

"You remind me of my computer," mumbled Larry as the canine creature switched on the console. The machine had denied its two primary programs in order to save their lives. One, its safety, and two, its permission to fire. It seemed like the old coot Palsy-Drake had managed to shove feeling into his creation. He had succeeded in getting Mess to think for itself, acting on the basis of emotion, opting for a noble sacrifice instead of continued existence.

The ship rose slowly and moved into the bright Destiny sky. The interior was far smaller than the ship was made to look from the outside. There were eight seats before a small hallway leading to four small cabins and a combination bunk room and eating area. The chairs were in two rows of three with two seats by the piloting console.

Napoleon stood beside the pilot, her hand on her weapon while Hana sat behind Larry, her face averted from the ripped corpses behind. Larry plopped down in the seat beside the foozle.

"How did the guards get to us?" he asked.

"They have a loading area below," Napoleon replied. "They dropped them out on the other side of the trees."

Larry surveyed the mass of forest on the screen, his face grim. He could have asked the foozle's name. He could have asked how it got involved with Bishop-Fortune. He could have asked it where he got its flying training. He didn't. He did not feel like it.

"Do you have a communication system?" he finally inquired.

"Sure," answered the foozle, pointing to a boxlike compartment on the console near Larry.

"What does this use?" Larry asked, eyeing the group of buttons. "Voice or code?"

"Code. It's a standard Jackpot issue code."

"I know that," exclaimed Hana, rising out of her seat.

"Get on it, then," said Larry. "Try to raise Harlan. Tell him about the fleet on the other side of the planet."

"But," her voice quaked. "But Bishop-Fortune said he was destroyed."

"What does Shemp know?" Larry said. "Shemp is dead. I'm betting Harlan isn't. I'm betting the skill that he was always bragging about has kept him alive this long. I'm betting we can still do something to save this planet."

Larry turned to the pilot as a shocked Hana hunched over the communication device.

"What was your next stop?"

"The Mile Long Palace," the foozle replied quickly. "In the central city."

"Take us there, then," said Larry with certainty.

"Not a great move," said the foozle. "You're outnumbered. They'll kill you."

Larry felt like crying. Such waste, such absurdity. All in the name of greed and conformity. But he didn't. His face showed only confidence.

"Take us there," he repeated quietly. "Win or lose, we're playing this game out to the end."

Harlan sped up, then around to the right. In his wake silent thunder rolled, accompanied by multi-colored lightning. The vacuum of space was filled with the soundless buzzing of dozens of space bullets, all moving with stunning speed in complicated geometric patterns. And all were trying to destroy.

All but one. Their target. Their target had little interest in fighting back. He was flying a defensive pattern, the finest of his career, the finest in Destiny's history. Brilliant maneuvers based on mathematical theories concerning a space bullet's shortcomings. No matter if they faced him in number or one on one, he would arrange that their killing blasts would take in their fellows. And if they employed weapons not powerful enough to hurt their kind, then they couldn't hurt him.

So they tried to wear him down. For hours they sought to tire him, to make him careless. By the time Harlan received the coded signal, the tactic was working in reverse. Two other space bullets had collided and had to be towed by two more. Before he received his sister's transmission, Harlan had thought of it as "four down—ninety-six to go."

But now, with infinite care, finesse, and cunning, Harlan Trigor began to lead his brothers to the other side of the planet.

EIGHTEEN

"One hundred space bullets," said Ministic, by the throne. "One hundred space bullets I sent into the sky to kill your brother." She took a moment to stab one metal-tipped arm at Hana as she paced back and forth on the upraised section of the royal room. "And they all failed. Harlan Trigor kept them at bay for half a day. Half a day!"

Larry, Napoleon, and Hana stood among a throng of Mantases in the mile-long throne room, a stone-and-wood-mesh palace now awash with the quivering blue, black, and gray of the entire Destiny insectlike population.

There wasn't a foozle in sight.

Upon landing in a small area reserved for the royal craft, the Mantases had swarmed onto the ship, disarming the trio, and taking the three remaining to face the Queen and Queen's aide. But at great cost. The Mantases had died in great waves at the hands of the three survivors. When the guns had been ripped from their grasp, they had used their hands, tearing at the mass of aliens until they were borne away before Ministic.

She stood there, her royal robes a kaleidoscope of swirling colors, billowing off in every direction as they curled around her body. The aide's pendant reflected the sun's light as it streamed in from the row of windows set high in the walls, stretching out of sight from the center of the throne room.

The Queen herself was still, dressed in a royal dressing gown. She was strewn in her chair, eyes closed, mouth hanging open. She breathed shallowly, her rich red hair piled clumsily atop her head, strands curtaining her face. But through the makeshift bangs the humans could see a dark bruise on her temple.

Ministic stopped pacing before the throne, standing to glower at her prisoners.

"Do you want to know why I had you brought here?" she asked with intensity. "Do you want to know why I did not allow my brothers and sisters to rip you apart? Because I wanted you to see our final victory. It is important that you know that my race, my rule, even in the face of defeat, even unallied, is stronger than anything you know."

Ministic shook uncontrollably as she talked, vibrating as if she were wracked with fever. Beside her, two other Mantases worked on a square block of machinery about three feet by three feet.

"Why go on?" asked Hana. "It is finished. My people will know of your treachery."

"No!" Ministic screamed. All around them the Mantases chattered, waving their arms, the deadly mandibles slicing the air. Ministic's were totally covered by metal gauntlets reaching from her first arm joint to the tip, leaving her with one thick steel finger on each appendage. "It is not over. With or without your people, Destiny will know The Rule. Where there is one Mantas there are all Mantases!"

The room reverberated with the cries of the aliens. All arms were up, all eyes aglow. All one with some shared inner fire.

"The space bullets have destroyed Bishop-Fortune's fleet," Hana pressed. "Harlan has led them to it. Even now they are returning. You have nothing to gain. Surrender!"

"We do not surrender," Ministic said quietly, calmly. "We plan ahead. As soon as Isenraid informed me of Bishop-Fortune's demise at your hands, seconds before his own death, we altered our strategy. This eventuality—yes, even this—had been considered. We were aware of this possibility. Even before your brother escaped, even before you were taken, the situation had been analyzed.

"As we had considered that your brother might escape. As we had considered that he might acquire allies. As we had considered our moves to fit all eventualities even if the allies were one million in number! This is one of millions we calculated. All the variables, all the variables were considered."

The Mantas' voice had risen to a shriek, then slowed to a deep crawl, its body hunched, the tone gentle. Suddenly it reared to its full height again, its arms up, metal glinting in the illumination.

"Oh, creation! Why do you always leave us? We long to be with you!"

All the Mantases looked in the same erect position. Larry and Napoleon exchanged glances. Here were the worst sort of conquerers, the sort who would commit mass suicide to achieve their ends. When they had no respect for their own kind in life, they had none for any other living race.

Then the spell was broken. The huge mass of creatures began to disperse.

"Go!" cried Ministic. "Prepare!"

The trio watched incredulously as the room emptied except for Ministic and the two Mantases by the cube. The Queen's aide pointed a metal-tipped arm at the trio. "I have been chosen as the assassin. I will kill the Queen. The space bullets will be destroyed by their own weapons. My people will turn on the residents of Destiny. They as yet know nothing of what has transpired. They will soon be dead or helpless. We will put out a message to the other worlds. Then it will only be a matter of time before the first Ruler arrives."

"It is a waste," Larry said passionately. "You're wasting all your lives. You're killing for the wrong reason."

Napoleon stared at Ministic, the former's voice a savage ripping sound in the cavernous hall. "There are no wrong reasons in murder. There are only different ones. Death is death. Life goes on for the killer. For the dead it is over. We, out of all in the universe, should know that."

Larry turned to his friend. "We killed for a reason, yes. The Mantases are killing for no..."

Napoleon leaped in the air before Larry's sentence was finished. But the ploy did not work completely. Ministic was taken by surprise but not soon enough. Her arm swung and a white bolt struck out from her metal point, catching the feline in the side, spinning her around and hurling her back onto the floor. She fell in a slack pile, her limbs smashing sickeningly against the stone and wood, her fur smoking.

"Nap!" Larry cried, pulling her prone body into his arms. Her eyes were closed and he could not see whether she was breathing.

He laid her down softly and checked her heart. It did not beat. Larry's torso rose, his fist spinning toward the ceiling. With a terrible scream he brought it down to her chest. Then again, and again, and again, each time screaming with all the power he could push through his vocal cords and his muscles.

Then he sobbed, his head sinking to Napoleon's prone figure. His tear-streaked eyes sank into the fur of her chest. When he rose, his face held a terrible smile. He turned to face Ministic.

"A weapon, as you have observed," said the Mantas as if Napoleon had never attacked. "A poor one versus the one we have prepared here." She motioned to the Mantas-tended block. "But effective for our purposes. You will be killed, as will the Queen, but only when we are ready. You shall see. The Rule will be served."

As she finished speaking the wall a half mile down blew inward. The explosion sounded like a clap followed by rainfall at such a distance, but Larry could see clearly the group of space bullets in formation speeding down the high-ceilinged room, tearing the ornaments from the walls and ripping the rugs from the floor. Ministic did not move as this occurred. She stood, still facing Larry, Hana, and the fallen feline, the metal tip pointing.

"Prepared?" she asked of the pair beside her.

"Yes," answered one.

"When I say," said Ministic.

"Agreed," said the other.

The room began to throb with the power of the space bullets. Dust, long since wedged in uncleanable cracks, flew up and swirled in the wake of the stone army. Larry saw them growing larger and larger in number in the hall, more and more screaming in from the hole beyond. They roared forward with no sign of slowing.

"Now," Ministic spoke.

The Mantas pressed a button. All the roar suddenly ceased. A moment later it was replaced by the whistling of the bullets losing all power and altitude. Then the noise of destruction boomed as the nine-foot rocks crashed to the ground.

Their momentum was such that they sped down, hit the floor at high speed, and either sank, bounced, or rolled. Wood chips flew everywhere. Floors and walls smashed open as the rocks collided with them. Human boulders bounced end over end until they slowed and crashed heavily down.

Some spun in the air like rotor blades, dropping to the floor and spinning. Most just hit the floor and stopped jarringly as the wood and earth surrounded them, some sinking as far as eight feet. The castle shook as if in the hands of a large earthquake. The raised platform gave with the rolling shocks. Ministic remained standing and the two other Mantases gripped the block of machinery.

In the space of seconds the room was littered with dozens of stone monoliths. Larry and Hana rose slowly from the floor. The shaking was so intense that the thought of escape was impossible.

"They are now entombed," said Ministic. "They cannot sense or move. The power of their suits has been nullified. Here they will starve, die, and decompose. Their ashes will remain in their suits forever. Some may suffocate. Some may go insane. Some may experience unbelievable hallucinations before death. Some may even be preserved, mummified, held in eternal night."

Hana stood by Larry, her arms at her sides. She wanted to do something, but what could she do? All during the space bullets' defeat Ministic had not turned, not even glanced away as a falling rock missed her by inches. If Napoleon with all her speed and agility could do nothing, what could Hana do? But she had come too far to die. She had to do *something*.

Larry stood, facing the Mantas with the same odd smile. Inside he felt doom clawing at his heart. His fingers tapped each other nervously, the thumb rubbing the forefinger, then tapping, rubbing, then tapping.

"Now I must kill the Queen," said Ministic. "Then I signal my people. Then I send the message to the stars. But I cannot do this and keep you captive. So ...now you must die."

Hana couldn't bring herself to charge or even run. She felt the energy of Ministic's emotion. She felt the end coming near. She felt as if she had but a moment left to give her death meaning. Her arms reached out and encircled Larry's waist. His arms encircled hers without his even turning. It was natural, not subservient, not desperate, but natural, easy. Necessary.

Ministic paused. "You will never know The Rule," she said sadly, as if it were the worst fate imaginable.

"We know ourselves," said Larry. It was a long, hard road, but he could die now. Given several more moments he would not want to, but at this moment he could. He wouldn't really mind. Now, do it now!

Ministic's weapon emitted its bright beam. Even though it traveled, it moved at such high speed that its emission seemed to materialize in the shape of its path. The beam made a giant L when it should have made an I. The top moved from Ministic to Larry, then the bottom moved away from Larry.

All three were stunned. Even as the beam destroyed part of a wall, Ministic fired again. The same thing happened. The beam arced away from the humans and buried itself in the floor. Larry didn't know how it happened, but he wasn't going to stand around figuring it out. He leaped up the steps toward the Mantas.

Ministic managed to back up one step and fire twice more before the human was upon her. The beams sped away from Larry with a crackle as if they were frightened of him. With a push, Ministic was hurtled off the raised platform. She crashed onto the wooden floor, breaking an antenna. Larry turned and charged the remaining Mantases.

"The machine," he yelled to Hana. "Destroy the machine!"

She ran up the steps after him. The pair moved in to grapple with the remaining creatures.

"Watch out for the mandibles," said Larry.

Then he jumped into the air and kicked out with both feet, the way Harlan taught him on the way to Jackpot, catching one creature on the shoulder, knocking it away. It toppled down the steps as Larry fell heavily on his back.

The other Mantas swung an arm down to pin him with its mandible when Hana hit it on the side of the head. The alien's blow was deflected enough to miss Larry and it lost its balance. Larry kicked up between the Mantas' arms and slammed it backward off the platform. It crashed down on its back.

Larry jumped up and gripped the block of machinery. He pushed and pulled but it wouldn't budge. He pressed every button he could find but nothing happened. He heard a noise and, looking up, saw Ministic on her feet, her arm pointing at them.

"Look out," he warned, pushing Hana down as the beam moved. Again it turned away with a crackle. Suddenly the answer occurred to Larry. The weapon was not crackling; he was. It was the communication device under his fingernail, the one with which Palend supplied him. It somehow was counteracting the weapon's electrical current, like two magnets repelling each other.

"Larry," Hana shouted. "The Queen!"

He broke out of his thought to see Ministic moving around the platform to get a clear shot at the unconscious monarch. Without thinking Larry ran two steps and leaped, his hand outstretched. The beam shot out and arced away as Larry's hurtling body crashed into the throne.

Ministic turned her aim to Hana as the chair rocked and Larry fell.

"Down!" he yelled from the platform floor. "Get down behind the machine!"

Hana ducked and the beam shot harmlessly over her head. Ministic dared not try another for fear of destroying the weapon that kept the space bullets in check.

But Larry had jarred the throne when he fell against it, shaking the Queen from her position. Before Hana's horrified eyes, she slipped from the seat and tumbled down the stairs, rolling to Ministic's feet.

The Mantas looked up in triumph. Her arm lowered. Larry stumbled up, knowing he could never reach them in time, His hands gripped the throne and Hana looked in horror as behind Ministic Napoleon rose.

Her chest was singed, the fur black, streaked with long red cuts. But her wound had nothing on her face. She looked totally alien as she stepped soundlessly up behind the Mantas. Her eyes were thin strips of black on a red background. Her mouth was open wide in a devilish smile, her teeth dripping saliva.

With a screech she was on Ministic's back, tearing. The Mantas' beam cracked into the floor between the Queen's outstretched arm and curving hip. The Mantas' face showed shock before a paw ripped across it, opening the head up in four long cuts. The feline's feet moved up and down along the insectlike body. Napoleon's head rose over Ministic's shoulder and sank her teeth in the creature's neck.

Larry watched, his fingers clenching and his shoulders hunching as the Mantas stumbled back. The veins in Larry's neck stood out as he sent the heavy wooden throne sliding across the platform. Hana dove out of the way as the solid chair crashed into the three-by-three-foot metal block.

Napoleon's head snapped up as the two items slipped from the platform and fell toward the floor. She leaped off the Mantas, scurrying away on all fours. Ministic tripped forward, her body flapping like the remains of her gown. Inner liquid drooled out, darkening the rainbow colors. She managed one alien scream before the block of machinery shattered on the floor.

Her arms jerked up in surprise as fourteen space bullet beams immediately converged on her body. With an otherworldly ripping sound her top half spun away, borne on the prismatic hues of her dress. Her legs fell over lazily afterward.

Somewhere on the planet, one hundred and one space bullets began to rise.

NINETEEN

Larry found her sitting on a rock by a rolling stream of water. She was unclothed, a red body suit lying beside her, crumpled on the ground. A shaft of sunlight spotlighted her head and torso, the heat feeling good against her healed chest wound. Yellow-orange hair had begun to grow there again, but it created a dish effect on her as the new fur tried to catch up with the unaffected coat. Her eyes were closed, her face at peace, but she was not smiling.

He sat down on a tree trunk that had fallen across the small river and let his legs hang down over the clear and dazzling rushing water, which seemed to be covered with cut diamonds. He wore a Destinian outfit made from material spun by tree worms on the other side of the forest. It was rare and expensive, but he couldn't bring himself to wear the hide of the tree creatures, not after what he had been through.

Napoleon opened her eyes and looked at him, the sun creating a halo effect around her face. She stretched her arms and legs, the muscles tightening with attractive curves. She mewed with pleasure, then turned out of the sun.

"Hello," she said.

"Hello," he replied.

"How did it go?"

"Well," he said, bouncing slightly on his wooden seat. "It went well. The Queen voiced her appreciation yet again, then filled the air with all the difficulties there would be in changing their system and dealing with the tree creatures—they still haven't given them a name yet—and how the planet couldn't afford any further strife at this time.

"I reminded her, tactfully of course, about the fact that the tree creatures proved to us that they were intelligent. I humbly recommended that Destiny had better make peace with them before they decided to make pieces of Destiny."

"She must have loved that."

"Not at first, naturally. She reminded me that the tree creatures' meat constituted a great deal of their diet. I inquired as to whether they had showed any signs of cannibalism. They had not, so I proposed that the tree creatures must eat something too. It would behoove Destiny to find out what.

"It's amazing, you know, how a planet can rationalize a less than moral existence. They had learned from Earth's mistakes, all right, but when it came to a choice between morality and expediency, the people chose meat.

"I further advised that the human population on Destiny was still small enough to make certain changes in their lifestyles without crippling everybody."

"It's not like they haven't had to go through some hard changes already," Napoleon interjected.

"Yes," agreed Larry. "Every Mantas wiped out. Total search and annihilation. As soon as Ministic died they tried to scatter, but it seems that the space bullets were faster. Except for Harlan, of course."

"Has anyone seen him recently?"

"No, he just stays inside his old home. Every time Hana comes out, she says he's thinking."

"Any foozles found?"

"Not a one."

He fell silent and returned his gaze to the water. Napoleon scratched the healed patch of skin, feeling the peach fuzz of her regrown fur.

"So that was it, then?" she inquired.

"Basically," he replied. "I've been inducted as an aide to handle the tree-creature situation since I've already proven myself...." His voice faded away. Napoleon knew already that he had accepted the position.

They sat on the rock and the tree trunk for a while, drinking in the leafy surroundings, feeling the warm air on their skin. Then Napoleon rubbed her thighs, stood up, and walked over to Larry's side.

"We started as strangers," she told him. "I don't want us to end that way."

He turned to look into her face, his hands in his lap, his legs still hanging down. He stared into her eyes for a moment before speaking.

"What do you say, Nap?" he asked with pain in his voice. "Have a good trip? Nice to have known you? Stop by if you ever come this way again?" His vocal cords constricted and his vision misted, making his eyes sparkle in the sunlight. He looked back at the water, ashamed of himself.

Napoleon walked into the water just above her ankles. She placed her paws on Larry's knees, looking up at him.

"I don't know," she said tenderly. "I don't know

what you can say. But I can say thank you. Thank you for saving my life and for being my friend. You have a good life here. You have a home and challenges and a partner that are worthy of you. You're an extraordinary person. You'll be happy here."

Larry looked down at her, tears forming in his eyes, his voice breaking. "But you were always my partner, Nap. I don't want to lose you."

His head bent and the sobs came, unashamedly.

"You'll never lose me, Larry. You'll always be with me," she said. "But this is not my place. I don't know if I'll ever find it, but I have to go and look. I would never be happy here."

"I know," he said, looking beyond her again, letting the tears drop onto his shirt. He wiped his eyes with the back of his hands but couldn't keep from crying again. Before the torrent came he managed to say, "I'll miss you, Nap."

Then they were in each other's arms, standing in the little river. Napoleon held him, feeling the pain she hadn't felt since the last of her sisters died so many years ago. But now as then, she didn't cry. Her face was twisted in love and loss, but she didn't cry.

She took his head in her hands and kissed him on the cheek. He took her into his arms again and rubbed her back slowly, her paws on his chest. Then they took one last long look at each other, his hands on her shoulders, hers on his waist. They walked out of the water and headed back toward the central city.

The great ship *Felidae* was ready. The citizens of Destiny had built a new intergalactic vehicle for Napoleon out of gratitude. It was outfitted with an O'Neil Light Drive and a dazzling array of weaponry and sensors. She originally did not want it to be so spacious, but the Queen had insisted, giving the feline enough room to really move about. Larry had built the computer personally and it was rumored that Harlan had calibrated the engines.

The citizens had gathered for her departure. The Queen, Hana, and Larry stood before the crowd, decked out in rich, royal finery. Napoleon herself wore a leotard Hana had made for her of a deep rust color, a brown and green patch on the left breast signifying Destiny. Words below it spelled out in the ancient space traveler's language, "Seek long enough and you will always find your Destiny."

Larry moved up to her at the last minute, reaching under his tunic. He pulled out a red plate covered with microcirquidity. He gave it to the feline, telling her to push it in the slot he had left in the compubot console. Then he had to avert his gaze, his eyes misting again.

Napoleon smiled at him warmly as he returned to the crowd. She had already said her good-byes. So, with a final wave, she entered her ship, the door closing behind her automatically. She felt sorry Harlan had not come to see her off, but everyone knew he wasn't the same since the Mantas massacre.

She walked to her pilot's console, not really noticing the particulars of the ship. She already knew it inside and out, having designed and helped build it. She sat in the custom-fitted seat and turned on the screens. She saw Larry and Hana crying in each other's arms. Before she broke down she initiated lift-off.

The screens were off. The red plate lay uninstalled on the computer console. The universe rushed around the ship, the computer handling the navigational chores, even without a personality.

Napoleon's figure lay hunched over her controls, her head in her arms. Two channels of black wetness had appeared beneath her eyes—the mark of feline sorrow. She cried and cried. She had felt the tears growing as the last of Destiny's lush greenness gave way to the black space beyond.

For the first time she felt totally alone. No more friends, no future, no God. She, too, had thought she could live without love, not truly knowing until she had left it behind. She wished she could have told him before she had said good-bye. Her body wracked with unknown emotions.

Then her head jerked up as the clear voice boomed over the communication speaker.

"Greetings. What language do you speak?"

"Harlan," she cried. "Harlan, is that you?"

"Yes," said the voice, echoing her emotion.

"What? What are you doing?" she laughed through her sorrow, choking on the words. "Why are you here?"

"I couldn't stay," he said in anguish. "My parents are dead. My sister has her own life now. My planet betrayed my trust. I had to leave. But I could not move inside our galaxy. We both have too many enemies. I followed you. You are the only other person I know who has shared my pain, who has lost as much as I have."

His voice turned hesitant, hoping.

"Can I join you . . . for a little while?"

"Yes," she said happily, blinking with the tears. "Yes. For a little while."

The feline and the space bullet sped into the unknown, side by side.

> From the womb we are born,
> It is what we must be.
> We're divers for glory,
> And the sky is our sea.